Reviews for other books by this author.

The Planet Dweller

Jane Palmer's first novel Is a real find -definitely a specimen of higher lunacy. The Planet Dweller appropriates all the furniture of TV sci-fi and duly stands it on its head, with a wonderfully pragmatic absurdity - that's been done before, of course (Terry Pratchett, Douglas Adams), but not quite this way.

Mary Gentle *Interzone*

A hilarious story in which the Earth is threatened by the deadliest life-form in the universe: the Mott. Diana, a menopausal mother, and Yuri, a practised drunk, are the two humans destined to fight them

SFF Books

Palmer has more in common with Muriel Spark than Marge Piercy. Her alien invasion of Earth takes place among the kind of people who cause havoc at the supermarket checkout.

Jane Solanas *Time Out*

Jane Palmer's novel, The Planet Dweller quite unashamedly a good sci-fi adventure,

Liz Adams *Chartist*

The Planet Dweller is a much more traditionally sf novel, and also funny in a Tom Sharpe/Douglas Adams sort of way:

Paperback *Inferno*

Jane Palmer's first novel The Planet Dweller comically (and Britishly) juxtaposes menopausal female reality with a farcical chauvinist SF subplot about the Molt and their plan to rule the galaxy.

Guardian

The Planet Dweller has more in common with Dr Who . . . including a sense of humour.

David Sexton *Sunday Times*

Jane Palmer spins a confused but amusing tale of
earth menaced by extragalactic baddies. Her heroine,
Diana, a menopausal housewife and administrator of
an architectural museum, is original, sympatico and
fun.

Sunday Times Supplement

The Drune

As in her 1985 debut novel The Planet Dweller, Jane
Palmer likes to confront wildly eccentric but plausible
humans with alien weirdness, producing offbeat SF
comedy containing the occasional serious barb ...
Palmer's narrative bubbles with frivolous inventiveness
and unhinged dialogue, and has a gentle sting in the
tail.

David Langford Amazon.co.uk

Palmer has some points to make about humans,
civilization, and civility. The fact that she works them in
to a wild, through-the-looking-glass adventure eases
the lessons into the most resistant brain, with little or
no pain.

Lisa DuMond SFF Site

Jane Palmer's fabulous and complex universe is
pleasantly refreshing ... [this] lively, bubbling and
buzzing universe is a gentle call for a more
harmonious, tolerant and generous society.

Martha Fumagalli WiPlash

And the story itself is the most remarkable blend of sci-
fi, fantasy, the self-defeating effects of bigotry, power,
control, love, self-sacrifice - and the ending is simply
perfect.

Joules Taylor WordWrights

NIGHTINGALE

by

Jane Palmer

DODO BOOKS

First published in Great Britain
by Dodo Books 2008

ISBN 978-1-906442-09-5

Other science fiction books by this author

THE PLANET DWELLER
THE KYBION
MOVING MOOSEVAN
BABEL'S BASEMENT
HUNDER

Fiction

BALD WENDY

PRELUDE

'Four legs!' snorted Tino, the strong man, 'You never saw an alien, it was probably a goat.'

'I know what I saw.' Ponder reeled a little. At any other time they would have said it was a surfeit of home brew. Now the tent master was too ashen to be anything but cold sober. 'On the top of the downs - I thought it was coming after me. If I hadn't taken that tumble I wouldn't be here now.'

Bernice laughed and pulled some burrs from his jacket. 'What would it want with you? I've been married to you for fifteen years and still can't see the point.'

Despite his impressive bruises, Ponder knew it was useless trying to make the performers and crew take him seriously. 'All right, all right. If this is where you want me to pitch the tent, then I'll do it, but don't say I didn't warn you.'

Hector, the ringmaster, straightened his top hat and waved a batch of handouts under Ponder's nose. 'We're not moving on after delivering a ton of these things to the district. Out here, we'll have days before anyone comes asking to see our licence.'

Angela petted one of her rather plump performing dogs. 'Well, it's not as if we use wild animals.'

'Yeah,' grunted Tino. 'Those things are so well fed it's a wonder they can get through the hoop.'

'Alright!' Hector bellowed in his stentorian stage voice. 'No aggravation! There's too much to do. Get your compressor working, Ponder. We want the tent ready for an evening performance.'

'Trapeze as well?'

'Of course.'

'But Chas Tharby is still on the North Sea ferry,' Sandra reminded him. 'He won't be here before midnight. With a test pilot for a wife, you know what he thinks about beam ships.'

Tino was unable to comprehend how anyone capable of performing dangerous stunts high above the arena could be afraid of flying. 'As soon as his child's born, he said he was leaving the high wire to do a tumbling act.'

'Freelancers,' murmured the disconsolate Ponder. 'You can't rely on them.'

Hector twirled his waxed moustaches like a benevolent demon barber and placed a paternal hand on Sandra's shoulder. 'This is the night of your debut, my dear.'

The young acrobat should have been elated at her sudden promotion, but had just prepared a huge bowl of spaghetti and all her tights needed mending. Her digestion could easily recover from a mere tumbling act and ladders in the hosiery of an acrobat performing with the clowns were quite acceptable. In the harsh spotlight above the audience, sequins, straight seams and a pinched waist became obligatory. Sandra should have cursed Chas Tharby. The man was entitled to his idiosyncrasies, though. He had come to the rescue of many small circuses like theirs at the risk of losing his performer's licence. She hoped his child wouldn't become a test pilot like its mother. Wrong moves in that occupation tended to end up in permanent closure.

Under a leaden sky dotted with circling seagulls, the tent was pumped up to sit like an inviting raspberry blancmange on the rolling downs. It used to be bright pink and was easily picked out from the air by patrolling community police. Though happy to let the circus carry on, they were obliged to turn over all their surveillance footage to the National Security computers. It would have been difficult to pretend they had missed a brilliant pink tent sitting on the landscape like a boil on the backside of a slumbering hippo. If it weren't for government control of the entertainment channels, the population would have been happy to stay at home and watch television.

However, most people can only take so much brainwashing and mental pap. Circuses may have been mindless and lowbrow, but they were exciting. The authorities were suspicious of anything that was not soporific. Having reduced all the theatres to performing works of spectacle with the lowest common denominator which only a few could afford, there were no alternatives to small troupes like Hector's.

As Sandra, in tights borrowed from the knife thrower, somersaulted and span through her practise routine on the trapeze the clowns, dogs and trick cyclists went through their acts beneath the safety net with surprisingly few collisions. The opening night would yet again be snatched from the jaws of every performer's nightmare. Ponder felt mellow enough to put the sight of the monster on the top of the downs to the back of his mind. It wasn't an apparition any sober brain wanted to dwell on for too long anyway.

The audience began to trickle in with their toffee apples, popcorn, crisps, and bioplastic bottles of lemonade that collapsed when emptied; a precaution taken to prevent anything rolling under the feet of the clowns who could get very annoyed about taking unintended pratfalls. Only a dozen strong, plus four musicians, the company were an energetic team and always gave of their best, whatever the size of the audience.

One school had risked forfeiting their term's funding by hiring an airbeam ship to bring several classes that should have been studying social discipline. It was also necessary for Ponder to remove some seating to accommodate a retirement club who had streamed along the valley in their monofloats.

Surfeited on the smell of sawdust, acrobatic stunts that had been outlawed for years and dazzled by rhinestones and sequins, the audience roared for encores and clapped until their self-correcting watches forgot what time it was. Hector's troupe was riding on the crest of adulation that made all the hassle worth while. How could anyone in such a state of exhilaration have anticipated the hideous incident that would torment them for the rest of their lives?

It began with a sound.

Sandra was first to hear it as she took her bow from the trapeze. It was a high pitched whine which penetrated the top of the tent like a needle.

She dropped into the safety net.

The applause died away and everyone listened.

During the catastrophic plague years that decimated the human race and deluges that tried to wash the survivors away, many different warning sirens had been used. Some to remind people to wear their filter masks when a new pneumonic infection appeared, others to get to high ground before a flash flood. This sound was like none of them. Having lived with alarms for so long, it could not be ignored. The floods had now settled at their optimum level and the plagues that couldn't be treated run their course. After so much trauma, everyone expected a new horror to present itself at any moment.

Tino put down the four acrobats he was supporting and darted out of the audience entrance. Ponder and Hector followed him.

A globe of brilliant ultraviolet illuminated the brow of the hill. Ponder dashed off to arrange some light while Tino and Hector bounded up the slope in the thin moonlight.

A stream of people from the tent followed, their way lit by the floodlight Ponder had redirected.

Seconds later, the air was filled with screams.

* * *

The only warning the circus troupe had of Nightingale's approach, was when one of Angela's dogs heard the faint purr of her powerful Amethyst. Bernice, who was on lookout, was first to see the sleek

4

body of the gleaming car as it wound its way down the narrow road like a magenta serpent.

Hector couldn't guess how the strange woman had found his troupe furtively huddled in the old Dutch barn due for demolition. The local community leader had promised to give them time to get away before they were obliged to call in the authorities; time to roll up the tent, pack the equipment onto their antiquated trailer, and recharge the gas cylinders that powered the circus from one secret location to another.

The visitor was no normal woman. Nightingale was long, lean, lantern jawed, and looked too scary to put in a sideshow. She may have appeared as dangerous as an old tiger act but at least she hadn't brought a security team with her. Not only was Nightingale as long as an anaconda, she was a very strange colour for a human. That was not the troupe's immediate concern.

They watched apprehensively as she pulled out an identification card. Billy Bloggs, the clown and one-time master forger, examined it. Satisfied, he handed it back to Nightingale. Only then did they relax.

Hector played with the rim of the top hat that he had been carrying around like a security blanket ever since it had happened. 'What is Group Indigo then?'

Nightingale slumped onto some bales of straw. 'We investigate unexplained phenomena. I understand you have one for us?'

Bernice was suspicious. 'Who told you?'

'I have contacts.'

'Security contacts?'

'Not if I can help it. I have to be careful.'

'Why?'

'World Government set up Group Indigo to investigate these occurrences. Security would soon become interested if they thought anything threatened the planet.'

'For pity's sake!' blurted out Ponder. 'That bloody

creature snatched Tino!'

'He was your strong man?'

'We always thought so.' Ponder calmed down. 'I saw the thing earlier in the day, but no one would have it. I thought it wanted to snatch me.'

Nightingale stretched her long legs and the black zipped body suit faintly creaked. 'What did this creature look like?'

'Horrible. Large glowing eyes like a fly's and four legs! Four legs! I ask you, what creature needs four legs?'

'What happened?'

Hector stopped toying with his hat. 'He dissolved. Tino rushed towards the thing - I don't know what he thought he was going to do. And just as he reached this odd violet glow, he ... dissolved. Not like fading from view. He fell apart!' The ringmaster took a deep breath. 'Each particle - he was a big man - floated away. It was like an explosion in slow motion. Horrible it was! Never seen anything like it before, and I've seen a few things in this business I can tell you.' He looked Nightingale in the eye. 'Will we ever see him again?'

Nightingale paused. Despite her natural brevity, there was no point in being brutal. 'I'm sorry. We've had reports of this happening before, and there is no record of anyone ever being retrieved.'

'What was it, for pity's sake?' asked a trick cyclist.

'As yet, we have no idea,' she lied. 'Whatever you do, keep well away from the creature if you see it again and leave a message on this machine.' She handed Hector a card with a number, then rose.

'But?' protested Sandra. 'What about us?'

Circuses were a world away from Nightingale's priorities. 'What about you?'

'We're bound to be taken off the road,' complained the trapeze artist. 'They're not going to let this pass when they find out Tino's missing. I know the way they work.'

'Just as well Chas Tharby never turned up after all,' muttered Ponder.

'Shut up!' hissed Bernice.

Nightingale half heard him. 'Chas Tharby?'

'He wasn't here,' Hector quickly said.

She already knew the name. 'Wife's a test pilot.' Dangerous machines she could understand. 'Proto-aviation reckon it was bloody inconvenient of her getting pregnant like that.'

Nightingale reached into an inside pocket of her ankle length black coat and pulled out a small coder. After tapping in a few words, it printed a strip of plasticized card. She stamped the corner of it with an authorisation insignia on a small pendant hanging from her collar zip and then handed it to Hector. 'This will give you clearance for as long as you want, but get a few social awareness discs for the intervals. No need to show them. It'll just look better if you're searched.'

Sandra was exasperated. 'So what was the thing that snatched Tino? We've got to have something to tell his mother. The last rise in sea level washed away the family home in the Med. She's an old woman. She won't be able to cope.'

Nightingale handed her a very low-tech writing pad. 'Jot her contact code on here.'

The acrobat was apprehensive. 'Why?'

'Because it'll save me having to access her address from World Government files.'

'Why don't you?'

The tall woman shrugged almost girlishly. 'They tend to be suspicious of anything I do.'

Sandra's common sense tended to agree with them, though her instincts trusted the woman. If authority kept a cautious eye on Nightingale, she must have been a kindred spirit.

Sandra jotted down the contact code of Tino's mother.

Nightingale took the pad back without a word.

The company silently watched as she sped away in her Amethyst.

Hector carefully tucked the plasticized card in his wallet, then took a map from his briefcase. 'Well, about time we were back on the road again.'

CHAPTER 1

Ben watched in sour disapproval as thousands of bees swarmed in the branches of his favourite apple tree. It had the sweetest fruit and lowest branches. His father forbade him to climb trees. The eight-year-old was expected to keep wicket when the village's most ferocious spinners bowled, though was not allowed to chase butterflies through the nettles or explore anything more than a metre from the ground. Those activities were immature, even if the resulting injuries were less severe than being struck by a lump of wood and leather travelling at thirty miles an hour.

The bees belonged to Mr Humphreys. More swarms were busy in the stand of orange blossom which had sent perfume wafting into his bedroom as the sun rose that morning.

Out of sight of the French windows, Ben skipped with all the immaturity he could muster through the orchard to call over the hedge to the old beekeeper. Something attracted his attention before he reached it. A bonfire? There was a still smouldering pile of ashes in a depression near the compost heap. The gardener never burnt anything there. She claimed it frightened off the beasts making all that wonderful compost. Ben hadn't seen Bertha for several days. He would certainly have compelled the gardener into conversation if he had, even though she usually ended up telling him that such a wise head should be on wider shoulders because it was bound to be knocked off sooner or later.

The eight-year-old carefully poked the ashes to see what felony had been committed. As he was also forbidden to play with other children, his imagination was not yet prepared to accept the mundane. How was he to know that the remains of every bonfire didn't necessarily conceal a crime? It seemed that the culprit had incinerated all the evidence.

Then a sparkling jewel bounced off the end of his stick. Ben snatched up the hot glittering bauble - and quickly dropped it. He flicked his find away from the embers and waited until it had cooled.

Even when it was no longer hot, it tingled the tips of his fingers. Then Ben remembered where he had seen it before. When his mother had last visited, she had been wearing a pendant exactly like it. She had taken it off and placed it in the secret compartment at the back of her dressing table drawer with a bundle of letters.

The pendant was with a fine chain, which he rubbed clean with some dock leaves. The catch still worked, so he threaded the pendant onto the chain and spun it in the sunlight to watch the jewel's iridescence. It refracted the colours in a strange way, not like the cut crystal in the cabinet that Ben shone his torch through. Each facet of his mother's jewel had minute squiggles engraved on it, as though a millipede had been using it as an ice rink and lost control of its skates.

The eight-year-old was subject to spot checks and told to empty his pockets at the most unlikely moments. Where could keep the pendant? Being a scrupulously honest child, he would naturally ask his mother if she wanted it back. Until then, he decided to put the chain round his neck and tuck it under his shirt.

By the time he had finished exploring the rest of the orchard for more treasures, Ben had forgotten he was wearing the jewel and didn't rediscover it until he was changing into his pyjamas, so he kept it on as an act of defiance.

The light slowly seeped from the chintz curtains. Eventually, the eight-year-old's fear of the dark could no longer keep him awake. Thinking up some dastardly prank he would never dare commit was a better aid to sleep than counting the sheep on his farmyard wallpaper. Fancy giving him a room with walls covered in cattle! Everyone knew he was terrified of anything that had horns or so much as bleated.

But weirder night companions appeared over the horizon of his slumber.

These creatures were not much taller than Ben and whispered amongst themselves in an alien language. Despite his father's efforts to drill any niceties out of him, he was an innately polite little boy and stood watching from a proper distance until they noticed him.

Because it was only a dream, he wasn't too worried about whose tea party he might have gate crashed, though he hoped that the spherical room they were floating about in wasn't surrounded by a herd of cattle. After all, the four creatures did have the same number of legs as a cow. Fortunately, there the difference ended. Their movements were far too deft to belong to something as clumsy as a cow. They were more like the centaurs in his "Stories of Ancient Greece". They had small pointed feet that resembled hooves in dainty cream boots and feathery heads that were an orangish gold. The same shade in the pattern of the front room carpet - in the spot where he had spilt the paint that Agatha had spent an hour trying to clean off.

It was odd to see the floating creatures tip toe about in mid air as though on some invisible floor. They might have turned off the gravity to assemble the machine they were working on because its components were so delicate. They made strange noises, but their eyes were even more puzzling. Three pairs of multi faceted discs that occasionally blinked were lined up above their mouths. Ben was surprised that with so many eyes, they never realised he was there. They were too intent on their task. With alien nimbleness, they passed the components of the machine to each other. After holding each item up to the six winking discs, it was replaced in the machine.

The creatures only become aware of Ben's presence when they stopped working.

The smallest of them lost its footing on the invisible floor and tipped over in surprise. The others reached for the tops of their heads and pulled off their three sets of eyes.

Then Ben tipped over.

Once upright, he reached out to try and pull off the smaller creature's mask, but his hand refused to make contact. However hard he tried, he couldn't grasp it.

Now he could see their real faces, it was obvious that they were laughing at him. Although very weird, he was able to make sense of them. Apart from the feathery hair sprouting eccentrically from the top of their heads, they had no ears, two huge faceted globes for eyes and tiny noses that looked as though they had been glued on as an afterthought to keep the eyes and mouth apart.

One of the creatures flicked a switch. The machine lit up and Ben heard a voice say, 'We have caught a fish.'

The eight-year-old was indignant. 'I'm not a fish.'

'Whatever you are, little minnow, your molecules are very uncertain of themselves.'

'What are molecules?'

'They are what this machine assembles.'

'Did it make you?'

'It is a very bright little minnow,' said the smallest creature.

'Shall we throw it back,' said the tallest.

'Oh no. It cannot do any harm. It would wake too suddenly and fall out of bed, wouldn't you, little minnow?'

'I'm a boy.'

One of the larger creatures interrupted. 'Do not listen to these jokers. What is your name?'

'Ben.'

'I am Tamble. The short one is Hysle, the tall one is Dey and the serious one is Datch.'

'But ... What are you?'

'What do you mean?'

'Boys or girls?'

'Oh. The small one, Hysle, is a boy, the rest of us are girls.'

'But that's not right. He should be taller than you.'

'We are big girls.'

'Oh.'

'The boys here are always smaller, little minnow,' added Hysle. 'There is no point in us being large as well.'

'Why not?'

'Then we would be expected to do all the work.'

'But my mother and Agatha do far more work than father, and he's taller than both of them.'

'Put together?'

'How could anyone be put together?' scoffed Ben.

'Oh, we do it all the time.' Hysle patted the machine.

'With that thing?' Ben took a closer look. Now he thought about it, the apparatus seemed more organic, like a complex colony of fungi, coil upon coil pulsating with a muted glow.

'Of course,' Hysle went on, 'we have to use a big box to keep the molecules from floating off.'

'Can you change things into something else? Like a bird into a bat?'

'It is possible.'

'Shut-up!' a voice in the background snapped.

Ben paid no attention. He thought hard as though confronting a genie willing to only give one wish. 'Can you change me into a ... a seagull?'

'What do you want to be a bird for?'

'So I can fly away from home.'

Hysle considered the suggestion. 'No, you would need a similar number of molecules. They can only be compressed so much.'

'You mean, you can't pour a pint into a quart pot?' Ben wasn't sure what a pint and quart were. One of his father's cricket team was always using that expression, and many others he only half understood.

The alien hesitated. He obviously had little idea what it meant as well. 'Why would I want to do that? I know I could not turn you into a rabbit - five rather plump rabbits perhaps.'

'Shut-up, Hysle!' scolded Tamble. 'Stop teasing the child.'

'Well, I am only a bad dream he will not remember.'

'I am not so sure. Do you understand what has happened to you, Ben?'

'I think I fell asleep.'

'Did you find a pretty bauble?'

'Why yes. How did you know?' Ben pulled it from his pyjama top. The aliens gazed at the iridescent jewel as though holding back their terror. 'It belongs to my mother.'

There was a desperate edge to Tamble's tone. 'Well, return it to her as soon as you can and say nothing about it to anyone else.'

'Why not?'

'Questions, questions - the child is full of questions,' complained Dey. 'That is your fault for encouraging him, Hysle.'

'It is part of their growing process,' Datch explained. 'They have to struggle for every scrap of information they absorb, not take it for granted as we do.'

Hysle laughed. 'He is cute, though. Can we keep him?'

'Do not be absurd. He would be unable to understand anything useful to us.'

'He managed to operate that "pretty bauble".'

'Why can't I stay?' asked Ben.

'We do not want you to be upset.'

'Upset? Why should I be upset?'

Datch hesitated. 'There are things here you can never comprehend.'

'But I like it here, even though you are so strange.'

Dey sneered. 'Perceptive as well.'

'And I don't know where my mother is anyway, so I can't give her the pendant. My father will probably find it and put it back on the bonfire.'

Hysle was puzzled. 'Why?'

'He doesn't like Mummy very much. I don't know why.'

'He sounds quite a shark.'

'And he parts his hair in the middle.'

'How did you end up in the same pond, little minnow?'

'I don't know.'

'It is important you return the pendant, Ben.'

'But I don't know where she is.'

'We will tell you.'

'No,' cautioned Datch. 'He is too young to wander about unaccompanied.'

'It is only a short distance.'

'I do not like it. They can face dangers we are unable to comprehend.'

Despite everything, Ben was an innately helpful child. 'Oh, I'll do it.'

'You could remember us when you wake,' Tamble warned. 'You may not be frightened by our appearance now ...'

'Oh I won't be, I promise. I want to see Mummy.'

Tamble adjusted the machine, and the creatures discussed something in their own strange language. As he listened, the eight-year-old fancied that he could make sense of the odd word.

Eventually Tamble asked, 'Do you know Bellwood Farm, Ben?'

'Yes, we often take our Sunday walk in that direction. One of the cricket team owns a real pub near there.'

Tamble indicated a map projected onto the far wall. The child recognised it. 'Just a little way down the farm lane is another road. It is quite narrow and not signposted.'

'Oh yes, that leads to the hayricks.'

'If you follow it past the hayricks you will come to some locked gates. On the other side of them is another road.'

'I didn't know that.'

'If you turn right and follow the road for twenty minutes you will come to a high wall. This is the place where your mother works.'

Ben was silent for a moment. 'But I thought she was a long way away?'

'Not even your father knows this. You must promise not to tell anyone else.'

'I promise.'

'He is far too young to walk that distance by himself,' said Dey.

Tamble disagreed. 'Given how honest he is, he needs to be tough.'

'His father might punish him.'

'Oh, he's going to Scotland and Agatha won't be back from her sister's until tomorrow morning,' Ben explained.

'He leaves you on your own, little minnow?'

'Quite often.'

'Yes, he is a tough little fish,' agreed Dey. 'Perhaps we should keep him.'

'How do I get over the wall?'

'There are several breaks in it,' explained Tamble. 'You should not have any trouble finding the large house. There is no need to knock the door. A voice will ask why you are there. You must say that you want to speak to Nightingale.'

Dey gave a hard laugh. 'Oh that will please her.'

'She will be even angrier if that transmitter key is not returned.'

'Who is she?' asked Ben.

'The Senior Controller.'

'Is she in the army?'

Tamble laughed. 'Oh no. She does not care much for soldiers. You will be quite safe as long as you do what I tell you. When you have returned the pendant, you will forget everything and never dream of us again.'

'There, little minnow, we cannot keep you after all,' Hysle sighed.

'All right,' Ben yawned. 'All right ...'

Ben rolled over and saw the early morning sunlight glowing through the curtains. The scent of orange blossom wafted into the room and the bees busily buzzed. He lay thinking for some while, and then his hand automatically reached up to grasp the pendant. He quickly took it off and reached over the side of the bed to tuck it under the rug. It was only five o'clock. His father wouldn't be leaving until eight. But what if he finished his research and decided to come back early?

'Oh, who cares,' Ben thought to himself. 'I'll stay in the big house with Mummy and that woman called Nightingale-'

Suddenly Ben remembered the sinister night creatures. They hadn't been conjured up on his teaching screen - they had been real!

He leapt out of bed. Had he really been talking to them with the same familiarity he used on Mr Humphreys' dog? It must have happened. The child was too young to deceive himself that it had only been a dream. The aliens had been so friendly. He could hardly dash out and return the pendant to the ashes of the fire.

Ben sat on his bed and thought. Should he risk the rage of an already wrathful father for their sake? The aliens insisted it was very important he returned the pendant. He picked up his well-worn teddy bear and hugged it. Now Ben was eight, he would soon be parted from the toy. He would need another friend.

CHAPTER 2

Jeff Devlin noted the thermometer reading then deftly confused the mercury with a flick of his wrist. There was no point in shaking the antique so brutally, but every movement he made had to have a cavalier flourish about it. After nine years of infatuation, Sally was just beginning to see her colleague for what he was.

Devlin had an eagle-like glamour and, when thwarted, his brow furrowed with a predator's cruelty. No one was sure why he had given up his smart Space Security uniform to join Group Indigo. Even Nightingale hadn't been told. As she was obliged to take at least one assistant selected by World Security, there was nothing she could do about it anyway.

The awareness of Jeff Devlin's true nature had come as a perverse relief to Sally and she no longer had any qualms about him standing hostage at the next encounter. If someone had to run the risk of having their molecules disassembled and reconstructed in a different dimension, Sally preferred them to be those of her self-obsessed lover. No alien was likely to be conned by his stunning good looks.

Jeff replaced the thermometer in its case and they once again paced the well-trodden grass to check the layout of the proposed location. Although the Lictana were the ones who controlled things, a little pointless preparation helped steady the nerves.

'How do you think they do it?' Sally asked.

Jeff stopped pacing to patronise. 'Well, they align their atomic structure with our dimension, don't they.'

'I didn't mean that.'

'We'll ask them the next time we meet.'

'Nightingale is the only one who understands.'

'Then she should be risking her atoms instead of ours.'

'You know what the regulations say about her

taking risks.'

Jeff laughed loudly. 'Given the way she looks, I bet she took quite a few.'

'Shut-up! You know she can lip read.' Sally darted a glance at the tall angular figure watching them.

'So what? Any woman who looks like that must be used to having comments made about her.'

A cuckoo made its presence known a short distance away.

'Damn, that bird scarer isn't working again,' cursed Sally.

'Leave it alone. It's only after crumpet.'

Sally was quiet for a moment, then suddenly snapped, 'You don't give a toss about what happens to poor little Ben, do you?'

Jeff was unfazed. 'Well, when the divorce comes through, your husband won't have any claim on him, will he?'

'Right. And nor will you!'

It took Jeff a few seconds to register what she had just said. 'What do you mean?'

Sally fastened her tunic belt. 'If I can't find him a decent father, he'll be better off without one.'

Jeff's disconcerted gaze fell on the golden buckle she had just pulled tight. He walked away without a word.

Sally pursued him, so he was compelled to turn and face her.

'You would like the aliens to carry me off, wouldn't you?' he accused.

Sally could now see that the tight frown she had always taken to be inscrutability was actually dangerous malice. 'It'd solve a lot of problems. You can't prove paternity without your body and, from what we already know, matter from each others dimensions breaks up pretty quickly.'

As well has the malevolent streak in Jeff Devlin's character, he was also full of clichés, bravado and bull. Sally wondered how he had managed to get into Group

Indigo as well as her bed. Even the military division responsible for World Security must have known what they were planting in the secret investigation group formed by World Government. Nightingale was very touchy about being compelled to take on anyone from a military division. Jeff must have looked very impressive in his blue and gold Space Security uniform. Nightingale, however, believed that it took more intelligence to be a civilian.

Though not much older than Sally, Nightingale had clocked up a record in energy research that awed other scientists with twice her experience. It was her success in fuel cell development that now maximised the advances in renewable energy. With a windmill and solar panels on their property, householders could store as much power as they needed and be independent of such monsters as the old fossil fuel suppliers. None of them knew that they had Nightingale to thank. Even the grateful World Government she had freed from one of its greatest problems, only reluctantly allowed her to pursue her new obsession. Chasing aliens.

The authorities assumed that her eccentric interest was a side effect of genius. Also, Nightingale was safer where they could keep an eye on her. No alien could be more dangerous than this scientist with a grudge. Nightingale was to be indulged until the next catastrophe when she would be needed again.

World Security had been aware for several years of interdimensional alien intrusions. They had been insignificant compared to the decimation of the human race by antibiotic resistant plagues and climate change. Nightingale would have been more useful researching weather control. When her credibility was eventually compromised by her pursuit of extraterrestrials, the scientist would have to return to the fold of conformity, and no one else was willing to risk their integrity to investigate reports of ghostly aliens and missing people. The military would prefer to lock away anyone who reported such encounters and bury the evidence in a restricted file, even though there could be no doubt that the Earth was in collision with a planet from another dimension.

No one else understood Nightingale's research, any more than they understood the disastrous fuel cell experiment that left her brown skin with a purplish patina which blocked out ultraviolet and scared small dogs.

As Nightingale was playing around with dimensionally volatile atoms, Group Indigo carried out their research in an HQ isolated at the centre of a large country estate. They had insisted she take Jeff Devlin as an assistant and Sally, because she would be near to her son, was the only molecular biologist willing to join the mad scientist. Nightingale eventually tired of her assistants bickering. 'That's enough you two. Inside.'

More used to obeying orders, Jeff turned without waiting for Sally. He marched up the steps into the large house. She followed on thoughtfully, oblivious of the impatient Nightingale waiting for her.

'What's the problem?'

Sally hesitated. 'You don't have any children, do you?'

'Wouldn't recognise one if I met it.'

'Seriously?'

'No. Given how much you worry about yours, it can hardly help anyone's peace of mind.'

'Just how safe is this encounter?'

'There's no reason not to trust them.' Nightingale always put on a taciturn front, but could tell someone needed reassurance. She stopped climbing the steps two at a time. 'What do you want me to do?'

'If something does go wrong, there's no one to look out for Ben. The mutated virus he inherited from his father may only make my son a carrier, like him. Then there is a chance it could attack his mind. No doctors I've consulted know enough about it. I don't want him to live with that. He must have proper treatment. My husband would just give him tranquillisers and tell him that it was all a figment of his imagination.'

Nightingale pondered for a few seconds. She didn't need to meet the child to understand his mother's problem. With a deceitful philanderer for a father and gullible flibbertigibbet for a mother, Ben needed all the help he could get. Nightingale had enough access to World Government database to destabilise nations. She might as well use it for something positive, and the luxury of being generous was seductive. Despite her ruthless persona, Nightingale never saw the point in doing harm if she couldn't do good.

'I'll see what I can do about it,' the Senior Controller announced. She strode inside.

Sally gave a sigh of relief. No down payment in any of the world's four currencies could equal the value of her superior's word.

When they caught up with him, Jeff was on the roof irritably pacing up and down by the photovoltaic panels as though trying to prevent the sunlight from reaching as many cells as he could. A light deep in the cellars may have flickered, though little else made note of his annoyance. He sensed that the two women were talking about him or, even worse, perhaps they weren't. By the look of relief on Sally's face and the enigmatic expression Nightingale perpetually wore, he was unable to confirm or dismiss his worse suspicions. He had always believed Sally to be the best catch of his many affairs. Now her ardour had cooled, he could only see a cunning woman trying to outmanoeuvre him at every turn. Nightingale, her long, dour face framed by mass of tightly curled hair, was just another unexploded bomb.

'Is the perimeter secure?' she demanded.

Jeff looked through some binoculars, then at the

small screen that mapped out the grounds. 'Few rabbits. No breaks in the current made by anything larger than that.'

'Good. Get Perry to reset the current and put down the flags.'

'Not expecting an alien invasion are you?'

Nightingale gave Jeff a long hard look that unsettled even Sally. On the verge of hearing the detonator ticking, Jeff quickly made the call down to security.

Nightingale scanned the grounds with the binoculars.

'Is everything clear?' asked Sally.

'Too much wildlife.'

'Well, Conservation's done a marvellous job over the last fifty years.'

Nightingale slowly lowered the glasses. 'I hope this sudden bout of sarcasm from both of you is due to nerves and not a cluster of loose molecules somewhere? At this moment in time, every atom needs to be in the right place.' She sometimes wondered how safe Group Indigo's valuable equipment was in their hands. Sometimes it was like trusting a couple of marmosets at the wheel of her state-of-the-art Amethyst car.

Nightingale glanced at Sally's belt. 'Loosen that buckle, it's too tight. Not metal is it?'

'Resin.'

'And lose those earrings.'

'Resin and amber.'

Nightingale grunted. 'Can't understand what you need jewellery and tight clothes for?'

Nor did Sally, so she never replied.

Nightingale turned to Jeff. Although she counted on him to check out the wildlife, she trusted him with little else. 'When Perry's team have finished resetting the flags, tell him to mend the bird scarer and flush some of that fur out. We don't want anything interfering with the signal.'

'The aliens said it wouldn't make any difference to them.'

'I'm damned if the first creature to witness the success of an experiment this important is going to be a hedgehog. Do as I tell you!'

Jeff obeyed.

Sally sighed. 'I can't understand why they wouldn't allow the materialisation inside the house.'

Nightingale did. 'They still don't trust us. How are they to know we don't have some sort of containment portal to trap them?'

Sally paused. 'Do they really believe that the disappearance of my transmitter key is some sort of plot?'

'By the last message they sent through, they didn't seem unduly bothered by it.'

'I got the impression they already know.'

'What?' Nightingale was uneasy. Sally was an expert communicator. Though often irrationally sensitive, she had an agile mind able to use language comprehensible to the alien's translator. She wasn't likely to be mistaken over something like that.

Jeff waved the receiver of the roof's intercom. 'Perry wants to talk to you on this line, Controller.'

'What's wrong with his phone?'

'Doesn't have voice security.'

Nightingale swore at herself for restricting the number of secure lines to stop the staff bothering her.

She leaned precariously over the parapet to call five stories down. 'You'll have to wait!' then muttered under her breath, 'He'd want the end of the world announced in triplicate.' She turned to Sally and Jeff. 'Now we've established the whereabouts of the wildlife, you can go and check your kit.'

'We still don't know when they're coming through,' protested Jeff.

'As the aliens are the ones operating the portal, we'll have to wait around until they're ready. Not having any more "bowel problems", are you?'

Jeff flushed in anger and left the roof.

Sally giggled.

'And how is your problem caused by his "bowels"?' Nightingale asked.

'Heggarty's tablets worked. I haven't had a bout for five months now.'

'Might have more to do with you keeping away from the source.' Sally opened her mouth to protest. 'I wasn't being moralistic, just practical.'

'What else?' Sally had no idea that the rare virus Jeff had infected her with would prove fatal and Nightingale saw little point in enlightening her. 'You might be more inclined to watch your ex inamorato with a less infatuated eye.'

'Watch him?'

'Very closely.'

'I don't understand?'

'You don't need to.' Nightingale pulled on her driving gloves. 'Let me know as soon as they make contact. I won't go too far.' She then descended the fire escape to see the officious Perry and take her Amethyst for a brief spin.

CHAPTER 3

Ben carefully slipped past the hayricks without catching the attention of the farm equipment sensors. He darted towards the large five bar gate at the end of the manure-covered lane. After scraping the muck from his shoes, he climbed through the gate's bars and onto the road the other side.

The countryside was suddenly different, as though he had passed through an invisible curtain. To one side was a vast water meadow where the stunted remains of a town built on a flood plain had been undermined and allowed to crumble. Come autumn, they would be immersed yet again.

Ben had to go in the other direction, where the countryside undulated up and away from the river's clutches.

He strained his eyes to try and see the ubiquitous power generating windmills or solar sails that usually peppered the land. The child had often wondered whether such a plethora of the machines speeded up the rotation of the Earth or slowed it down. But here all the land's furniture was totally natural, bar a tiled road. He gingerly picked his way along it and the smell of manure gave way to the odd pocket of perfume wafted from foliage he was unable to identify.

Distracted by the wonder of what he had trespassed into, Ben didn't hear the purr of a car's engine behind him. Its sudden warble made the eight-year-old freeze to the spot in fright. As she stopped, the driver slowly removed her polarised glasses and looked at the small, fair interloper with more curiosity than annoyance. Ben gazed back at the angular mauvish-brown features of the woman with a huge shock of tightly curled hair. There was something fierce about her and she drove the sleekest vehicle he had ever set eyes on. The battery for the Amethyst must have had at least four charging units that needed a whole windmill's worth of power.

The woman's features creased into a tight smile and Ben discovered he could move after all. He scrambled up the buttercup-covered bank and the car sped off.

Ben reached a grassy verge that made his journey much safer. On either side, downland peppered with bright flowers rolled away like an ancient French tapestry. He half expected to find knights, damsels and dragons woven into the landscape and, sure enough, a huge unicorn had been carved into a distant chalk hillside. It must have been near the virtual fantasy park Agatha had promised to take him to. Ben was tempted to go there instead, but he only had one entertainment token and packet of biscuits in his pocket and, of course, was on a mission as bizarre as anything he was liable to find in a virtual reality cubicle.

The tiled road led to a long, high stone wall. What if that strange woman in the car was on the other side? What would he say if he met her? She was very intimidating, even though she hadn't tried to run him over.

Ben looked up at the stone blanketed in ivy. He was frightened. There must have been hungry wild animals on the other side.

He cautiously trudged through the weeds outside the perimeter. Even though he had braved a field of cows to reach here, things that no campaigning zoologist would be willing to pluck out of the grass by its whiskers and conserve must have lurked on the other side of that wall.

The eight-year-old was growing weary. He knew it wasn't possible to put off the mission any longer. Ben gingerly clambered up the ivy and into the estate beyond at the next section of crumbling stone.

It was like stepping into one of those ancient fairy stories from his grandmother's collection. Though the regular world Ben lived in was green and buzzing with life, it was also organised, cultivated and cared for. Here, he half expected the fearsome sprite and her sleek car to suddenly come charging out of the undergrowth at him. This was the unruly world he had been taught to fear in social awareness classes. "The disorganised is wasteful, the undisciplined dangerous and the imagination a wild beast." The child hadn't understood what it all meant of course, even though he was shown pictures. He was very good at organisation, though suspected that an undisciplined imagination would be the death of him.

'Oh well,' Ben sighed fatalistically, 'at least I can't be told off when I'm dead.' He jumped down into the mysterious wood.

He felt a tingling sensation as though something had registered his presence. Alarmed, Ben bounded for the cover of the bracken. As he ducked out of sight, a bright orange flag snapped up from nowhere. Realising that this meant discovery, the eight-year-old plunged deeper into the thicket.

By the time Ben stopped to look about he was lost and very scared. It was becoming difficult to remember the odd dream instructions, so he sat at the foot of a tree to organise his thoughts. He had run in a more or less straight line away from the wall that was probably circular. So, if the large house was in the centre of the grounds, all he needed to do was keep moving in the same direction. He was bound to reach it sooner or later.

Ben struck out through the bracken again. At times, the tall fronds totally obscured the eight-years-old's view and made him wish he had brought his pocket compass.

He heard the murmuring of voices. Ahead, a lattice of sunlight patterned a small arena of closely cropped grass. Spotlighted in the centre was a man wearing a magenta suit. He remained still for some while, listening to instructions coming from his lapel receiver.

Then he strode to where a machine sat on a pedestal. There was a similar device quite near to where Ben hid. The sight of it filled him with inexplicable terror.

Another figure, also wearing magenta, walked in from the other side of the clearing. She silently made her way to the machine near Ben then turned to face her companion.

The woman was his mother.

Ben nearly called out. She was obviously doing something very important, so he stopped himself.

His mother and her companion placed their hands on the alien looking machines and synchronously turned two keys. The devices began to thrum loudly. Ben covered his ears.

'Translator engaged,' a metallic voice droned over the din.

Eventually the sound stopped pounding Ben's eardrums. He carefully moved closer as a third figure started to take shape in a busy, ultraviolet cloud. The softer the thrumming grew, the more distinct the strange creature became.

It was standing quite near his mother.

The prickling terror of recognition combed Ben's scalp.

The alien had four legs. That bizarre feathery hair and large facetted eyes - it was one of the creatures he had met in his dream!

He now knew for sure that this errand was no flight of his own fancy. What sort of trick had these alien creatures played on him?

And what sort of trick were they playing on his mother?

The creature was now quite solid and moved from foot to foot to foot as Ben's mother held a conversation with it. Suddenly the child became tearful. The experience was overwhelming him, even though he could tell by the relaxed way his mother stood that she was quite enjoying the encounter. For fear of her hearing him cry, he silently pushed his way through the bracken and round to the other side of the clearing.

The man by the second machine was watching the meeting with a tense, twitching expression. Ben studied the intensely handsome face. The eight-year-old didn't like him. About the same age as his mother, the man had a cold look in his eyes. Having been sheltered from normal human contact, Ben could see into the depths of a depraved psyche which social conditioning would have blinded anyone else to. He also noticed something familiar about him. That was more terrifying than anything alien.

Ben shuddered and quickly returned his attention to what was happening.

The alien and his mother were enclosed in a large bubble that curved the ultraviolet light about them like a lens. Inside it, the air seemed to buzz as though fine sand was being whipped up by a vortex. She was treating the occasion with such nonchalance that they might have been discussing the new fuel cell she wanted for her car.

As though he had just been about to leap away from his post, the cold gaze of the man in the magenta suit suddenly fell on Ben. He was startled and hesitated. For a second the man was frozen in mid air. Then suddenly dissolved!

As that happened, there was silent explosion. Ben's mother and the alien were shattered to pieces. The bubble disappeared. Fragments of his mother and the alien lay strewn about the clearing.

Nothing moved.

Ben suddenly missed the bird song. He heard himself whimpering. That bloody mass of dismembered limbs must have appeared from nowhere. That had to be it.

The eight-year-old felt sick and couldn't stop trembling.

He was moving. He didn't know how and was

hardly aware of climbing back through the gap in the wall.

As Ben tumbled onto the road, he heard voices calling. They must have been on another planet - this one had become a blur.

As the eight-year-old ran, the tapestry landscape was transformed into a realm of dreams where he could escape the brutality of recollection.

He had to reach his room and hide under his duvet. Only there could he be safe -safe behind the bolted door of the new compartment in his mind. Anyone trying to drag him from it had to be fought off at all costs.

Ben was inexplicably calm by the time he reached his front door. He went to the kitchen and poured himself a glass of milk. Agatha had left him a meal, so he microwaved it and sat down on the living room sofa to eat. His father would have been furious if he knew.

The child slowly placed his knife and fork on his plate then realised that he had forgotten what his father looked like. It didn't matter.

Ben went to the picture window to stare at high nacreous clouds and dangerous dimensions buzzing outside his secure sanctuary.

CHAPTER 4

Perry pushed the orange flag back into its slot. The scanner's needle indicated that it had been activated by something heavier than a muntjac. Whatever it was, trespassing wildlife was nothing compared to the tall savage human he had to go back and report to.

The security chief ordered his team to methodically pace every metre of the estate. They only found body parts. The remains they had collected added up to one human and a rapidly dissolving alien with four legs. Jeff Devlin, or his remains, was probably further away than Perry's organised brain could imagine. Nightingale knew. If he was that cynical, Perry would have realised how pleased she was at the prospect of never having to see his glamorous good looks again. This was not a logical deduction for a uniformed mind like his to make. The explanation had to be spelt out for him in the secrecy of Nightingale's basement laboratory.

'He was a plant.'

Perry's jaw dropped. 'What makes you say that?'

'He couldn't have been anything else. When you see an urban rat, you can be sure the sewer isn't too far away.'

That made sense. Being an uncomplicated security man, Perry had easily comprehended Jeff Devlin's true nature. It was the machines, laser tools and circuits Nightingale was forever tinkering with he couldn't make sense of and he hardly dared look into the anteroom where she kept her biological samples. The place had that odd antiseptic smell of the cheap mortuaries that had once prepared the dead for quick cremation. Since the plagues, nobody would handle bodies without enough disinfectant to wipe out the region's cockroach population. For all Perry knew, Nightingale was creating a human species resistant to all the mutated viruses, germs, and bacteria that had devastated the immune systems of the old one. Given the massive range of technology the survivors had inherited, the Chief of Security supposed somebody ought to make use of it.

Perry was suddenly aware that Nightingale was waiting for a response. 'Plant?' He darted an uneasy glance over his shoulder to make sure none of the equipment was listening.

'World Security planted Jeff Devlin when Group Indigo was being formed.'

'How can you be so sure? World Security were the ones who set us up. They've access to everything we do, so why should they need a spy?'

Nightingale lounged back in her chair and swung her feet onto a bench. She had a far worse suspicion than the one that she was prepared to admit to Perry. It would endanger him and his family if she aired it. 'They are beginning to realise that these aliens could be dangerous and that they have invested the safety of this planet in Group Indigo. When World Government decided we should be a civilian organisation, World Security found it difficult to swallow.'

'Well that's the way it had to be. There are still plenty of regions who refuse to trust uniforms after the clampdowns. It's not as if this is some natural disaster or nuclear waste clearance that only the military can tackle. They would go crazy if they suspected that aliens had managed to penetrate our defences.'

'And now these aliens believe that Group Indigo blew up one of their agents, we probably do have something to panic about.'

The admission coming from someone as adamantine as Nightingale was enough to daunt Perry.

He took a short intake of breath. 'Can't we contact them again?'

'Devlin's key is damaged, Sally's is still missing, and mine was destroyed in the explosion.'

'Did you find out what happened to hers?'

'She thought her husband took it. He probably keeps it with the wax effigy of me stuck with antique hypodermics.'

'That bad is he?'

'Like Dracula with a toothache. He'll sink those fangs into her child if he isn't stopped.'

Perry looked worried. Nightingale was no child snatcher. She was more likely to put a silver bullet through the Dr. Harold's brain.

'Surely he won't make a fuss over parting with the boy?'

'The housekeeper reported him to Social Concern centres twice. You know what they're like where the medical profession is involved. Prosecuting a doctor doing research for a popular provincial government is like trying to slice a slug with a feather. No, I'll work something out.' When Nightingale told Sally that she would look out for her child, she didn't think it would involve adoption. Wriggling out of that commitment without breaking her word would take more working out than the blueprint for her revolutionary fuel cell. Dealing with people was more difficult than mathematics.

Perry always found her calculating expression disconcerting. There was the inevitable fallout to clear up afterwards. 'You will be careful, won't you boss?'

Nightingale looked up. 'Careful? I'm always careful.'

Perry resolved not to mention the word "doctor" for at least six months. With a little luck and her preoccupation with damage limitation after the disastrous alien encounter, premeditated murder might somehow slip the Senior Controller's mind.

'Have you any idea what caused this explosion?' he asked.

'No,' Nightingale lied. The only thing which puzzled her was why Devlin was willing to stand as surety, only to miscalculate the time of the detonation and not jump clear.

'It must have been someone who knew Sally well,' Perry went on. 'As far as we can tell from her injuries, she was carrying the explosive in her belt, probably disguised as a buckle.'

'Little present from an affectionate "friend".'

Perry had no idea what she was driving at. 'There's not much left of her torso, though ...'

'All right, all right. We'll have to think up a cover story for her husband. Something to do with radiation. That'll ensure he doesn't ask to inspect the remains.'

'Lead coffin?'

'Largest you can find. There must be plenty in government storage since they over anticipated the casualties from the last nuclear accident.'

'Thank God we're now driven by wind, waves and sunbeams.' Then Perry inwardly groaned as he remembered the car that had been crushed for being a serious pollution hazard.

'The worst thing a windmill can do is whine when it needs servicing, although too many neat sunbeams can give you a complexion like mine?'

Perry feigned ignorance. Some things Nightingale consistently lied about. 'Thought that was genes?'

'Playing with the wrong end of the spectrum. Luckily I was brown to begin with. The other two were white and turned cobalt violet.'

Against his better judgement, Perry believed her. 'How the hell-?'

'Never mind, Perry. We gave up that line of research when the ozone renewal plant in the Antarctic was put on stream and it became evident that we weren't going to lose the ozone layer after all.'

Perry shook his head. With her fuel cell research and the Natural Energy Grid she had helped to bring on line, she had enough qualifications to comment on the state of the planet. He had no intention of asking what there were. He knew he wouldn't like the answer.

'I'll see what the database can dig out in the way of lead coffins. What about the alien?' he asked.

'She's still breaking up. We've got her remains in a vacuum but the molecules won't be stable in our dimension for very long. By the time we get her companions to speak to us again, we'll be able to hand her back in an egg-cup.'

The grisly always brought out Perry's longing for the security a military uniform had given him. He had an overwhelming urge to salute Nightingale as he left, before remembering her reaction to any form of forelock tugging.

The Senior Controller paid no attention. She was deep in thought.

As soon as Perry had gone, she leapt up and flicked the cover from the machine that had transmitted Jeff Devlin to another dimension. She threw the lever on her console and thick lead screens slid into place, sealing the laboratory in an airtight shell.

With some difficulty, Nightingale wriggled the distorted crystal that had been Jeff Devlin's transmitter key into place.

She hardly expected anything to happen. The Lictana were the ones who controlled their encounters. It was somewhat optimistic to hope that they still wanted to talk.

There was no sound for some while, then an erratic whirring.

It rapidly built to a crescendo.

With controlled desperation, Nightingale tried to pull the key free. It had jammed tight.

Before she could take cover, an almighty "crack" lashed out from the machine and sent her sprawling. It was like colliding with the blade of a rotating windmill.

Feeling more like a stunned Don Quixote than Senior Controller, Nightingale tried to regain her senses. It was obvious by the machine's furious reaction that she had managed to raise something.

An alien voice activated the translator. 'Who is there?'

The scientist gave her temple a swift rap to make her name come. 'Nightingale.'

'What do you want?'

'To talk to Tamble.'

'Not possible.'

'Who is that?'

'Datch.'

Nightingale daren't hesitate in case the translator cut out. 'You know what happened?'

'No. We assume you do?'

'We're still trying to find out.'

'You are aware that we have your agent hostage?'

'Keep him. He probably planted the explosive on Sally.'

Datch sounded less mechanical. 'Why?'

'Someone in World Security obviously doesn't want Group Indigo to fraternise with aliens.'

'We understand that they set Group Indigo up for that purpose.'

'That's what I thought. Now it's apparent they're worried about us making too much progress.'

'That sounds like a problem even you cannot solve.'

Nightingale chuckled. 'Oh yes I will, even if it takes the next hundred years. This situation is too serious to trust to authority.'

'You realise that if your agent is to remain molecularly intact, we will have to keep him in suspension?'

'Spread him on toast if you want. It wouldn't bother me if his molecules did drift apart. There's nothing much left of your agent, I'm afraid.'

There was a brief silence.

Nightingale sensed the calculation in Datch's next question.

'Was the missing transmitter key returned to you?'

On hearing that, a chasm opened up in her carefully laid plans. Nightingale was plotting even before she found out what the Lictana were up to. How could the aliens know where the transmitter key was? As it wasn't molecularly stable in their dimension, they shouldn't even know that it was missing, unless... If Jeff Devlin didn't take it, there was another player in the field! Someone else without a name or identity recorded on her database. Nightingale's scars tingled in terror at the thought.

She tried not to sound alarmed. 'Should the key have been returned to me?'

'The incident probably interfered with our plan.'

'What plan?'

'I have said enough.'

Enough to worry the wits out of the Senior Controller. 'If there is another agent I know nothing about, you do realise what that means? Perry can keep his mouth shut. I can't speak for anyone else.'

'We control the link and will be prepared for further sabotage.'

'You seem sure that I'll never make it a two-way system?'

'That, Nightingale, will take you longer than a human life span.'

'So how many years will our planets remain interdimensionally linked? How many more alien sightings can we expect to hear about?'

'You sound as though you do not trust us?'

'People have disappeared.'

'Some other aliens nearer to home, perhaps.'

'Yes, I suppose there are bigger monsters than you walking the Earth. Before I do anything else, I have to pay one of them a visit.'

'Do not take our willingness to negotiate with you for granted,' warned Datch.

'We've never been any threat to you.'

'While our dimensions overlap, you will keep trying to cross into our world as easily as we can cross into yours.'

'Group Indigo are the only ones able to contact you and I protect the system like a basilisk with a platinum egg.'

'Is this another aspect of your perverted diet?'

Nightingale wasn't taken in. 'Don't try to kid me you don't understand irony after the amount of "research" you've done on humans.'

'We could learn more.'

'What for?'

'Our own security. What else.' Despite the translator, the threat in Datch's tone was unmistakable.

'I'm the only one you can make contact through. I'll decide how much you need to learn.'

There was a pause. Datch was conferring with someone else.

'You will have no choice but to come to an arrangement with us before long,' the Lictanan eventually announced.

'Don't try and blackmail me with Jeff Devlin.'

'Nothing could be further from our wicked alien minds. But we will keep him all the same.'

Nightingale was silent. Behind the creature's familiarity was a culture she couldn't visualise, though she knew that the Lictana were testing the resolve of the human species.

Then she remembered the missing transmitter key. Datch knew who had the device. Nightingale had to get to it first. She would sooner shake the truth out of Sally's husband than discover what "arrangement" Datch had in mind. Although the aliens had been cooperative so far, that could change if they had found a human able to operate the key.

CHAPTER 5

Although he was a physician, Colin Harold had never been able to fathom the chemical reactions that had conspired to give Nightingale her purplish brown complexion. He had only ever seen the woman once, and that was early in his marriage when he had arranged to meet Sally at a restaurant on one of London's park domes.

Dr. Harold had stowed his car half a kilometre beneath the green turf, next to one of the City's main arterial roads. He took the lift up to the pure food restaurant and saw his wife step from an alpha licensed vehicle. The Amethyst was being driven by Nightingale, of course.

It was hate at first sight.

Nightingale needed only one look at the man to confirm the suspicions she had about Sally's taste in the opposite sex. Dr. Harold immediately realised that the Senior Controller had been the one to try and talk his wife out of the marriage. Most people now thought that the concept was a decadent arrangement and the legal contract that catered for all combination of genders was quite adequate. Dr. Harold liked order in his life, though. Knowing his wife was involved in important secret work that she was not allowed to discuss with him only added to his resentment.

On that occasion, Nightingale had not stepped from her car to further daunt the doctor with her height and taciturn manner. Now, ten years later, Dr. Harold looked out of his study window and saw every inch of that towering purple affront to his ego. He had just arrived back from Scotland where, ostensibly, he had been doing research for a government report on the hazards of living in sealed air conditioned housing.

But Dr. Harold had gone out of his way to find other masters. Given his wife's important status, his ego demanded he approach World Security. He had gleaned enough from Sally to realise they were a massive bramble in Nightingale's secret garden. The doctor also craved that magic pass which would let him through doors bolted against the usual hoi polloi, and the sense of knowing that, although he may not have been on the right side, he was on the winning one. It was a comedown to learn that they were only interested in his wife.

When Colin Harold had learnt about Sally's death, he cut short his trip to Scotland, which was probably the excuse World Security used to keep him out of the way. They assumed he would ask too many awkward questions about why his wife was killed. With all the evidence safely salted away, her husband would have to take Nightingale's word for what had happened. She was unlikely to tell Dr. Harold that a World Security agent had blown up his wife while she had been in conversation with an alien.

They had badly miscalculated. Dr. Harold had been more annoyed by the early morning mists and several checks by conservation squads for the odd hitchhiking bear than distraught at losing his unfaithful partner.

The doctor knew why Nightingale had come and saw no reason why he should he part with Ben. Legally he was responsible for the boy, if not biologically. She would only have him fostered out to some comfortable family circle with enlightened attitudes and solar powered toothbrushes. That was certain to announce to the world that the physician's wife had cuckolded him. In fact, the world had too much on its mind to worry about his private life and probably forgotten what cuckold meant.

Dr Harold summoned Agatha and asked her to send Ben in. She told him that Ben wasn't well enough to come down so soon after his mother's death. The housekeeper was disconcerted by the child's remote behaviour as though he hadn't taken in what had happened. She would have called in a therapist to investigate Ben's dissociated state of mind, but the doctor refused to allow it. All Agatha could do was humour the eight-year-old.

She went to the stair cupboard where Ben was hiding and gave him a glass of orange juice and several biscuits then persuaded him to go to his room. As soon as he was out of sight, the housekeeper opened the front door to see what manner of creature was casting the weird silhouette on its stained glass.

Throwing a steepling shadow into the hall, over two metres of lean, mean, secret scientist peered down at the homely pink housekeeper.

With mutually amazed curiosity, Nightingale noted Agatha's apron and rolled down socks. Given the advances in domestic technology, it had never occurred to the Senior Controller that people were still employed to do housework. When Sally had mentioned what a blessing Agatha was, Nightingale assumed she had been referring to some domestic appliance.

There was even more to wonder at inside the house. Its interior had stopped evolving over a century ago. Instead of a positive ion counter and humidity dial, there was an antique barometer by an equally old-fashioned coat stand. Neither of the hall windows was triple glazed, though judging by the amount of stained glass, there was no lack of funds. Every door had a gap of at least a centimetre below it as well as being hinged instead of sliding. Dr. Harold might have had some exemption on grounds of preservation so Nightingale went on to count a dozen more transgressions she could have had him prosecuted for. It was hardly surprising that Sally had been trying to get authorisation to place Ben in a more civilised environment.

The Senior Controller stiffened. She felt a pang of guilt for insisting that Sally live at Group Indigo's HQ where no pets or children were allowed. Even watching Perry scream at the wildlife and his security team would have been less traumatic for the child than having to contend with an emotionally stunted guardian and illegal draughts.

Agatha dawdled off to see if Dr. Harold was ready to meet the visitor.

As Nightingale waited in the hall, she noticed a movement at the top of the stairs. Sitting there was a fair-haired child with a solemn expression and large blue eyes. His gaze was motionless. Unlike many eight-year-olds, who all tended to look the same to Nightingale, this was not an easily forgotten face. It was the same boy she had encountered on the road leading to Group Indigo's HQ.

The truth dawned like a supernova.

Immediately all the plans the Senior Controller had so methodically calculated to confound Dr. Harold and the Lictana started to unravel. The aliens knew where the transmitter key was. In all probability, so did Sally's son.

Still mentally reeling from the revelation, Nightingale was escorted with old-fashioned courtesy into Dr. Harold's presence. As he set eyes on the tall purple creature in the long black coat, both noted that their mutual dislike had not waned.

He hardly seemed overcome with grief, so she never bothered to offer her condolences over Sally's death.

Nightingale towered over the doctor like a Norway spruce, so he insisted she take a seat. She slumped into a wicker chair without moving her gaze from the sternly handsome face just beginning to be pinched by intolerance. Again she wondered why Sally had always set so much store by the way her men looked without bothering to analyse those embryo lines of meanness. Given her late assistant's intelligence, there must have been some deep-seated aberration learnt in babyhood that had not shown up in a personality scan.

Harold flicked a strand of black wavy hair from his

forehead. 'What can I do for you, Senior Controller?'

'I understand that our provincial government has commissioned you to undertake the research for a report of a delicate nature?'

He smiled smoothly. 'Yes, though there's nothing secret about it. Unlike projects some other people are engaged in.'

'It will ensure you are away from home a good deal.'

'Quite possibly.' So she didn't know about his connection with World Security. An idea started to form. 'Some intensive interviewing will be necessary. Very few subjects are local.'

Nightingale couldn't tell if he was lying. He would have sounded just as devious if he was telling the truth.

'Your wife was concerned that, if anything happened to her, Ben should be brought up in a family circle.'

'Yes, I know. After Ben has recovered from the shock I think the matter should be looked into.'

This was too easy. Something was wrong. Nightingale was unable to work out what. 'I have approached various agencies. You will naturally be consulted about the home he goes to. For the boy's sake, things should not be left too long.'

'I will contact you in a couple of weeks.'

The man could have got up to anything in that time. 'I'll contact you. How is the child?'

'Agatha tells me that he hasn't been able to take his mother's death in.'

'You prescribe for him yourself?'

Dr. Harold sensed that she was dangling a noose in the hope he would put his head into it. 'I've never treated any of my family. If his condition deteriorates I will take him to a colleague. He should be all right, though.' The doctor was obviously not going to acknowledge the condition that Ben had inherited from his true father.

Nightingale recalled Ben's motionless gaze and

wondered if the man really knew how serious the boy's condition was. 'A very active child, is he?'

'Not very. The furthest he ventures is to the far side of the orchard. Wouldn't go into the fields. He's terrified of cattle.'

'So he would never wander off by himself?'

'He wouldn't dare. Courage has never been one of his strong points.'

'I see.' Dr. Harold knew even less about his "son" than Nightingale had suspected. 'Oh, by the way, your wife was entrusted with a small transmission device. You may have seen her wearing it? It looked like a pendant.' By the expression Harold tried to suppress, it was obvious that he had assumed it to be a gift from a lover. 'We must have it back as soon as possible. I will naturally expect to hear from you as soon as you come across it. My ferrets are well trained, but tend to mess up any burrow they're let loose in.'

Her threat certainly had an electric effect on Dr. Harold. Unfortunately, it wasn't the one she had intended.

Nightingale rose. 'I'll contact you within the week. Can't leave you my number I'm afraid.'

'Of course not.'

The Senior Controller left without another word, grateful for a few days grace to work on a new scheme. Though she felt guilty about it, Sally's child had now assumed an importance that wasn't necessarily going to help his welfare.

Before Nightingale could step outside, Agatha caught her arm. 'When does the child go?'

'Within the fortnight I hope.'

'He agreed then?'

'Yes. Why shouldn't he?'

'He's up to something.'

'Why?'

'That's the sort of man he is.' Agatha rummaged in her apron pocket for a stub of pencil and shopping pad.

'Give me your number.'

'It's not possible to contact me.'

'Then give me a number I can leave a message with.'

'Why?'

'I know that man. You may just dislike him, but beneath that efficient exterior beats the heart of a medieval torturer.'

'Sounds eerily quaint.'

'Now his mother's dead, someone's got to look out for Ben. I thought you were going to do it.'

'You were listening at the door,' Nightingale accused.

'So what?' During her time, Agatha had stood up to bigger tyrants than Nightingale. The young now counted more than ever and she was determined to do what she could for Ben. The child was swimming with sharks without a flight reflex left in his brain.

Faced down by the scruffy, middle-aged woman with the pitted pink complexion, Nightingale relented. 'Ring X line 20ZA7. There's a tape you can leave a message on. It's checked every hour.'

Agatha scribbled the number down. Nightingale strode back to her Amethyst, which

purred off through the tidy patchwork countryside.

CHAPTER 6

Ben tried to get a closer look at the clucking creatures in the lollipop-shaped trees. There was a whirring in his ears and lights throbbed behind his eyes. He wanted to wake up but couldn't turn back now. There was something he had to know.

The child concentrated and found himself back in the spherical room with the Lictana.

'Why?'

'Why what, little minnow?' asked Hysle brightly.

'You said everything would be all right.'

'We did not know someone was going to sabotage the meeting.'

'What's sabotage?'

'The explosion. It killed one of our best communication agents.'

Ben was outraged. 'It killed my mother as well! You have to catch who did it!'

Hysle sighed. 'We would need help to do that.'

'I want whoever killed her punished! I'll help you.'

'Would you, little minnow?'

'Of course I will.'

'Perhaps you would,' humoured Tamble, 'but you are very young.'

'I don't want to grow any older. I don't like adults.'

'I am sure all human adults cannot be that bad, can they?'

'I don't know many others apart from Agatha and Bertha, and they're all right.'

'You live a very sheltered life, little minnow,' laughed Hysle. 'Would you like to know the Lictana better?'

'Lictana?'

'That is what we are called.'

Ben hesitated. Just because the four-legged aliens were very odd, it didn't mean they shouldn't have a name. Knowing it somehow helped him see them in a clearer light. Strangely balletic, the Lictana weren't half a human grafted onto the body of a horse and were as carefully designed as any creature he knew; they probably never had back trouble. It must have been difficult to make their four-legged overalls with so many fringes and pockets.

The eight-year-old was also little suspicious. 'You don't really know that much about us, do you?'

Datch was quick to mollify him. 'Not as much as we would like to.'

'Why do you want to know about us?'

'We are close neighbours.'

'How close?'

'Closer than most humans would dare guess.'

'As close as ... Jupiter?'

'Closer than that.'

'The moon?'

Dey decided to join the game. 'Even closer. From here we can count the welds on that new base being built on the moon.'

Ben gasped. 'I didn't know they were building a base there!'

'Right next to the one that decompressed suddenly and killed all its occupants. This new base has a double pressurised shell. The air in the outer one collects the sun's heat during the day and it is used to keep the hydroponics dome warm.'

Ben gave sour look. 'My father said that now there's a world government, we'll never know what's going on.'

Hysle laughed. 'You are an old-fashioned little thing, aren't you.'

'Very proper,' agreed Tamble.

'Would you like to stay the same age, Ben, yet know everything an adult does?' Datch suggested calculatingly.

He would have liked nothing more. However, he lived with a doctor whose patients died more frequently than on average. This made him a realist on the subject. 'It's not possible.'

'Oh, it is. Can you guess how old we are?'

How could Ben know what the signs of ageing in a Lictanan were? They might have grown even more legs for all he knew. 'No.'

'We are all over two hundred of your years and will probably live to twice that.'

'But I don't want to live to be four hundred; I just don't want to grow any older.'

'We could help you do that.'

Datch's serious manner didn't intimidate Ben. If anything, he trusted her because of it. 'Would you really?'

'We can teach you everything you want to know while you are asleep,' Hysle added.

Datch gave him a disapproving glance.

'Would it be a sort of swop for all the things I can tell you?'

The small Lictanan laughed. 'My goodness, you are a quick little minnow.'

'But I don't know that much.'

'Do not worry. We will tell you the sort of things we are interested in.'

His suspicions addressed, Ben felt more comfortable. Though he would never see his mother again, he had found some friends in a place nobody else could find. He knew there was no world closer to the Earth than the moon, and they would easily explain that when they were ready. He needed someone to depend on too much to worry about elementary astronomy. He felt so comfortable he started to fade.

The Lictana switched off their translators.

'Damn,' cursed Datch. 'What is he doing?'

Tamble turned on her and Hysle. 'What do you two think you are up to? How could an eight-year-old human know anything that would be useful to us?'

'Nightingale is in a corner. She might be prepared to take a gamble to maintain contact,' Datch explained.

'What sort of gamble?'

'The sort their World Security would kill her for if they found out.'

Hysle laughed. 'She does not seem to be the sort of human easily killed off.'

'Can't you take anything seriously?'

'Earth's small mammals, pond life, and children.'

'You may know more about those subjects than anyone else, but they will not be any use if Nightingale manages to build a portal and Earth's military finds out.'

Dey realised what Datch was driving at. 'If we use Ben as a spy, we will have something to blackmail Nightingale with. She is not to know whether he can tell us anything useful or not.'

'Neat,' agreed Tamble. 'How do we go about it?'

'We are going to be very nice to an eight-year-old human as soon as he comes back.'

* * *

Ben briefly woke to smell the orange blossom scent filling his bedroom. The rays of the rising sun shone through the chintz curtains. Someone was thumping about downstairs. It was too early for Agatha, so it had to be his father. The child pulled the duvet over his head and returned to the safety of that room in the back of his mind.

* * *

Ben glanced out at the puzzling Lictanan landscape. Nothing was the right colour or had shapes he was familiar with. He felt like a hamster escaping from the known world of its cage and quickly returned to the spherical room.

'Where did you go, little minnow?' asked Hysle.

'Nowhere. I just looked outside. That's all.'

The other Lictana froze in alarm.

They turned on Hysle.

He had forgotten to switch on his translator!

Datch was the first to say something, albeit under her breath. 'What an adept.' She just hoped that Ben hadn't overheard them plotting.

'Not many Earth's small fish would be capable of doing that,' agreed Tamble.

Hysle felt protective. 'He has just had an awful shock. How about frightening you out of your skin in the name of science.'

'Do not argue you two. He is important to us.' Datch scolded.

'Oh now we must keep you, little minnow.' Hysle was thrilled at the prospect.

Tamble took Datch aside. 'Do you think there is a chance we could stabilise his molecules?'

'He could never become solid.'

'He is able to communicate without the translator. That is more than we ever managed to do before disintegration set in.'

Hysle skipped about the sphere like a cartoon centaur. 'I want to see if he can move away from the transmission portal.'

Datch wasn't enthusiastic.

'Oh he will be all right. The worst thing he could do is wake up.'

'Oh yes, I would like to explore,' Ben joined in.

'I will go with them,' said Dey.

Datch was worried that her careful scheme could be scuppered by Hysle's ebullience. 'I am concerned about the effect on his mind. If he is fully conscious, it might be traumatic.'

'What could be more traumatic than seeing his mother killed?'

'All right. Do not take him past the perimeter.'

Ben had no idea why Datch was being so stern. In his excitement, he tried to grasp Hysle's hand. His fingers passed through it.

Hysle and Ben fell about laughing.

'Calm down you two,' Dey warned.

'Where shall we take him?'

Ben remembered an ancient book he had seen. 'Have you got a zoo?'

'A zoo?'

'A home for different sorts of animals. The last one was closed down long before I was born.'

'What did you need zoos for?'

'Oh, that was when there were far more people. They took up all the space the animals used to live in. Putting the ones that were left in cages was the only way to keep them alive. Now there's much more space they could go home to the wild. Not many people get to see them, except on holiday. Daddy would never take me on holiday, and now that Mummy's ...' Ben sniffed. 'I've always wanted to see a zoo.'

Before the idea appealed to Hysle as well, Dey quickly suggested the next best thing. 'Let us show him the Spacers' canteen. There is always a weird bunch in there.'

'Spacers?' echoed Ben.

'Space travellers,' said Hysle.

Ben wasn't sure whether it was right to stare at other people, even if they weren't in cages. 'Space travellers?'

Dey couldn't comprehend Ben's limited existence. 'Lictan is a busy place. It is at the centre of what you would call a throbbing civilisation.'

'Why would any civilisation want to throb?'

'Oh come on, little minnow.' Hysle guided the eight-year-old outside.

Ben immediately found himself tumbling out of what looked like a huge toadstool.

Hysle flapped his arms mockingly in mid leap then landed daintily on a lift platform. 'He does not fly very well.'

Dey refused to see the joke. 'Not many minnows do.'

Ben tried to slow his fall by clutching at a wall of

leaves. 'Stop calling me a minnow!'

'Poor Omcrom,' laughed Hysle. 'Stop pulling its scales.'

Ben floated to the ground. He looked up to see that the leaves belonged to a massive creature with no interest whatsoever in his presence. It had a huge, doleful expression as though resigned to the fact that it would eke out its existence being mistaken for a hill of foliage.

Ben was amazed. 'What is it for?'

Hysle stepped from the lift platform and joined him. 'For?'

'What does it do?'

'Interrupts the view mainly. The Omcrom has a remarkable digestive tract that wastes nothing it eats. Consequently they can go on for ages, browsing the foliage about them, and not need to stand up for anything very much. They can make dents in the lawns when they move, but nobody really minds.'

'Now I know you've been telling fibs.'

'Why do you say that, Ben?' asked Dey.

'There's no creature like that on Earth and, if you're closer to us than the moon, then we must be somewhere on Earth.'

Hysle was perversely pleased that Ben was beginning the bite back. 'What impeccable logic, little minnow. What do you say to that, friend Dey?'

Ben had hoped to provoke them into telling the truth, but Dey evaded. 'He is too young to understand.'

The child was used to the response. 'That's what Daddy always says.'

Dey hoped the eight-year-old would find something else of interest. Ben was more disciplined than that and his expression demanded an answer.

'Oh very well, I will try to explain.'

'Go on? '

'How would you travel to Jupiter?'

'On a spaceship.'

'In what direction?'

'Towards Jupiter's orbit.'

'How would you travel to another star?'

'The same way I suppose, though it would take much longer.'

'Another galaxy?'

'Even longer. By the time we arrived, it might not even be there any more.'

'Oh very good,' chuckled Hysle.

Dey hesitated. 'How about another universe?'

Ben thought. 'I don't really know what another universe is.'

'He must be the only one willing to admit it,' Hysle murmured.

'Well, what is another universe?'

'We are in another universe, Ben,' explained Dey.

The child had some trouble with this. 'Like ghosts, you mean?'

'Not quite. If you went to another star, do you believe you would travel in a straight line?'

'I suppose so.'

'But you cannot travel in straight lines through space. You just think in straight lines.'

Ben was puzzled. 'So everything's really curved?'

'Everything. Now, imagine what is a solid to you as curving in one direction, and what you cannot feel, like us, curving in another. Two dimensions in collision where none of our atoms can touch. This is how our universes are overlapping.'

'How odd.' Ben would have to take this conundrum home and give it some thought. The auto teacher could probably explain it. 'Can we see the Spacers now, please?'

'Do you think they are ready to meet our little minnow?' asked Hysle.

Ben was irritated. 'Why does he have to keep calling me a minnow?'

'Humour him,' said Dey. 'In the selection tests for

our unit, he came first in your Northern Hemisphere's pond life. We only took him on because he makes us look so efficient.'

'Oh,' said Ben.

Ben was no longer interested in where Lictan was or why Hysle glowered at Dey. He darted enthusiastically ahead towards a spot of bright orange in a wall of shimmering stone. It was the oval entrance to a huge hall. Inside, the large sun's rays shone through a concave roof.

As they entered, Hysle caught sight of some frantic attendants clustered about an inflated spacesuit. 'Oh look, there been a decompression.'

Dey ushered Ben away from the sight. 'They never learn.'

'What's a decompression?'

'Usually fatal and always messy. We would rather you met people who at least had the wit to remember to check their life support suits before they disembark.'

'I thought only very intelligent people were allowed to be astronauts?'

Hysle laughed. 'Hardly, little minnow. Who, with any intelligence worth using, would want to spend at least half their life asleep and the other half talking to computers?'

'Our spaceships have only gone as far as Jupiter, and the crews didn't sleep all the way.'

Dey was impressed. 'These humans sound positively advanced at times.'

Hysle murmured. 'I only hope Nightingale does not manage to become as advanced us.'

'Shut up you fool!'

Ben only half heard. He was too busy looking at the visitors in the Spacers' canteen. Now used to the alien, they all seemed quite mundane - nothing green, slimy or bug-eyed about any of them. Inside their thermal and atmosphere suits, they appeared to be a friendly enough bunch.

Dey noticed his disappointment. 'Seems our charge can stand more stimulation.'

'Shall we ask the Omcrom if it is hungry?' Hysle teased.

'Oh, a minnow would get stuck in its throat.'

'No, no, that's a stickleback.'

Ben had a better idea. 'Why don't we ask it to eat one of you two instead?'

Hysle was delighted. 'I think I hear the murmurings of rebellion.'

In this safe, surreal world, the nightmare of his mother's death no longer troubled Ben. 'I think it's about time I woke up. If I'm not downstairs for breakfast before eight there's always trouble.'

'What does that monster make you eat? Gruel?'

'No,' snapped Ben. 'Pondweed!' and he woke with a start.

Dey and Hysle knew he would be back soon enough.

CHAPTER 7

Agatha dashed up the drive to meet the sleek Amethyst car.

Nightingale had been sending out a scout every evening for the past week to keep an eye on Dr. Harold, and the housekeeper's urgent call had not been expected.

Nothing about the house and grounds looked any more eccentric than when the Senior Controller had first called. Local officialdom had made a half-hearted attempt to serve an energy conservation notice. That had been left pinned to the gate in its clear plastic envelope for all the world and its goat to read - apparently it was the third attempt. The prosecution of doctors was fraught with difficulty. Nightingale assumed that the man had somehow escaped the obligatory social conditioning as a child that produces responsible, homogeneous citizens. She certainly had.

She strode over to Agatha who was flapping about in agitation.

As they reached the antique front door with its stained glass heat waster, Nightingale guessed the worst. She followed the housekeeper inside.

The bookshelves in Dr. Harold's study looked like so many rows of gappy teeth where he had hastily snatched his most essential volumes.

Very little else was missing. He obviously had a furnished home to move into. But where? Dr. Harold had plenty of time to make good his escape. Nightingale wished that there was still such a thing as an old fashioned passport. Under World Government, it had fallen into disuse, being regarded as an affront to a person's self esteem. Now, with far fewer people to keep tabs on, the individual was allowed freedom from carrying such demeaning documents and this, on the whole, encouraged better behaviour from a population being cosseted back from the edge of extinction. There was the fingerprint pass. All air and seaports insisted on them for casual travellers as identification in the event of accidents or anti social behaviour. Civilian ranks like lawyers and doctors were exempted. It was politely assumed that their agents would know their whereabouts. Unfortunately, Dr. Harold only answered to provincial government.

Nightingale lifted the receiver of the ancient phone on the desk and tapped out a complex code. Then, Nightingale. Request voiceprint pass. Her voice signature approved, she was connected to a department deep in the hive of government records. 'Check: - Harold, Colin; medical doctor. Should be registered under research.' Agatha could hear the clicking and bleeping of an electronic index file. 'Discharged.' Nightingale sighed. 'Fully paid up two weeks ago.'

'Well I never!' gasped Agatha.

'Damn!' Nightingale replaced the receiver.

'But he was researching something.'

'Probably how to evade minor agencies, like World Government.'

'Why didn't I realise he was going to take off like that?'

Nightingale was light years away from Agatha's self-recrimination. 'Perhaps he knew that his wife was going to meet with an "accident".'

The housekeeper registered the sarcasm in her tone. 'Accident?'

'You don't seriously believe it was a radiation leak, do you?'

'Well, that's what Dr. Harold was told?'

'The last nuclear reactor was buried in radiation proof silicon over ten years ago.'

Agatha had to give that some thought. 'So you think he had something to do with Sally's death?'

Nightingale shrugged.

'You can't be serious?'

'Wiring a miniaturised bomb does have some similarity with micro-surgery.'

'Well, that lets Dr. Harold out. He still uses the needle on his patients. You ask Bertha about her wart.'

Bertha's wart was the last thing on Nightingale's mind. 'You're probably right. Sally wouldn't have given him the chance to plant explosives on her.'

'Harold was an ill-natured sod, but he wouldn't take those sort of risks.'

'Have you been paid?' the Senior Controller suddenly asked.

'Oh yes. Left what he owed me, but no discharge bonus.'

As the doctor had flouted every other rule, he was bound to have ignored the caffeine regulations. 'Make me a cup of real coffee and I'll make sure you get it.'

Agatha padded out to the kitchen.

Nightingale returned to the phone and tapped in another number.

'Jock ... Yes, Nightingale ... I know I always mean trouble, but this is only a fraction of the favour you owe me ... "Who knows who" this time. Rack that gin soaked brain of yours. "Dr. Colin Harold".' There was a lengthy pause. 'Are you sure? ... That's right, antique in every objectionable sense of the word.' She gasped in amazement. 'Hecuba? That's World Security's number two code. If he's had access to that I'm not surprised he could vanish off the face of the Earth ... No Jock, that doesn't make me just the person to go and look for him. He must have a totally new identity by now ... Business? Not so good. Communication problems ... What new communications base on the moon? ... No, of course I didn't ... Four years ago ... Well, seems we're quits now. I'll have to see that the right applicants apply for some of the posts there ... What do you mean? Only one? It's not possible for just one person to crew a moon base. I'll believe that when it's announced, you old soak ... Cheers.' She replaced the receiver just as the housekeeper came back with a large mug of coffee.

'Didn't leave a note or anything with my money,' Agatha said. 'So he couldn't have gone for good.'

'Oh, he's gone for good. Neither of us will see Ben again.'

The pink flush left Agatha's pitted cheeks. 'But ... Goodness knows what will happen to that child.'

'It's worse than you think. Ben has inherited a clinical condition that could affect his mind without competent treatment.'

'Well he certainly won't get it from that quack.'

'And without knowing his whereabouts, there's no guarantee a community therapy unit will find him in time.'

'Oh dear,' sniffled Agatha. 'I knew I should have done something a long while ago.'

'If it'll make you feel any better, we could search the house for clues. I've no doubt an estate broker will walk in any minute and take possession.'

'Yes, there's a lot of Sally's stuff lying around.'

That was what Nightingale had in mind of course. It was her only hope of finding the missing transmitter key.

'I don't know what we should do with it though?' worried the housekeeper.

'I'll hold onto anything of value, just in case we eventually do find her son.'

Although Agatha was already reasonably familiar with the contents of most cupboards and drawers, Nightingale noticed her badly suppressed glee as she riffled through them as though they were a diamond merchant's lucky dip.

'Little Ben's,' she would say, putting an article of clothing or toy onto a neat pile, then, 'That's Sally's,' as she found some diaphanous item to put into another beside it. Agatha's grandparents had no doubt told her about the 21st century. Perhaps she was entitled to empathise with her late employer's decadent tastes.

The frills and jewellery her late assistant had hoarded over the years puzzled Nightingale. Some of the fabrics were made from ancient petroleum based synthetics which shimmered against her black coat.

By the time Sally's wardrobe lay strewn over the bed, Nightingale was craving her black zipped body suit made of fabric so dense it could block out infra red. She wondered if Group Indigo had been nursing some closet 20th century female. Sally hadn't displayed much tendency towards feminine exhibitionism when working. The condition was probably related to her disastrous tastes in men. She could hardly blame her for that, as one epidemic had made sure there were now so few of them.

Nightingale examined each piece of lace and embroidery with a forensic investigator's eye. There was no sign of the missing transmitter key amongst the trinkets and exotic fabrics.

Agatha packed everything of Ben's into a case. Nothing belonging to Dr. Harold interested Nightingale, though she did pick up several items in the hope of collecting traces of hair and skin for DNA mapping or a genuine clairvoyant.

She left Agatha to sort through the rest and wandered out of the back door.

A flurry of frogs dived into their pond and a diamond-eyed cat gazed from the roof of a small shed. Someone must have had a licence for it because there was a defiance in its manner not seen in feral cats liable to be shot as vermin.

The garden contained an inordinate amount of early lavender which, combined with the orange blossom, could have purged the emanations of a sewage recycling plant from the air.

Nightingale suspiciously eyed the odd pot of datura. She recalled that the shrub had been banned because everything about it, from scent to foliage, was toxic. They could have been forgiven mass poisoning for the beauty of their starched handkerchief flowers. The sunflowers were as impertinent as the cat, and tall enough to return her two metre high gaze.

Dr. Harold's garden was as decadent as his house. The blooms were like candles that refused to be extinguished by the coming of electricity. It contained no hybrid orchids, miniature Wollemi pines, or giant jasmine. Everything here had been grown from genetically unaltered seeds and cuttings with no help from plant plugs and their own self-contained ecosystems.

Nightingale wondered if she had spent too long in her basement of bizarre gadgets. She strode down some irregular steps crowded with stonecrop and briefly toured the orchard. After kicking the ashes of the bonfire and watching the bees swarm in the apple trees she had a short conversation with Mr Humphreys about his honey.

Nightingale had turned to go back to the house when someone called to her.

'So they've gone then, have they?'

A short, youngish woman was leaning against an apple tree, a pipe clenched in her yellow teeth. She wore a much muddied and washed duffle coat and knee-length boots two sizes too large.

'Got a note this morning with me pay. Mean, surly beggar that man was. Wanted me to nail back anything overgrowing the paths and kept a cat because he didn't like birds shitting on the solar panels of his car. Did the neighbourhood a favour in shooting his bolt he did.'

Nightingale was fazed for a moment, so the woman announced, 'Gardener I am. Bertha Mooney's the name. Admit it; you don't often come across a handle like that nowadays.'

The Senior Controller joined her under the tree. 'Bit

like Agatha.'

'Reckon that's why he took us on. To him it must have sounded biblical, that and us both being the most broke around here. Old Albert reckoned he was more broke than we were, but Aggie and me both had children so got more employment credits. Never forgiven us, Albert ain't. Reckons a womb ain't no reason why anyone should get job preference - not that Aggie's still got hers. Sour old critter he is.'

'I don't suppose you know where ..?'

'Where Harold's gone?' Bertha sucked her pipe into life. 'Not a clue. I wouldn't wish him on diseased camels. Dracula's got a better bedside manner. Claimed he could cure my wart, he did. Bloody agony I went through with those injections. So's I eventually cut the thing off meself. Didn't half bleed too.' Bertha could tell that her pipe intrigued Nightingale. 'Not much of this stuff around now, eh?'

'I thought the trade was banned?'

'Grow me own, don't I. Grow anything if you know how. Weeds can cure anything - or kill you.'

Nightingale was aware that her purplish complexion had come under scrutiny. 'It's not curable. Was on the wrong end of an experiment to screen out ultraviolet.'

'Bet you can screen out light on any wavelength now.'

'I'm vitamin D dependent.'

'Pity they patched up the ozone layer. Might have come in useful.'

'If we had pursued that line of research, everyone could have ended up this colour.'

'Well, don't suppose someone your height gets that many remarks made about them. Not that it would have bothered little Ben. Wits like drawn cutlasses, that lad. Could cut any adult down to size and read their entrails. Pity he won't be about any more.'

'How perceptive was he?'

'Never met sharper. Blade of grass out of place. Cat

chasing the frogs. Tendrils growing in the wrong direction. They all got sorted out. Tartar for order he was.'

'Pity I never knew him. Sounds like the sort of assistant I need.'

'He'll survive I suppose. I know Harold's a tyrant, but Ben'll be a match for him before long.'

'If he's still got a brain to cope,' the Senior Controller said under her breath.

Bertha clenched the pipe in her teeth and hummed. 'If you do find Ben, you will let old Bertha Mooney know?'

Nightingale hesitated. 'Why not? Might take a long while, though.'

'I just want to see the lad once more, however long it takes. I'll always be around.'

Nightingale gave a half nod and muttered to herself, 'Oh, so will I. So will I.'

Forty years of tinkering to correct climatic imbalance was at last bearing fruit. The still declining population was not large enough to repollute the environment so Weather Control had inherited some interesting toys to play with.

It was decided to keep the world at a warmer temperature and control the weather patterns. The larger equatorial regions and deserts were reforested by introducing inland seas to produce cloud cover. With little left of the ice caps, Antarctica was now a popular holiday resort.

The Northern Hemisphere had suffered the most from the antibiotic resistant plagues and the centre of world power had shifted. The descendants of once starving nations could now dictate where and when the next monsoon, or light shower, would fall. Where there had once been encroaching desert, fresh water seas produced rich alluvial mud for their robot farmers.

Repeated inundations and meltwater began to interfere with the saline balance of the North Atlantic Drift and the UK should have been plunged into an Arctic climate. Weather Control restored the balance so successfully, only Scotland experienced winter - and that was through choice. To accommodate the confused wildlife, reserves with tailor-made microclimates were set aside.

* * *

On many plants, at the crucial junction of a sap-supplying limb, there often appears a blister. No creature worth the name of parasite misses the opportunity to fasten into the nourishment supplied by growths that are too large to notice their presence. Especially large growths like world bureaucracy, top heavy with facts about everything from ants' kneecaps to the ice terraces of Europa.

Four decades had passed since Nightingale asked her last favour of the gin melancholy Jock. As the power of World Government grew, her occasional mole was replaced by the professional sifter - an intellectual anteater with a mental proboscis capable of reaching into everyone else's secrets.

After forty years of dealing with her, no bureaucracy dare retire Nightingale, even World Government's. This intimidating, purplish-brown steeple had evolved into a formidable tower of clandestine alien knowledge Babel would have been proud to own. She may have aged; she certainly hadn't withered. The steely glance had been perfected and the shutter that concealed any chink from an intimated world was virtually impenetrable. One or two other women, and a hyper sensitive secretary, had managed to peer through the chinks. What they saw, they kept to themselves. Nightingale preferred to hold just enough empathy on stand-by to wrong foot anyone who believed they understood her.

After so long perfecting her espionage resources, the Senior Controller now needed more than moles or anteaters. She replaced them with parasites.

Newly installed in their blister, Hazlewood and Nichols scanned the equipment left in immaculate condition by their predecessor, Arachne. They had been waiting years for this chance. Arachne had been honest, diligent, and steady, showing no inclination to illicitly use the secrets gleaned in that blister on the junction of World Government communications.

Hazlewood and Nichols were not so scrupulous. Unlike in appearance, the women had the reflexes of hyperactive ferrets. Trustworthiness may not have been stamped at the top of their CVs, but they were able to solve computer crosswords without an encyclopaedia.

Hazlewood was a large, square-faced woman. Her

hair was tufted, like a badly knotted carpet, and her eyebrows unsure which way to grow. She was obliged to occasionally push them up to prevent them being tangled with her ridiculously long eyelashes.

Nichols was sharper featured. She moved with a cutting motion as though demanding the air part before her. Her tone could skewer any opposition. Hazlewood's pocked complexion could well have proved it.

Their natural habitat was below ground and they had no time for social interaction.

In dowdy overalls, they could have been taken for subterranean maintenance as they worked to reinforce the walls of their blister with enough security traps to keep out free-lance sewer rats. Arachne had used hundreds of security access codes at the heart of the complex and they had to break every one before picking up a spanner.

By the time the pair returned to their control, Hazlewood had suspicions. 'Do you think Nightingale arranged everything just to confuse us?'

Nichols was too busy retuning the satellite dish to bother with such imponderables. 'I doubt it. Check our access to World Security files.'

Hazlewood tapped out several different codes and watched her monitor. 'We have got access.'

'Good.'

'What next?'

'We need to go for a walk.'

'A walk?'

'To check the dish.'

They ascended in their secret lift to one of London's green domes. The fresh air struck them like a surfer's dream wave.

'I could get used to this,' coughed Nichols.

Floods had submerged Central London. At first, the Fleet had relieved the rising water of the Thames, but not for long. London was a natural flood plain.

Barriers had to be built to hold the river back. This left a large area of London below sea level. Historic buildings worth preserving had been surrounded by cofferdams and the water pumped out. Those ubiquitous turfed domes continued to cover the remaining wreckage of the City long after the water had seeped away. As a consequence, many facilities became subterranean, much to the benefit of troglodytes and people like Nightingale's spies.

Nichols briefly held her scanner up to check the satellite dish. 'No problem there.'

Hazlewood gazed at the sky as though she could see the signal being transmitted to them. 'What were you expecting?'

'Not sure. Having come this far, we cannot take chances.'

'Do you really think Nightingale is monitoring us?'

'It would not surprise me. She might have held onto a few moles.'

'What does she think we are liable to get up to?'

'We are her eyes and ears. She is bound to be wary.' 'This planet has not evolved much over the last few years, has it?'

Nichols shrugged. 'Regressed if anything. I will never get used to this clean-minded indifference to everything.'

'We are so isolated down there we do not need to.'

The two women sauntered past the remains of a major accident that had happened earlier that week.

Hazlewood peered into the cavernous depths where the neighbouring landscaped dome had collapsed onto an office block. The building had been renovated after the floods and thought sound enough to store old records salvaged from the water.

'Looks as though someone's moles went berserk.'

'Probably molecular reversion.'

'Molecular reversion?'

'Rust.'

Casualties were still being brought out of the underground complex. The manner in which the corroded buttresses were being hauled away suggested that there were no plans to rebuild it. Another victory for The Natural Living Campaign. That small, dedicated band had spent decades arguing that, as traffic and industry were no longer pollution threats, there was no need to bury either and court such disasters. Pushing workers and commuters underground so hills could drop on them was no way to restore the population.

Those living on the equator had the right idea. Now climate controlled, more temperate and with unlimited solar power, they let their machines do the work while they went on airbeam ship cruises through the rainforests to watch wildlife. The only fun anyone seemed to have in the Northern Hemisphere was gratifying weird dietary cravings and watching the sentimental soaps regional governments made to reassure the population that they would never need to think for themselves again.

Nichols and Hazlewood dawdled on, comfortable in the knowledge that their complex was effectively reinforced.

'Does anyone realise that Nightingale is actually able to operate the other transmission portal at her HQ?' asked Hazlewood when they were out of earshot of the rescue workers.

'No,' Nichols said. 'Not even her chief assistant.'

'Good. Then the only other person who knew was Perry.'

'And he died fifteen years ago.'

'Nightingale has the uncanny knack of outliving everyone. I wonder how she manages it?'

'Grim determination, a good medic, and no rust.'

'When does she want us to set up the next contact with Lictan?'

'As soon as we have settled in.'

'Are you sure that she is the only one who knows about us?'

Nichols had her suspicions about Nightingale, but she was predictable. 'She has no reason to trust assistants.'

'Those agents were killed over forty years ago?'

'And it has taken her much of that time to make up lost ground. If Jeff Devlin planted that explosive for World Security, she is unlikely to trust anyone close to her again.'

'I still do not understand why they did it?'

'Might have been to warn off the wicked aliens. Why bother to negotiate when you can blow them up.'

'Not a very subtle way of managing the planet's affairs. Even Nightingale has a lighter touch than that.'

'World Security were scared. If they found out what she was doing now, they would be terrified.'

After touring a couple of reconstructed churches, Nichols and Hazlewood returned to their subterranean complex. This time they entered through the tunnels where the apparatus tapping the communication lines of World Government was installed.

The planet was no longer bombarded by signals from satellites because plenty of radio bands were available: they were easily intercepted, so allocated mainly to astronomers. Digital connections fanned out from their meridian to the network that linked World Security control points about the globe. Flame, flood and impact proof, the engineers had not taken into account Nightingale.

The discovery of aliens so many decades ago had concentrated authority's mind wonderfully. They still didn't trust Group Indigo, but there was no one else with the expertise to deal with it. Nightingale should have told the agency that renovated old radio telescopes to scan the stars that they were looking in the wrong place, only then she would have been scrutinised even more closely.

Nichols and Hazlewood made a cursory inspection of the communication junctions before returning to their control room.

'What is bothering you?' Hazlewood eventually asked.

'I don't know.' Nichols began collating information on uniformed security movements. 'There is something fishy about World Security.'

'That is what Nightingale has been saying for over forty years. They might sabotage her again.'

'Well, we had better make sure they never find out that she is doing something worth blowing her up for.'

Hazlewood went to her monitor and started to flash up information on "Occurrences - Inexplicable or Unexplained."

'What are you doing?' asked Nichols.

'I thought I might dig out a file to keep that chief assistant of hers happy.'

'Nothing short of abolishing the monthly "Happy Morning" would cheer him up.'

'He cannot be that miserable?'

'He is not miserable. He is virtuous. He would make the hedgehogs at Group Indigo's HQ carry phosphorescent passes to give beetles without flash torches a chance,' said Nichols.

'It is surprising that Nightingale does not have the grounds patrolled by tigers.'

'Given her achievements in biochemistry, I am not too sure I would trust the hedgehogs.'

Hazlewood remembered something. 'Nightingale said Sendall was ill. Sudden losses of co-ordination.'

'You mean he keeps falling over? Not very often. Nightingale's secretary is medically trained. He maintains a close watch on him.'

'Nightingale has a secretary?'

'You know, the pink pudding with vanilla perfume who doubles up as Sendall's assistant.'

Hazlewood laughed. 'That is her secretary? I thought he was Group Indigo's hairdresser.'

'Comes from a line of jugglers or whatever. I know there was some connection with circuses.'

'Circuses?'

'You know, before the human dignity legislation was passed. Nightingale probably picked him up in a job lot.'

'What a pair. The more we can keep Sendall occupied, the less chance of him discovering us, and I certainly would not fancy being upwind of his assistant.'

Nichols sighed. 'Oh find something to keep them happy then.'

Hazlewood pushed her heavy eyebrows back into position before settling down to concentrate.

'I wish you would stop doing that.'

'I am sorry.'

'It just annoys me.'

Nichols left Hazlewood to search for a credible UFO sighting and turned on the surveillance monitor to watch mere mortals go about their mundane lives. It was always boring up there. With everything safely homogenised, there wasn't any scope for adventurers and eccentrics. Nightingale was an aberration.

Most people lived in their self-contained bungalow units with their own private parks where they could operate a work terminal without having to set foot over a neighbour's threshold. In their ample free time, they were able to wander from cafe to play to exhibition over the rolling green domes that covered the capital. They seldom had to risk being inside one when the collapse sirens sounded or the flood barrier holding back the Thames sprang a leak. It was one of the few rivers you could see at its best by looking up through the safety screens.

Nichols switched to the moon monitor. World Government's base there had been fully operational for over thirty years and was still top secret.

Few people wanted to go to the moon any more. After the decompression disaster on the old moon base, it wasn't surprising. Why travel all the way there to see Neil Armstrong's footprint when a virtual reality unit could rerun the highlights of the landing with you as the astronaut? No wonder people could be fooled into believing there was nothing left to achieve: all diseases and genetic aberrations cured, free energy forever more and criminal behaviour eradicated.

The plagues had necessitated rapid advances in medicine and technology. As a consequence, a small population had inherited some very sophisticated engineering without the creative imagination to use it. All people really wanted was someone to blame when things went wrong. A scapegoat for all their ills was worth giving up a few freedoms for. World Government had no choice but to take up the reins cast aside by a population unwilling to believe that they had brought so many disasters on themselves.

When Nichols began to see authority's point of view, she knew she should have stayed at home. But World Government was growing into a double-headed beast. She needed to dig a little deeper into their restricted files. They went deeper than Nightingale realised.

CHAPTER 9

JB Sendall, Nightingale's chief assistant, was everything Nichols believed him to be. Though, if he did ever fall over, he made sure it wasn't in public. He was a careful man and behaved as if, when God realised most of his congregation were now indifferent about Him, the first bolt of lightning would part his silver-white hair. In a previous century he would have been incarnated as an army general with an emotionally traumatic home life or a celibate priest wishing he had one. Nightingale's number one had subconscious reins that always jolted him back when he at last seemed on the verge of contentment. When Tim Tharby tried to give him therapy, the medic found that he was the one going into a trance. JB's pale eyes could be as motionless and penetrating as a calculating shark's.

Group Indigo ostensibly investigated unexplained phenomena, from drunks' pink-booted Venusians with North Pole accents to flight controllers' lucid descriptions of triangular traffic floating in formation fifty feet from the ground. It was JB's brief to check out the most credible. He discovered that the latter were real enough and did remarkable things to motorways with ancient Tarmac, but secretly wished he could just once meet a pink-booted Venusian. Fortunately, Tim Tharby had the medical authority to forbid him alcohol.

At times, JB Sendall wondered who was the greater blight on his life; the short, tubby secretary medic or towering Nightingale, still as lean, angular, and upright as she was forty years ago. He often amused himself with the thought that the Senior Controller had once been a beautiful, sympathetic paragon before being blown up by her own fuel cell. Rationale insisted the idea was wide of the mark. JB's subconscious, very deep and seldom mined, was a mystery, even to him.

He hoped he never talked in his sleep. Nightingale was bound to have his rooms at HQ monitored. Any fine sentiment on his part for the woman, however subconscious, would have caused more suspicion than outright espionage.

Sometimes JB yearned to become just another member of the homogenised hoi polloi. Regrettably, his severe manner intimidated the most ambitious of Group Indigo's personnel and the friendliest of drunks ever likely to see a pink-booted Venusian. All except Tim Tharby, that is. JB might as well have shot arrows at steam. Providing JB with an assistant who would have been better planted out with the pelargoniums must have appealed to Nightingale's sense of humour. When together, JB and Tharby looked like an Antarctic inspection robot and its pink penguin. If he weren't so dependent on medication, JB could have happily bribed some unexplained phenomena to carry the medic off. Given Tim Tharby's strange tastes, he would have probably enjoyed the experience.

JB Sendall walked through the cluttered corridors of the HQ Nightingale had used for the last forty-five years to reach the sanity of his own methodically arranged office.

A paper dart spiralled down from a landing above.

'Just testing the description of a new UFO sighting,' a voice sang down.

JB glowered upward with a gaze that could have penetrated lead, then went on his way.

Nearer the central basement of the large building, the fittings started to look more like those of a scientific establishment. Nightingale's laboratory was overlooked by a circular gallery. This was where World Security had installed their own control console. In it, communication links idled in readiness for a major incident. As they had insisted on having the emergency terminal at Group Indigo's HQ, it was obvious who they believed would cause the disaster. Nightingale's lab was below the gallery and contained a transmission portal. As soon as the portal was activated and some alien placed its foot over the interdimensional threshold, that gallery would swarm with World Security personnel. Nightingale was not flattered by their high regard for her apocalyptic potential and resented all that equipment, however inactive, looking over her shoulder as she worked. There were other World Security installations dotted about the planet as a precaution against an alien pre-emptive strike. The one overlooking Nightingale was the largest.

JB didn't like the place. He resented the threat of uniforms that could usurp his authority, those doppelganger generals of his own nature, the might-have-been mirror images of his early potential. Fortunately they would never have any authority over Nightingale. That tough, purple totem pole had carved out her empire with the accuracy of a political fretsaw and her tentacles now reached into everyone else's database.

The Senior Controller was not in her laboratory so, with an uneasy glance up at the World Security console surrounding it, JB passed on to his own domain.

He had hardly made the sanctuary of his office when the ebullient Tim Tharby bounced in.

'How are we today?' the medic demanded in remorselessly jovial tones.

The hyperactive glove puppet seemed to spend his life on a permanent high. JB was tempted to push him out, but the small man had the strength of a medium sized yak and could have easily flattened him against the wall to take his temperature.

'I feel as though I've been kicked in the head by a deranged diplodocus, and it's obvious that you are your usually obnoxious self.'

'Sorry I had to give you such a large dose - it was a rather bad turn.' Tharby took out a stethoscope and hypodermic from his pocket. 'Need your pressure and another sample.'

'What are you doing? Starting up a blood bank? That's the third syringeful this week.'

'Well I need it to make up your treatment, don't I. Without a bit of you to help it, that biology of yours would probably spit it out, sweetie.'

'Don't call me that.'

'Ooh, we are in a lugubrious mood aren't we? What's been depressing us then?'

'I am not your sweetie.'

Tharby was just being annoying. He knew full well it was what his wife had sometimes called him. She was a wonderful woman who had divorced him because of the frost factor. The union had survived the eagle-eyed attention of Nightingale, only to founder when Melony met someone more animated than JB. She thought she could cure JB of his detachment from everyone else's reality, only to fall for the very doctor who agreed with her that it might be possible. Now JB's state of mind was in the care of an insubordinate, pink, bouncy toy.

Tim Tharby knew JB would never be anyone's sweetie. His body sugars were too low and taste buds as active as icicles. He could have frozen the knickers off a polar bear.

JB groaned. The dizziness he had been fighting off all morning suddenly engulfed him. Tim Tharby bodily caught him before he hit the floor. Tharby's father had been a trained acrobat and taught his son many useful things people their limited height needed to know for self-preservation.

'Let's have a little rest, shall we? We can't see the big boss while you're in that condition. She'd drop you into a jar of formaldehyde and put you on the shelf.'

He lowered JB onto a couch. Despite every instinct

telling him he had work to do, he fell asleep. Lights above flickered and were imprinted on his retina. Then the usual cast of characters, noises, and ridiculous creatures that regularly clattered through his subconscious pushed him off the cliff into blessed oblivion.

Nightingale watched Tim Tharby take his patient's blood pressure. 'How is he?'

'Quiet enough.' Tharby pulled a blanket over JB and settled his head more comfortably on the pillow. 'The last dose was too much for him.'

'There wasn't any choice.'

'What if he'd driven off somewhere before checking in?'

'His car's batteries were put on faulty charge and I've got his ID card.'

Tim Tharby may have looked like a Victorian bridesmaid's posy, but he was not easily daunted. His parents had no fear of heights and some innate cussedness often persuaded him to the edge of precipices, some of them as high as Nightingale. That was a very long drop.

The medic fearlessly glared up at the intimidating woman. 'Think of everything, don't we?'

The Senior Controller took a deep breath. She hated the way the only person she trusted couldn't be unnerved. 'Don't start feeling sorry for Sendall after all this time.'

'Having pumped him full of drugs for over twenty years, I should start worrying about his emotional state now.'

'I know you, Tharby. Inside that steel Easter egg, you're as soft as a half-cooked soufflé. If you want to keep your patient, you'll do what I tell you.'

'There are times he should have been in intensive care.'

'You are his intensive care. You're all the machines any human body needs to stay alive against its will, and machines don't get emotionally involved.'

'You're a callous old crow!' Tharby suddenly snapped.

Nightingale peered down at the token insubordination. 'That's right. Just you remember it.'

Looking over the edge of the purple precipice, Tim Tharby pulled back. Why should he feel sympathy for that emotionless iceberg? He did, though. If he had one splinter of the frost in JB's character, he might have been more detached. Tim Tharby had been weaned on heightened sensations, though. His father had just retired as one of the last touring variety turns and his mother had been the last but one test pilot before robots took over. By the time he reached adulthood, all the occupations he was suited to were either banned as dangerous or obsolete through technical progress. Now even astro pilots found their lives routine. The sight of Earth from space no longer awed. It had been used too many times to remind the remaining members of the human race what several insidious plagues had managed to snatch from the jaws of over population.

Tharby sighed. Living and working so close to Nightingale and JB Sendall made him feel as though he was in a pantomime with the Wicked Witch of the East and the Sphinx.

'All right,' he heard Nightingale snarl somewhere in the background of his wandering thoughts. 'Say what you're thinking.'

He couldn't face another bout of verbal combat. 'Is it really true that they've discovered another hominid species in the Amazon?'

Nightingale was hardly expecting the truth. 'Why? Isn't it enough you have to work with us?'

'That's just what I was thinking.'

'One day, Tharby, I am going to pick you up by your pink-rinsed perm and feed you follicle by molecule through the transmission portal to the Lictana.'

'I'd be careful if I were you. You don't know what they might send back in return.'

She paused. 'Have you been eavesdropping again?'

'It was an accident. I just happened to be outside your office door when you were on the line to the gruesome twosome. You should remember to shut it if you don't want anyone to overhear.'

Nightingale glowered.

'It's no good putting the evil eye on me either.'

'Got a cure for that as well, have you?'

'There's only one thing I can't treat.'

'Oh yes?'

'Curiosity.' Despite common sense telling him not to, Tharby demanded, 'What are you up to?'

'I'll tell you when I'm ready.' She indicated JB. 'Keep him quiet for the rest of the week. I've got work to do.'

'On what?'

'I said I'll tell you when I'm ready.'

'So what if you have another accident?'

'I haven't had one that's killed me yet.' Nightingale strode out of the room.

'So what fatal accident would dare happen to you?' muttered Tharby.

Now the medic had to turn up something interesting to occupy JB Sendall. Perhaps he could find an inexplicable sighting for him to investigate. JB liked nothing more than teasing apart the reports of manifestations spotted by easily duped mortals.

Unfortunately the "IN" file was empty. There was always the progress report on Nessie, but JB had never thought the Great Orm worth fishing for. There was now a popular theory that the creature had become so fed up with microphones, cameras, and divers dropping on its head, that it had taken up residence somewhere else. At least, the local security near a neighbouring loch had been sending the occasional resident to recuperation centres for seeing the beast. In this quirky, conforming world, everything had its place, even phantoms and monsters. Few people admitted to seeing things where they had no right to be. Those that did were usually oddballs.

With a little help from some spiked oxygen, JB slept on until two. Tharby still couldn't find any report dramatic enough to keep him occupied. So, taking his life in his hands, he walked the patient outside before he was awake enough to know what was happening.

In showing him so rapidly to other Group Indigo staff, as well as the fresh air, in that condition, Tharby risked the wrath of both JB and Nightingale.

JB Sendall's wrath leapt into third gear as soon as he realised that he was standing under the lunging branches of a holly tree in the ancient jungle surrounding the listed HQ.

'What the hell are we doing here, Tharby?' he snapped.

'I just prescribed you some fresh air, buttercup. Pollen included. I know you're too stubborn to contract anything as simple as hay fever.'

'How long was I out?'

'Several hours or so.'

'Several? That was those bloody drugs you gave me last night!'

'I warned you not to get up so early this morning.'

JB beheaded a thistle with his bare hand.

Tharby flinched. 'There are easier ways to garden, you know.'

'Go and powder your freckles.'

Tim Tharby wandered off and turned his attention to the arguing squirrels and thistledown floating free from the decapitated seed head, occasionally casting a concerned glance back at JB. Despite his superior's condition and the fact that he was middle-aged, the man had a degree of stamina that Tharby found quite puzzling. Perhaps Nightingale was right, and he was beyond normal sensations.

JB abruptly stopped in his tracks. Tharby thought he was on the verge of another attack. He bounded back through the bracken towards him.

Sendall's eyes were motionless, staring at a rebuilt section of the estate's high wall in the distance.

'What's the matter?' Tharby demanded.

'Nothing,' JB said too faintly to be convincing.

'Hell,' Tharby swore. 'You should have come out of that cycle by now.'

'Leave me alone.'

'Tell me what's wrong?'

'Nothing. Leave me alone.'

'No chance.' Tim Tharby took JB's pulse. It seemed normal enough.

If the medic insisted his patient return to the house, he would probably demand to know where Nightingale was, so he left him staring at places peopled with blankness. It was only a minor relapse and best left to wear off. JB could stand there for hours without being seen by anyone else; a motionless statue offending the unkempt grounds with his immaculate presence.

CHAPTER 10

At last, Nightingale had given Nichols and Hazlewood something worthwhile to do; controlling a transference from Lictan to Earth in their secret bunker's transmission portal. In her HQ, Nightingale watched on her monitor. The computer linked to theirs counted molecules as alien equipment unstitched atoms and reassembled them in another dimension. It was frustrating that not even the most sophisticated space telescopes could pinpoint the whereabouts of the other planet. Being able to see Lictan, if only as a photon of light, would have given her something to metaphorically aim at, but the Cosmos never intended overlapping universes to see each other.

A lifelong commitment to dealing with the Lictan paradox meant that Nightingale had been too busy to turn to other things. As the world's climate was now under control and there was plenty of eco-friendly power, there was no need for more revolutionary fuel cells, ozone producing plants, or carbon capture platforms. She might have incited the Natural Living Campaign to bring down World Government. That was probably why she had been allowed her to keep her HQ in the middle of nowhere and chase aliens.

Even though it was only happening on a screen, Nightingale was still awed by the transmission process. So much so, she only dared utter the name of the creatures who had created the matter transference system in front of Tim Tharby. Unfortunately, the only human she could totally trust was a highly-strung, rebellious package not interested in anything beyond the medicine cabinet, Group Indigo's filing system and grey roots. Despite his pampered, powdered appearance, Tim Tharby was a tough little character with a pragmatism that must have embarrassed him by the way he tried to conceal it. An alien machine knitting together living flesh was not quite the same as patching up human tissue, even JB Sendall's, so Nightingale didn't invite him to watch.

She was horribly fascinated as Nichols and Hazlewood continued to supervise the operation down in their secret burrow. They were on top of the unworldly fleshing process and no doubt relished every moment of it. The weird pair were the only others with the expertise to organise a transfer. Expecting them to be totally trustworthy as well was asking too much, but somebody else had to have a working transmission portal. Nightingale couldn't use hers in the centre of her crowded complex and had persuaded everyone it was not operational. Also, restoring an agent who had not aged one day after disappearing forty years ago would have begged too many questions she didn't have the patience to invent answers for.

Forty years was a long time for even Jeff Devlin to be unconscious. Nightingale would have been happy to never set eyes on him again, especially from the inside out. She was running out of ways to spread disinformation and needed the glamorous lecher, though. World Security was always trying to recruit spies in Group Indigo. The least she could do was give them one, even though he would be forty years out of date. Assuming the molecules of his brain had been reassembled in the right order, that could easily be sorted. Jeff Devlin was a devious opportunist, not stupid. Nightingale was counting on it.

At last the handsome features of the treacherous philanderer appeared in the buzzing cloud of particles. Sure enough, he looked the same as when the Lictana had snatched him so long ago. Nightingale doubted that his habits would have changed either. However, in the modern world, even the lowliest rubbish could be recycled into something useful.

Nichols and Hazlewood called to confirm that the transference was complete. Nauseous, Nightingale switched off her screen and wandered back into the relatively humdrum world of JB Sendall and Tim Tharby.

* * *

Hazlewood wiped some condensation from the portal chamber with her overall sleeve as she gazed at the body inside it. 'I wonder what he is like when he is awake?'

Nichols shrugged. 'According to Nightingale, we are seeing the best side of him now. Cannot understand why she wanted him back?'

'If anyone understood what Nightingale did, the Universe would be safer place.' Hazlewood stepped back to take a more subjective view of the ivory-skinned body hanging in mid-air like a wax effigy on an abattoir hook. 'Do you think he is good looking?'

'I do not know.'

'Wonder what he will make of this new world?'

'Who cares? All we have to do is ensure that his grey cells are intact. What conclusion they come to after that is no concern of ours.'

'You think that so long in suspension could have caused any damage?'

'Who knows. It is time for lunch. We can say hallo to him later.'

'I thought..?' Hazlewood started.

'Do not worry. I will make sure he does not remember us.'

'Nightingale will be furious if he does.'

'She is probably feeling too sick to worry about anything at the moment.'

'Well, it was a messy transference. Why do human beings need so many internal organs?'

'They seem to be all there. He will go back to her in the same pristine condition as when he was snatched, mutant venereal condition included.'

Hazlewood grunted and pushed up her eyebrows.

* * *

As Tim Tharby passed Nightingale's office, a long hand caught him by the collar.

'Anti-nausea pills,' she demanded.

His mind was on other things. The medic didn't have time for stomach upsets. 'What for? Fancy food, poisonous inhalations, or nasty fright?'

'My digestion, you little prat.'

Tharby shrugged off her grip, hardly expecting his superior to be more specific. 'Well, given what you get up to at your age ...'

'I want something to settle my stomach, not a sermon on what a lively geriatric I am.' Nightingale's pallor was tinged with a pale magenta, a sure sign she had been up to something a thirty-year-old would have thought twice about.

'Come into my medicine cabinet.' Tharby led her into his office.

The patient obviously wasn't going to elaborate about her symptoms, so he rummaged through the phials and bottles in the no-hope cabinet for inspiration. Tharby discovered some pills exactly the same colour as Nightingale's skin and dropped a couple into her hand. Having been intensively trained in every form of medicine, from herbal to radiological, he should have known better. At least they weren't poisonous and would only clear out her system.

While he was tidying the cabinet, Nightingale flushed them down the sink.

Then she noticed that something was missing. 'What have you done with Sendall?'

'Left him in the grounds staring at goodness knows what.'

'Not another relapse?'

'No. Could be burgeoning interest in the flora and fauna for all I know.'

'It wasn't near the old transmission point, was it?'

Tharby stopped rummaging. 'Why? Is something

extra-dimensional liable to leap out at him?'

'Not that we'd notice. Only hope he doesn't either.'

Tharby thoughtfully closed the cabinet doors. 'Something stopped him dead. His pulse wasn't irregular, so I left him.'

'Just how bad is he?'

'How bad are you prepared to let him get? I'm the one who's been trying to cure him for the past twenty years.'

'Now he's going to have a real assistant, it probably won't matter so much.'

Tharby scowled in his owlish way. He was already everyone's assistant. 'I'm not happy with JB's alpha and beta rhythms.'

'Why not?'

'They don't seem that human to me.'

'What do you mean?'

'His brain is active where most peoples aren't.'

Nightingale knew what he was driving at. She evaded. 'Could it be a growth?'

'No. It's cerebral agitation. Isn't it about time you started taking it easy?'

'I need his mind. Just keep it intact.'

'I'm a medic, not a fairy godmother. I only hope this new assistant of his is sane enough for both of them.'

'Well, he's certainly different.'

Tharby didn't like Nightingale's tone. He said nothing. He was warming to the idea of getting back to his less traumatic secretarial duties. Nightingale's office sense may have been a bad dream, but watching JB Sendall was like trying to keep reins on a claustrophobic polar bear.

'So, what are this new "assistant's" qualifications?' he asked.

'Spent eight years in the Space Security Corps.'

'What? I thought you wouldn't have anything to do with uniforms?' Tharby hesitated. 'Hold on, weren't they disbanded twenty-five years ago?'

'Yes.'

Tharby was puzzled. He wasn't going to give Nightingale any satisfaction by admitting it, though. 'Look, I don't want two geriatrics on my hands. You're enough to last any medic a lifetime.'

'Thought your father used to be a juggler?'

'The day I can lift you off the ground, World Security will start wearing tutus.'

Nightingale giggled to herself.

Now Tharby was suspicious. 'You don't know any ballerinas in the simulated brown leather brigade, do you?'

'If you're lucky, you may never meet her. And if you do, she certainly won't be wearing brown leather.'

'Who is this new addition to Group Indigo then? A double agent of some sort?' Tharby persisted.

'But of course. You know how attached I am to everyone else's data.'

'Beneath all those zips must be this planet's biggest spy network.'

There was a burbling noise from the sink and a purple froth bubbled from the plughole. 'That sink isn't very hygienic, Tharby.' Bored of the conversation, she strode out.

Tharby scowled after her.

CHAPTER 11

An assignment dropped from the UFO file slot.

Tim Tharby seized the brief before it was delegated by some office boy. After reading the details, the medic could hardly believe his luck. Nightingale's two new parasites must have known what fired JB Sendall's curiosity. Though a job more suited to one of the B pass beards, this assignment was guaranteed to take JB's mind off whatever was bothering him. The only snag was, the medic would have to go with him to make sure he didn't keel over.

The sightings came from reliable sources - no pink-booted Venusians seen by drunks - and were close enough to Group Indigo's HQ to be a security risk. Nightingale was certainly up to something the aliens would have been interested in. Tim Tharby stood a better chance of finding out what it was from them.

Nightingale already knew the first witness the brief listed, so JB and Tharby were curious to find what any friend of hers looked like.

The address was in a district reclaimed from a flood plain after the river had been diverted north for irrigation. It was now flat meadowland spangled with wild flowers. Amongst the stunted ruins of the old town undermined by persistent floods, were the odd looking homes of people who had chosen self-sufficiency. Despite the solar panels and windmills, they resembled the detached bay-windowed energy wasters of yesteryear. Goats and the odd wallaby meandered into the path of JB's electric car, no doubt to test its brakes, then ambled off into the field on the other side of the road.

In the middle of its own meadow, the faded house of the first UFO witness sat like an ornate rabbit hutch with marzipan tiles. It had once stood on stilts, but they had sunk into the ground. Now it was a raft on an ocean of rippling greenery.

Tim Tharby and JB had never encountered a garden like it before. An arch of jasmine, more needle sharp twigs than leaf, tried to inoculate them with its perfume as they opened the warped front gate. A pair of canary-yellow eyes watched from a bush of lavender. The only thing Tharby felt sure about was that they didn't belong to a canary.

JB found it a welcome relief to be engulfed by natural fragrances robust enough to overwhelm Tharby's perfume. Surrounded by such huge clumps of vigorous plants, Tharby's nostrils quivered uneasily in anticipation of the primitive compost heap they were bound to blunder into at any moment. This was only the front garden.

To the medic's concern, JB's sense of order appeared to be taking a rest. In his natural habitat at HQ, Nightingale's number one thought nothing of decapitating thistles with his bare hands. Here he reached out to delicately examine the barbarous looking spires of gorse.

Not being able to raise anyone by knocking the paint-peeling front door, they had to dodge branches and step over brambles to reach the back yard.

The unruly vegetation unnerved Tharby. 'I don't like it.' The land the house had been allocated was not large, but the garden at its centre was crammed with flowers and foliage only seen in ancient seed catalogues. 'This place is eerie.'

'Stop whingeing.'

'I bet this friend of Nightingale's is going to be as odd as she is. That woman has a weird sense of humour.'

'Oh go and charge up the car then!' snapped JB.

Tharby gratefully bounded away.

JB stood sniffing strange, somehow familiar, perfumes lacing the ramshackle back porch and burgeoning garden beyond. Tharby was right; there was something unsettling about the place. It was unlike the wildlife jungle at HQ where, at one time, Perry and his team had used high-pitched whistles to evict any animals or birds that took up residence. This garden was screened by tall hedges and probably populated by beavers, bears and badgers.

JB recognised the large leafed crop partly covered by thermal sheeting. Tobacco - a plant banned so long ago not many drugs officers would be able to identify it. Then the names of the different flowers flooded back to him. Borage, camomile, sweet peas, silver-pursed honesty, and towering sunflowers gazing down like lopsided Nightingales. They were hardly exotic enough for the modern gardener, who could grow exotics as easily as mustard and cress. Deeply buried memories so painful he almost flinched, would have surfaced if it had not been for a sudden voice from the porch.

'So you're Mr Sendall, are you?'

While he had been taking in her garden, the gardener had been summing him up from the concealing comfort of an old wing chair losing its stuffing.

He sent his memories back to their dungeon and turned to the porch. 'That's right. I understand you have a statement to make?'

'Oh,' the old woman leaned back thoughtfully. 'I've a lifetime of statements to make. Don't often get many to listen to them, though.'

'Your name is Mooney?'

'Call me Bertha.' The woman beamed, showing her yellow, gappy teeth. 'Young fellow with you don't like the old weeds I notice.'

'He isn't that young. He wears enough powder to fill the cracks.'

'Come and sit down a minute.' Bertha indicated a less dilapidated armchair opposite her then, to JB's amazement, took out an antique smoking pipe from her cardigan pocket, struck a match, and puffed it into life. 'Don't mind, do you?'

JB stifled back a cough and sat down.

'Ain't the smoke that worries most people, it's because I knows how to grow the leaves that bothers them.'

'I thought it was illegal?'

'So who's going to lock up a loony old woman like me? Loony Mooney, that's what they call me hereabouts, but none of them knows how to grow their own food any more. They think it sprouts up ready washed and packed in ecoplastic. People'd be useless if we were ever invaded. Last as long as an irradiated cauliflower.'

JB suddenly remembered why he was there. 'You reported a UFO?'

'Oh yes. Told your Nightingale I did.' JB opened his mouth in surprise. 'We got this small understanding from way back. Nothing you should worry your serious head about.'

'I never question Nightingale.'

Bertha raised an eyebrow, but believed him. 'Several folk have seen these things.'

'So I understand.'

'I'm the only one who reckon they don't come from outer space.'

'Why not?'

'What have we got that could be any use to someone able to travel at the speed of light? Irradiated cauliflowers?'

The jolly woman's lucid logic unsettled JB. If she could remember the desperate experiments to store food by irradiation, she was older than Nightingale. She looked it, though it could have been weathering. His prejudices were not tuned to cope with the implications if Bertha Mooney was right about the sightings not being alien. JB turned his attention to the plot of carrots, lettuces run to seed and wigwam of scarlet runners. She certainly had a point about alien motives. What use would their quietly conserved world be to a life form advanced enough to travel at the speed of light?

'If you're right, this would mean that the military have the resources to undertake a massive proto-aviation project.'

'Well, they're funded by World Government, ain't they? And you seem bright enough to know what a twisted load of bleeders they are.'

In her own eccentric way, Bertha Mooney shared Nightingale's view of the world. She just expressed it in growing things instead of causing uncontrolled explosions. Nightingale had often dropped hints that JB look over his shoulder more often. He needed a revelation like this to loosen the bolts in his neck. In Group Indigo's jungle, all matters seemed cut and dried. From Bertha's modest plot, the outside world took on a more sinister aspect. There were truths being cultivated here that resonated in a past he couldn't remember. The way Bertha gazed at him in that all-knowing manner was unnerving.

'What location?' he asked.

'Most of them were sighted out Twin Hills way, but I don't reckon they're anything to do with that old disused airstrip. Too many watercress beds now. Land's soggy. I think they come in from that restricted area twenty miles north of here.' JB's expression tightened. 'Ain't you got clearance for it, then?'

'It's a botanical reserve.'

'Always wondered what went on in that place. They do say they were the ones to grow the plant equivalent of a white mouse. Damn clever that! Some medical researcher wants to test her new drug, she just nips into the conservatory and picks a few vegetable rodents.' JB looked dubious. 'Nah, I don't believe it neither. Nearest I ever got to growing anything with a mind of its own was ground elder. That stuff must have been around with the dinosaurs. Probably what poisoned them.'

JB shuddered. He buttoned the top of his silver edged jacket. 'What's that smell?'

'Which one?'

'It's heady, familiar.'

Bertha laughed. 'Oh, that's the late philadelphus what old Den put in for me.'

'Philadelphus?'

'Mock orange. Ain't you got any where you come from?'

JB shook his head. 'It's more of a nature reserve.'

'You should try the great outdoors more often. Still patches of it that ain't had their smells glued to the nearest surface by an industrial negative ioniser.' The gardener sniffed the air. 'Storm coming up.'

The sky was almost clear, without so much as a breeze.

'How can you tell?'

'Can hear them seeding balloons. Threatened they'd do it some time this week if Nature didn't oblige. You better be under cover in the next hour. When them buggers do find a cloud, it won't know what hit it.'

* * *

JB Sendall and Tim Tharby sat in the auto caf watching the rain sheet down. It was as though God had opened the sluice gates, hell bent on washing away his disbelieving progeny once and for all.

Tim Tharby touched up his face where the powder had absorbed too much moisture. 'You'd think they would be able to control it better by now. After this downpour, the botanical reserve won't want any visitors.'

'It probably wasn't meant for them. You're not getting out of it. I haven't got an Approved Grower's or medic's card.' The rain suddenly stopped. 'Anyway, it was only a five-mile downpour. They wouldn't empty a deluge like that on so many delicate experiments.

95

Bertha Mooney reckoned it was to rot the roots of the illicit tropical vegetation grown in her area.'

'What illicit vegetation?'

'You'll be able to ask at the botanical reserve.' JB slid his credit card under the eye of the waiter as the unit trundled past. It bleeped irritably. 'Damn, the thing must have an overload.'

Before JB or Tharby could leave their seats, an agitated attendant in ankle-length overalls, hairnet and hygiene gloves blundered through the kitchen flap. 'Relax everyone; this always happens when it rains - damp connections.'

An ageing travel rep yawned in her regular corner and an illegal cat took the opportunity to escape from the food dispensary and curl up under the artificial flower display. The attendant deftly unclipped the waiter's lid, switched on its dehumidifier, slammed it shut, patted it on its way and bounded back to the kitchen. This time the waiter whistled happily as JB flipped his card under its beam.

When the machines went wrong and had to be fixed by a human being in a hairnet and hygiene gloves, it wasn't always a reassuring experience.

The road north was already dry. Hidden storm drains had carried the water from any potential fords, the electric motor's greatest hazard. Apart from a couple of single carriage trams and several tricycles, the route was quiet. No one noticed the Group Indigo agents leave the road and go to a collection kiosk.

'She wouldn't have had time to get it here, especially through that storm,' wagered Tim Tharby.

JB Sendall never underestimated Nightingale's delivery pods, small postage blimps with jet propulsion and attitude. He showed the kiosk scanner his ID and the lid yawned open. Inside was a large wildlife proof box. JB lifted out the scanning equipment.

'You'd better find something after all this hassle,' Tharby warned.

'I intend to.'

'How can you be so sure anything's out here?'

JB was about to say intuition, but didn't want Tharby to think he was going soft. The medic always had a sedative ready to jab onto his neck at the first sign of uncharacteristic behaviour.

With the equipment stowed, they drove on to the botanical research reserve.

Tim Tharby still objected. It was pointless. There was no way that his holographic ID could be mistaken for JB's. So through the unguarded gates he was sent with his medic's pass clutched tightly in his sweating palm as though suddenly producing it could ward off dragons. He puffed his way along the gravel path through the ordered criss-cross beds of plants no where near as threatening as those in Bertha's Mooney's garden. Nothing in the immediate vicinity grew over two feet so no dragons he would recognise could hide behind it.

Botanical research reserves were weird places. Tharby had been obliged to attend one as part of his training. Now researchers were not allowed to use animals in experiments, he was convinced that these sick geniuses had managed to grow plant-like creatures to take their place.

The deeper into the grounds the medic travelled, the more he wanted to be outside the perimeter with JB, trying to pick up atmospheric fluctuations with the equipment Nightingale had sent them.

Tharby grew more and more irritable as he felt he was being engulfed by a knee-high bouquet. If Nightingale knew everything that was happening on Earth, there shouldn't have been any need for all these inconvenient excursions. Their business was with aliens, not run-of-the-mill human beings with rampant gardens and research establishments cultivating plants that looked capable of trotting across the path at any moment.

'Hello there,' chirped a young woman. She was probing about behind some unnatural looking vegetation. Tharby would have noticed the gardener before if her hair hadn't been green and better permed than his.

'Hello. Group Indigo sent me.'

'Group Indigo?'

'Supposed to be secret. UFOs and all that.' He showed her his ID just in case she was a dragon.

'You look younger there?'

Tharby prickled with annoyance. 'That's because it's easier to produce a photo taken in the past as opposed to the future.' His sneer traced age lines in his powder.

'We're working on rejuvenation, you know. Don't fancy applying for tests do you?'

Tim Tharby wanted nothing more than to be twenty years younger, but wasn't flattered at being taken for an experimental vegetable.

'HQ wants to know if anyone here has spotted any UFOs?'

'All the time, but you'll find weirder things inside the labs over there.'

The Medic snatched a wary glance at the white domes fastened to the ground with short, sharp prongs like engorged ticks. 'You're joking?'

'No. Old Pentecost has managed to cross an apple pip with an octopus egg - got a tree that can pick its own fruit.'

Tharby groaned. 'How about taking me to your leader?'

'Can't leave nitrogen drip. Just follow the path left until you come to a yellow greenhouse. Spud is her name. Can't miss her - wears a red sun hat and striped overalls.'

'Spud?'

'Spudely.'

'Thanks.'

Relieved to escape any more bad jokes, Tharby went on his way.

Whoever thought up yellow for the long, high greenhouse had managed to produce a structure that could actually clash with sunlight. It was a glinting sore running through several beds of summer tulips.

Tharby didn't want to know what was inside it. Every fibre in his body rebelled as he compelled his feet to walk past a bizarre tree at the entrance. It had pushed its branches into the ground to resemble a massive, electrocuted spider. What few leaves it had were curled and singed as though suffering from a surfeit of self-inflicted ECT.

Several of the monster's pods opened fire on the medic at the vibration of his footfall. Valuable experiment or not, he brushed the wrinkled seeds from his pink hair and into the gravel where they were soon lost.

Inside the greenhouse there was a flurry of activity at the far end. Though the air was like hot tomato soup, there was no going back.

Tharby made his way to the woman in the striped overalls and red sun hat, keeping his elbows tucked in to avoid corkscrew tendrils.

Leader Spudely was in a rare state of agitation. Several trays had fallen from their benches during the night and the gardeners were trying to rescue each stranded seedling. Amongst the community of eccentrics and their bizarre flowers, Tharby's presence seemed quite natural. The gardeners hardly glanced at him.

'How did it happen?' he asked.

A naturally harassed person, Spudely looked as though worry had worn her contours away and embossed lines in her short, chinless face. The baggy overalls and red sun hat she wore reminded Tharby of an inverted flowerpot, the plant inside having wilted somewhat.

Eventually the horticulturist seemed aware of the stranger in their midst. 'Only the Good Lord knows, if he's still about.'

'Animals?'

'Everything was locked.'

'This happened before then?'

'Several times.' Spudely abruptly stopped as though someone had prodded her with a stick.

An explanation started to form in the unmappable labyrinth of Tharby's mind. He asked instead, 'Seems I'm bothering you at an awkward moment, but Group Indigo understands you've seen UFOs in the vicinity?'

Spudely instantly stopped bustling about. 'Group Indigo?'

'You know.' Tharby pointed upwards.

'Oh, meteorology.'

'No,' he sighed. 'Spaceships.'

'Oh those. See them all the time.'

For a harassed human, Leader Spudely was peculiarly nonchalant about extraterrestrial visitations. It made Tharby wonder if the rumours about the botanists' bomb hadn't been true after all.

'Couldn't they have set up vibrations?'

'To knock these trays off the benches? Perhaps.' Spudely's sudden diffidence was odd.

Tharby pursed his lips. 'No idea where they came from?'

'Outer space I suppose. Isn't that where spaceships are meant to come from?' The gardener returned to the precious scattered seedlings.

This was getting the medic nowhere. If there was anything more irritating than trying to get sense out of a crank who sees Andromedan UFOs lit up like galactic Christmas trees, it was trying to get information from someone who has no interest in anything unless it's rooted in terra firma.

There was no point in staying. Tim Tharby left to find the quickest way out of the sprawling grounds.

The beds of primulas lining the most promising path back to the main entrance appeared quite innocuous, even though they were probably being bred to feed killer hornets.

After walking for some while, Tim Tharby stopped to loosen his collar. Given that surveillance monitors must have picked up his presence, scanned his ID and counted the permed hairs on his head, it seemed ironical that nothing leapt from the foliage to point the way out.

Then his phone rang. Irritably he pulled the receiver from his breast pocket only to hear Nightingale.

'What are you up to, Tharby?'

'I'm lost.'

There was an audible groan. 'You should have checked in sooner.'

'Since when have you been interested in what hole I fall down? JB's the one with the expensive equipment.'

'You shouldn't have left him on his own. I hope you've come up with something worth reporting?'

'I can't go into that now, wallflowers have ears.'

'What?'

'At least they do in this place.'

'Where is Sendall?'

'No idea. Why don't you phone him?'

'He's not answering.'

'Hell, his implant must be playing up. So what am I supposed to do about it?'

'Find him!' Nightingale bellowed, then hung up.

Tharby span round to see where he was. The medic had somehow managed to strand himself in a sea of rippling rice and nasturtium like flowers. Way off track and without a soul in sight, he tapped the compass on his wrist and consulted the rough plan of the grounds HQ had transmitted. He felt sure he was being watched, and not by someone who would send help if he stumbled into a bottomless well.

There was nothing else for it. He pulled out his glasses and peered into the distance to see, just where the plan indicated, a small gate. Beyond its laurel hedge, the vegetation looked relatively benign and there was an undulation in the landscape that contrasted with the flat vista of the botanical research reserve. Only replacing his glasses when he was sure he could see the gate without them, Tharby jogged through some avenues of hybrid beans. He hoped his medic's ID would let him out of the place as easily as it had let him in.

* * *

Until then, JB Sendall had also believed that spaceships came from outer space. Now Nightingale's scanning equipment was nibbling away at this illusion. These manifestations had left very substantial dents in the atmosphere. They must have been using some banned nuclear fuel, perhaps even a fusion engine. These aircraft were no relation to the silent solar wings and airships that routinely sailed Earth's skies. Now the population of the world was too small to afford any conflicts, why were such powerful machines needed?

It was not often that JB allowed himself the luxury of being scared. That day, however, too many dormant sensations had been roused.

He drove in the direction of the trace on the scanner, only to lose it by a fence enclosing a strawberry field.

JB wearily stepped from the car to stretch his legs.

The air was heavy with the scent of overripe fruit.

'That's odd,' he mused to himself, 'all this produce going to waste and not a picker in sight.' The land was not inside the botanical reserve, so it couldn't have been an experiment. Definitely a matter for prosecution.

JB ducked under the fence. Though there was no voltage running through it, he felt a sudden sickening sensation. He had experienced it once before. It meant trouble.

As he was about to turn back, something even more astounding than the rotting fruit caught his attention. He missed his footing and stumbled into a metal furrow running round the field. This was no irrigation scheme!

JB darted for the safety of the fence. There was a resounding "crack!" as soon as he touched it and he was sent reeling back. His skull felt as though it had been delivered a blow from inside.

The last thing JB Sendall could remember was the overpowering smell of sweetly rotting strawberries.

CHAPTER 12

Ben peered into a tangled cavern formed by cup-shaped flowers balanced on large sepal saucers. By the way their stems arched and swayed they seemed to be sniffing the air.

'What odd flowers?' Ben said to himself. He was suddenly aware of Hysle standing beside him.

'They are the city sensors.'

'What do they sense?'

'Everything. They tell us about the atmospheric pressure, temperature, and amount of noise.'

'But they look like flowers?'

'Oh,' Dey joined in. 'We did not realise you called them that.'

'You're joking again. How can flowers talk?'

'The flowers on your planet must tell you when the atmosphere is being poisoned, or that there is too much noise?'

'They may do. No one ever listens to them.'

Hysle chuckled. 'What a primitive little creature you are.'

'Call me things like that and I won't tell you what I've found out.' Ben darted between the stems of the iridescent blooms and defied the Lictana to catch him.

A couple of six-legged creatures with rattling shells scuttled past, snapping at the dangling round leaves as they went. The eight-year-old wanted to take one home as a pet but couldn't pick it up. It was probably just as well. They looked quite capable of nipping his fingers off.

The child knew that Dey and Hysle had to humour him. Everything he told them seemed very important. He would part with his information when he had tired of the game.

Hysle and Dey sometimes worried about how much the boy could remember when he woke up. Ben was more adept at conversing with other alien life forms than any communications agent the Lictana had trained.

The eight-year-old defiantly remained amongst the silver foliage. 'I want to see Demsel before I tell you anything.'

'That old charlatan must be corrupting the child,' whispered Dey.

Hysle shrugged. 'The Trocan is harmless and will soon be gone.'

'Her species have an affinity with the young. Probably because they all look so decrepit themselves. If she realises what we are doing, she would try to interfere.'

'The child would be suspicious if we stopped him from going to her.'

'Oh all right.' Dey called to the floral sensors. 'You had better be quick. Demsel has to take her ship out.'

Ben emerged from the stems. 'Don't worry. She promised to show me round it before she left.' He sensed the apprehension of the other two. 'It won't do any harm, will it?'

'To the Trocan ship or you?'

'Will it?'

'Probably not,' conceded Hysle. 'It is not as if you can touch anything is it, little minnow?'

'I wouldn't. Even if I could.'

Next to Hysle, Demsel was the friendliest alien Ben had encountered and reminded him of his old teddy bear. That had been covered in long fur. It had spindly legs and arms because it was made in a part of the world where they never had bears, real or teddy. Unlike the Lictana, Trocans only had two pairs of limbs, which were long because their planet's gravity was weak. The captain moved rather like a ponderous giraffe and needed to wear a pressure suit in Lictan's denser atmosphere.

After the Trocan ship's airlock closed, Demsel removed her helmet and suit, throwing the garments to her third-in-command who tossed them into a machine which checked for flaws. The crew no longer paid much attention to the apparition of the eight-year-old human in a blue sweatshirt and loose striped trousers. Ben was never too sure whether he was wearing his pyjamas or best trousers and jacket. Any aliens meeting him for the first time were just amazed that he didn't need a life support suit.

Demsel's head was large and looked quite old. She rolled it from side to side as she spoke and the gold tassels of hair growing like a mane occasionally fell from their fastenings.

'I thought you weren't coming, Ben.'

'Dey and Hysle really didn't want me to.'

'They might be afraid of you learning too much.'

'I don't know why? Anything I learn here I never remember when I wake up.'

Demsel looked at him with a strange expression he couldn't make out. The amber eyes of the Trocan had darkened and her elegant snout wrinkled slightly.

'What's the matter?'

'Do you really like visiting Lictan, Ben?'

'Oh yes. Though I would like to meet Datch and Tamble again. I don't know why they stopped seeing me like that.'

'Whatever you know or are in your own world, you will always be a child here. Having this mental energy which allows you to jump to and fro between dimensions is perhaps not so good for you.'

'What do you mean?'

Demsel stepped into a hover shuttle. 'One day, when you have the strength, you may decide to break the link.'

Ben sat next to her; it would have been impolite to float beside the shuttle. 'But why?'

'Because, while you flit backwards and forwards like this, you belong to neither world.'

'Dey and Hysle wouldn't like it. I tell them so many

things they need to know.'

'Don't you ever want to grow up?'

'No!'

'One night, when you visit Lictan, you may start to remember who you really are. You must be prepared for that.'

'Does it matter?'

'Dey and Hysle may not want you to.'

Ben was puzzled. 'Why not?'

'Worse still, they may not want you to learn what they really are.'

'What are they then?'

'Not quite what you think.'

'Tell me?'

Demsel continued to tantalise Ben. 'They are very clever creations.'

'You mean they were made by some God?'

'Not a God.'

The folds in Demsel's face deepened into a smile. 'You wanted to see the ship before we left?'

This successfully distracted the eight-year-old. 'Can I see your planet as well?'

'No. Your transmitter key can only bring you to Lictan. The rest of the Universe is further away than you can ever imagine.'

Driven by some sort of biological impulse, Demsel's vast spaceship was cluttered with coils, pipes, tubes, and massive tanks. She had travelled hundreds of light years with her crew who were almost as wrinkled as she was.

The cargo bay was as large as an ancient international airport and deep as a canyon. It was filled with exotic minerals in crates with their own zero gravity so they had to be tethered to the bulkheads during transit. The small hover shuttle swooped about the sheer walls of cargo blinking with security codes.

Ben felt giddy.

Back amongst the coils of the engine chamber, he left the shuttle to float alongside Demsel. She found this funny. Ben was unable to imagine how he looked as he moved like a cartoon phantom through her dimension.

Just before Demsel ended the tour, she beckoned him over to a recess in the main bulkhead separating the living quarters from the engines. The Trocan Captain reached through a jumble of cables to unlock a small door. When she withdrew her hand, something was sparkling in her closed fingers.

Ben loved anything that glittered. 'What is it?'

'This is a tagging crystal. Its molecular qualities are so strange we have to keep the ones we don't use away from the machinery. We use them to tag small consignments that could break free from the main crates during transit. The crystals' frequencies are harmonised with the storage cases so we can easily find them again.'

'Why do you have to keep them away from the machinery?'

The Trocan's amber eyes opened a little wider. 'When they aren't tagging a consignment, they can develop a mind of their own - sometimes jump dimensions.' Demsel took an egg-shaped box from the storage cupboard and placed the small crystal inside it.

Ben was intrigued. "What are you doing?"

'I'm going to tag you.'

He squealed with delight. 'Does that mean it will hold me in once place?'

'Goodness no. It will just stay with you. Wherever you go.' Demsel completed the tagging code. 'There. Now it will only recognise your molecular frequency.' She removed the crystal from the coding device.

Ben immediately reached out, expecting the gem to sink through his hands as the Trocan captain passed it to him. To his amazement, he felt its solid warm shape. He stared open-mouthed at the crystal.

Demsel tossed the golden tassels from her face. 'There are some things not even the Lictana know. That crystal will now only recognise you. It might disappear for a while, but don't worry. It will crop up again when you least expect it. If you put it in your pocket they won't know you have it.'

'Because it will disappear?'

'Undoubtedly.'

'Thank you. I wish there was something I could do for you?'

'There is.' Demsel reached out to tap the gem. Her finger passed through it. 'When you next see this crystal, remember me. Then throw away that transmitter key.'

Ben stayed long enough to watch the huge Trocan cargo carrier lift away from its mooring clamps and ascend like a faceted asteroid to its launch point high above Lictan.

Dey and Hysle were too anxious to hear his latest intelligence to worry about what the Trocan captain had said to Ben.

The eight-year-old would have liked to tease them a little longer. He wasn't sure what the Lictana did to their own disobedient children, though. He hadn't seen any to ask, so decided to play safe.

It was very claustrophobic in their small sphere after being in the gigantic Trocan ship.

'Did you know that the engines of Demsel's ship work by some sort of biological reaction?'

Dey sighed. 'Yes Ben.'

'I know a place where they experiment with plants and other things like that as well.'

'Where is that, Ben?'

'Right next to the launch pad for these strange aircraft things.'

Hysle laughed.

Dey glowered at him. 'Go on, Ben?'

'They look like spaceships, but aren't really. They

must be some sort of weapon.'

Hysle now realised that this was important. 'I thought weapon development had stopped on your planet?'

'Oh it has. This is very secret. The factory is under a plant research place. They have made these devices which are so explosive that they took some of them above the atmosphere to test. The last one killed twenty satellites. They do most of the tests underground now. It shakes the ground terribly.'

Hysle's amusement had turned to horror. 'How did they manage to make these weapons without anyone knowing?'

'The research place is locked up at night when they carry out the tests. They make a lot of noise and the vibrations mess up a terrible number of plant experiments.'

Dey called up maps of the region on the curved wall. 'If there is a launch pad it must be visible.' She could find nothing.

'Oh no! It's hidden under a strawberry field.' Ben pointed it out. 'It grows over this lid which can be swivelled aside to let the launch pad come up. It's very well hidden. If anyone does go near it...' Ben faltered.

'Then what happens, little minnow?' asked Hysle.

'I don't want to remember any more.'

'Do you know what the weapons are for, Ben?'

'Yes, but I don't think I should tell you really.'

Dey tried not to sound desperate. 'You must.'

Ben became apprehensive. 'Let me think about it.'

'Why, little minnow?' asked Hysle.

Ben suddenly felt Demsel's warm crystal in his pocket. Then it faded from his touch. 'I'm frightened. I sometimes don't want to play this game any more.'

Hysle forced a laugh. 'But you have been so valuable to us. We should get the Central Council to award you with a cone of Soolain.'

'What's that?'

'It is not a thing, it is an energy field. It cures people.'

'Of what?'

'Broken spirits, broken hearts. It could even restore the courage of an eight-year-old human.'

Dey was irritated. 'Don't listen to him.'

'Doesn't it really exist then?'

'Yes, but the resources needed to activate the field are so complicated they have hardly ever been used.'

'It sounds wonderful. The sort of thing those ancient gods I read about would give to mortals.'

'The Lictana have the same feeling about the cones of Soolain.'

'A gift which can mend minds and sew souls back together,' Hysle added.

'How do they work?'

Dey sighed. 'Oh Ben, we do not know. They are pure energy. I doubt if the guardians of the cones know either. The reaction can only be triggered for an act of pure altruism.'

Ben would have asked what that was if Dey wasn't looking so serious.

'It must be about time for you to leave. When you come back, you must tell us about the missiles.'

'I don't want to go back yet. I'm not happy there.'

They needed to humour the child more than ever now. Lictan's survival depended on him.

'How about another trip round the capitol?' suggested Hysle, 'It might make you feel a little better.'

Much to Dey's annoyance, he took Ben on a short tour of Lictan's municipal centre.

Ben liked the glittering steeples that studded Lictan's skyline and landscape full of domes, archways, toadstool shapes, and gigantic globes. The Lictana never built underground and most of the toadstool-shaped buildings were only accessible by air lifts. Ben couldn't understand why they had evolved four legs.

They must have been inconvenient. There were so
many things it had never occurred to him to ask when
he was there. He had always taken it for granted that
he was only seeing what they wanted him to. Now he
craved to wander off into the forbidden zones that the
atmosphere seemed to draw a curtain around.

When the bright Lictan sun had set, Ben reluctantly
went back to the world where his molecules would feel
every bump and blister.

CHAPTER 13

Powder and mascara streamed down Tharby's freckled cheeks.

'Stop snivelling like an asthmatic rodent!' snapped Nightingale. 'Pull yourself together and get Sendall back on his feet.'

'But he's in a dreadful state,' Tharby sobbed into his phone. 'I can't make out what happened to him. He must have been lying there for hours.'

'Well, it never killed him you so won't need to invent an autopsy report.'

At that, the medic's marshmallow shell was punctured by the steel underneath. 'You callous old bat! Don't think I'm going to give JB any more shots.'

'He won't be needing them. Just make sure you get sense out of him when he wakes up.'

'He may not remember anything.'

'He'd better remember my name,' Nightingale threatened.

'And I'm not giving him adrenaline. Between us, it's a wonder that we haven't already killed him.' Tharby wiped away his ruined make-up then bit his thumb in frustration.

'He's tougher than you make out. Stop being such a sentimental sponge. Get the facts out of him! I want him back at HQ by the end of the week. And stop sucking your thumb!'

Nightingale hung up before Tharby could protest.

He looked in the washroom mirror at the streaked mascara and wondered why he bothered. Technology that could print the circuitry to power a city on a pinhead had allowed the last waterproof make-up to go out of production half a century ago. There weren't many political points to be made by actors swimming underwater in government sponsored dramas. Those who wanted make-up had to buy the chemicals and blend it themselves. They also had to regularly check their backs for stickers planted on them by members of the Natural Living Campaign.

Damned by the authorities and ecologists alike, Tharby washed his face and returned to JB's bedside.

A nurse was pottering about, happy to at last have a seriously ill patient.

'He's quiet now. About to come round I wouldn't be surprised.'

'Thanks.' Tharby pulled his stethoscope from a pocket.

'I took his pressure. Down to normal and his heartbeat's regular.' The nurse twitched a disapproving eyebrow. 'He hasn't been given stimulants of any sort?'

Tharby was annoyed. The nurse had been warned that only a Group Indigo medic could examine JB. 'Not by me,' he lied. 'What makes you ask?'

'Just wondered where he got the energy to become as delirious as that.'

Tharby was upset and paranoid enough to believe that that the man was laughing at his freckles. 'I'll stay with him now. Can you make out the discharge papers.'

The nurse hesitated as something occurred to him. 'Oh, of course, you two are "classified" aren't you.' He winked lecherously. 'I'll put a notice on the door.' Then he left.

Tim Tharby would have flown into a rage if JB's eyelids hadn't flickered open at that moment. He put an arm under the patient's shoulders to raise him a little.

JB was puzzled by his surroundings and his assistant's lack of powder. 'Tharby?'

'Who else?'

'I didn't recognise you with freckles.'

'I haven't had time to make up.'

'You've been snivelling.'

'Oh don't you start!'

'What's the matter?'

'All those wasted strawberries. The sight of so much crushed fruit is enough to make anyone cry.'

'What?'

Tharby sighed. 'You don't remember, do you?'

'No.'

'Well try. Nightingale wants a detailed account.'

After being unconscious for two days, reality's stiletto prodded JB Sendall back to sensibility. 'About strawberries? You look different without make-up, Tharby. Like a spotted prawn that's lost its whiskers.'

'That's why I wear make-up!' Tharby let JB fall back onto the pillow. 'I don't know why I should get into such a state over you.'

'You want me to stay unconscious so you can feel sorry for me?'

'I'd just like you to pretend to be a human being once in a while!'

'Where are we?' JB asked to stop Tim Tharby bursting into tears again.

'Nursing home used by that botanical research place.'

'What comes in here then?'

'Bruised grapefruit and premature dahlias.' Tharby fidgeted with a phial before announcing, 'You had better remember what happened you know. If you don't by the time Nightingale gets you back ...'

JB shook his head. 'After I stepped out of the car to stretch my legs, everything is a blank.'

'What the hell were you doing in a field of strawberries? You don't even like them. Any fruit that doesn't have the texture of hammered copper is too soft for your palate.'

'There must have been a reason.'

Out of patience, Tharby tossed the phial into his case. 'Can you get up?'

'Another walk?'

'I don't trust that nurse.'

'Why should they listen at the door?'

Tharby shrugged uneasily. 'He just made some saucy comment.'

'About what?'

'Never mind.'

A couple of hours later, as soon as enough sensation had returned to his legs, JB found himself in yet another garden. Unlike HQ's jungle and Bertha's mixed vegetable patch, this was a florist's festival. The botanical reserve's gardeners certainly knew how to regiment their plots into beautifully good behaviour. The elegant dells, banks, and beds wore a multi-coloured gown of no functional use whatsoever.

JB Sendall stood and stared for a moment at the foot of a small waterfall.

Tharby immediately drew the wrong conclusion. 'Don't go and have a fit here.'

'I was admiring the view. The water will mask what we're saying. Anyway, as this is a hospital, having a "fit" should hardly matter.'

'It'd take weeks to explain your condition to these turnips. They only understand root mould and stem infestation.'

'Why didn't Nightingale have me taken back to HQ?'

'That's why she's mad. I wouldn't let her,' Tharby evaded.

'Why not?'

'If you're unconscious, does it matter where you are? It's not as if you can talk in your sleep with a security chip in your skull.' The medic hesitated. 'Anyway, there's something bloody odd about the place. I wanted an excuse to poke around.'

'Find anything?'

'The resident moles don't talk to strangers.'

'Dig up anything on illicit experiments with animal tissue? Or even fish fertility?'

'So you can remember where you sent me.'

'Did you?'

'I didn't want to.' Tim Tharby sighed. 'Look, they're only hedgehogs out here. It's all botany. I doubt if Leader Spudely knows enough about biology to find her own backside. If you want to find out about animal tissue hybridisation, look for a bunker with high electrified fences that burns the lights all night.'

'Nothing even on space research?'

'To explain the UFOs?'

'Well?'

'They're dotty enough to grow asparagus on the moon, but that's all they'd be worried about.' Tharby hesitated. 'I did find something else out.'

'What?' snapped JB, nearly losing his balance.

Tharby steadied him. 'I think I'll save it for Nightingale, or when you remember what knocked you out next to a fence around a strawberry patch.'

JB had a faint glimmer of memory. 'Was it electrified?'

'It was wood. The worst you could have done was fallen off the stile.'

'Stile? I don't remember any stile. What about the scanning equipment?'

'Didn't record a flicker.'

'I'm sure I was picking up something.'

'The rabbits around here aren't allowed transmitting licences.'

JB was irritated with Tim Tharby, any reference to wildlife and himself. He unsteadily strode away from the muffling splash of the waterfall. Then stopped. His expression was tense. The medic reached inside his pocket, ready to give him a tranquillising jab. No longer noticing how much the beds of pinks and hanging fuchsias clashed with Tharby's hair, the cool pale eyes gazed into the distance at more profound implausibilities.

'I'm going back out there,' JB suddenly announced.

Tharby gasped. 'What? Now?'

'While it's still light. There's a bat colony near here

and I don't want any of them parting my hair.'

'Thought it was goats you couldn't stand?'

'Only ones that dye their hair pink.'

Tharby sneered. 'I'll get the car and see if your discharge papers are ready.'

The nurse seemed disappointed at losing his most important patient. The only other cases he had to care for were a poisoned finger and fungal infection on a hydroponics attendant's forearm. Tharby could tell that this nurse had the flickering eye of a voyeur and preferred to treat conditions below the waist. No doubt he and JB Sendall had disappointed him on more than one count.

It was a relief to drive away.

Everything looked idyllic. With the flat quilted colours of the botanical reserve on one side and field of strawberries on the other, it was the ideal place for a picnic. For all its sophistication, Nightingale's scanner failed to detect so much as a gravitational blip.

Tharby stopped the car and jumped out. Even the field voles seemed to be holding their breath.

JB wasn't taken in by the tranquillity. Something was wrong. He got out of the car as though expecting an ambush. The strawberry field looked very much as he remembered. There was a wooden fence and a stile. He didn't remember them.

JB knew Tharby suspected he had one of his regular blackouts. If a more sinister agent had caused the coma, all evidence of the crime had disappeared.

The tubby medic wandered through the strawberry plants picking and eating as much of the fruit as he could while the plundering starlings squawked at him.

'What do you think you're doing?' bellowed JB. 'Those things could be poisoned.'

'I'd rather be poisoned than starve.'

'Missing a meal would do you good.'

'If you don't eat something as well, you'll be flaking out again.'

'An appetite helps me think.'

'So that's where I've been going wrong all my life.'

'Go and watch the scanner.'

Tharby returned to the car, snatching another handful of fruit on the way. According to the scanner, everything was still holding its breath.

'Nothing,' he called back.

JB was standing stock still again.

'What's the matter?'

'This isn't the place.'

'Well of course it's the place.' Tharby came back to him. 'This is where we found you.'

'I was near another strawberry field.'

'Well just how many strawberry fields with overripe fruit do the authorities allow around here?'

Whatever else might have been wrong with JB Sendall, he never made mistakes like that.

Tim Tharby knew it. 'How can you be sure?'

'The birds.'

'Different colour are they?' the medic demanded, stained red hands on hips.

'There weren't any birds in the other field.'

Tharby laughed uneasily. 'So they're gourmets.'

'It was full of ripe fruit and not so much as a sparrow showed interest.'

JB turned to face him. They silently gazed at each other.

'Good grief. That wasn't a blackout. Somebody put your brain in a blender. What does it feel like? 'Tharby eventually muttered

'Get me back to Nightingale.'

'She'll go mad.'

'Why should she? My implant wouldn't have allowed me to say anything.'

'Well, you know what she's like.' Tharby faltered. 'And who the hell could have kidnapped you?'

'Only World Government has the facilities to develop a secret aircraft and they charged World

Security with setting up Group Indigo. So why should either of them need to access my brain?'

Tharby was silent and wished he had become an acrobat like his father.

CHAPTER 14

Nightingale listened with uncharacteristic patience to Tim Tharby's outpourings before interrupting.

'I'll have to let you out into the big wide world more often.'

'I was so worried about JB's condition, I had to do something to take my mind off it.'

'How can you be so sure there's an engineering complex under this botanical reserve?'

'I just followed the paper trail Nichols sent me. Given the amount of heavy engineering equipment delivered to a spot in the middle of nowhere over the last twenty years, it couldn't be anything else. And your scanner detected a large enough cavity.'

'Now why would they shift proto aviation research underground?'

'You tell me. You're the one with the devious mind.'

'Careful, Tharby.'

'Want me to go back?'

'Christ no! It's a wonder they never saw you the first time.'

'I toned down the blusher and wore a headscarf. It must have been vibration that made those trays of seedlings fall off the bench.'

'Have you told Sendall what you found out?'

'Nearly. Then decided to keep it to myself.' Tharby was suddenly suspicious. 'You didn't already know about this, did you?'

'Nichols and Hazlewood haven't come up with any intelligence on it.'

'Given all the info they sent me, they couldn't have thought very hard about it. But then, I don't trust those two gargoyles. Whenever they come up for air they give daylight a fright.'

'I don't trust the pair either, but they'd be no point in them keeping anything like this from me.'

Tharby wasn't convinced. 'What do you think these

UFO things are anyway? Strawberry picking machines?'

'Must be missiles.'

'What for?'

Nightingale smiled icily. 'Aliens perhaps.'

Tharby felt the roots of his pink hair push out a little more grey. 'You think World Security has discovered how far we've got?'

'They have one or two good guessers and the information Jeff Devlin must have passed on before he was snatched. They've had forty years or so to work it out.'

'But ...' Tim Tharby started to sniffle. 'What are we going to do?'

'Bring back Jeff Devlin. What else.'

Tharby's tears evaporated in a surge of rage. 'So that's what you and those two trolls have been up to!' he exploded. 'Why didn't you tell me?'

'You look like an angry puffin, Tharby.'

'That man was a spy! And probably a murderer!'

'I've no doubt he's both, and forty years in deep freeze will not have changed him at all.'

'You can't let him near JB.'

Nightingale's expression was becoming more and more reptilian. 'What's the matter? Jealous because he's becoming Sendall's assistant?'

'You are mad, aren't you!'

'I know what I'm doing.'

That was no consolation to Tharby. 'A murderer, though? JB won't like it.'

'Sendall isn't to be told anything. Not even that the transmission portals are operative.'

'Devlin will know that.' Tim Tharby could usually second-guess most of Nightingale's moves but sometimes her reasoning was beyond even his comprehension. 'Just what are you up to?'

'How do you think I've managed to keep the reins on this place for so long?'

Tharby saw cobra and backed off. 'I don't speculate about things I can't prescribe for.'

Nightingale rose. 'I've spent enough time listening to you.'

'Where are you going?'

'To collect Jeff Devlin of course.'

'I want to see him.'

'I'm not letting you out of the bag until I'm sure his molecules came back in the right order. Just take my word for it; you won't like him at all. He passed the audition for the pustule on World Security's posterior. Not even you could lance that.'

* * *

Alison Spudely pulled off her red sun hat and mopped her brow. It wasn't the hothouse humidity making the gardener sweat. It was the presence of a small, dark woman glittering amongst the hybrids and wondering why it wasn't possible to grow a flower with sequins.

'And what else did you tell him?' Gita Medlock asked in her sweetly disarming manner.

The World Government official was a short, well-upholstered woman punctuated by the full stop of a brilliant gold bindi mark on her bronzed forehead. Sometimes she used a ruby or emerald that sparkled like a third eye. Gita Medlock had the aura of a well-fed vixen waiting in the corner of the chicken coop until her appetite kicked in again.

Leader Spudely was mesmerised by the woman's chandelier earrings. 'I told him that we all see the UFOs. I couldn't very well deny it, could I? That would have made him even more suspicious. How was I to know he would walk in at that moment? We can't afford to have someone watching security monitors all day.'

'Of course.' Gita Medlock could make two words sound like a sentence of execution.

'There were no other options. He might have come

to the right conclusion if I hadn't said something.'

The senior official's diamond nose stud flashed as she gave a china white smile. 'I wasn't criticising,' she lied. 'How much do we owe you for the breakages this time?'

'I haven't calculated.' Spudely went along the bench pointing out rows of precious, decimated seedlings. 'We lost about thirty per cent of the bean cross trays that time, but I'm more worried about the date hybrids. They don't like being shaken about.'

'Goodness, my dear. We can import them.'

It was Alison Spudely's turn to employ the disconcerting glance. 'They are for overseas growers. Their plantations are too temperate now. If you lot stopped messing about with the weather, there wouldn't be any need for places like this.'

'And you would be out of a job, Leader Spudely.'

'I'd prefer to push an allotment wheelbarrow. How was I to know I was becoming over qualified?' The gardener was no longer able to resist asking, 'What are your lot doing down there?'

'World Security experiments. You know the sort of thing? Comes of having access to more money than sense of reality.'

'So why doesn't Group Indigo know anything about them?'

'They only investigate UFO sightings. World Government has always pursued the policy of keeping intelligence and engineering apart. Once one starts interfering with the other, minor cogs start getting illusions of technology.'

'That pink-haired fellow looked as though he came from outer space.'

Medlock chuckled at her sour expression. 'Well, red sun hats and striped overalls aren't exactly standard issue.'

Alison Spudely started to automatically tuck the roots of half potted specimens into their cartons.

'What if he comes back?'

'Just smile and lie, as you've always done.' Then Gita Medlock remembered something. 'Oh, the eastern strawberry field needs tidying up. All that rotting fruit. Looks bad. Not to mention the smell.'

'I'll send out the jam makers.'

'Good.' She wandered up the isle of the long yellow greenhouse to several baskets of bright orange flowers. 'How beautiful.'

'Yes, we keep them for the wasps.'

The official's glittering smile faded. 'Wasps?'

Spudely grinned maliciously. 'They only sting the white fly. Like a basket?'

'Er - no thank you.'

Medlock pulled on her lace gloves and bustled outside. Spudely strode leisurely after her.

'Looks as though the weather's changing.'

The gardener sniffed the air. 'I hope so. We're getting near the end of our water ration.'

'Oh don't worry about that.'

'In that case I'll get the rice/corn hybrid bedded out.' Spudely hesitated. 'I thought the water table was supposed to be going down?'

Gita Medlock examined the flowering shrubs for a suitably garish corsage. 'You don't want to believe all the stories we put about. That was just a ploy to stop people watering their three-acre lawns. When the Saharan Sea is at its maximum level in two years time, the tides will probably fall about three centimetres. Could mean land reclamation and perhaps no need to tour Venice in a submarine any more.'

'Some meteorologists say that the Northern Hemisphere could get colder if Africa becomes any more temperate?'

'That's only a theory. It's not obligatory. Anyway, we could do something about that as well.'

'There's not much World Government can't do.'

'Without all this hassle from the Natural Living Campaign, we could make this the happiest planet in the galaxy.'

'Going to shove something in the water are you?'

Gita Medlock found a bright lemon tree daisy. Making sure there was nothing living inside it, she asked, 'May I?'

'Take a bunch.'

Carefully beheading the flower with a small jewelled knife, she pinned the bloom to the lapel of her violet jacket. 'If your pink, permed visitor turns up again, remember what I said. If he brings his frosty friend with him, lock them in a greenhouse and call me.'

'More breakages.'

'We always pay, Leader Spudely, we always pay.'

* * *

While a field of strawberries was electrocuting JB Sendall, Jeff Devlin had been regaining consciousness and wondering what had happened to a sizeable chunk of history.

He was in no hurry to recover. Although puzzled by his condition, the nurses waiting on him were female and attentive. Patients with reassembling molecules were rare at the convalescent clinic situated on one of the islands that was all the rising North Sea had left of East Anglia and Zeeland. Not knowing he was in fact over seventy, Devlin couldn't make out why he was with the geriatric patients. Nichols and Hazlewood had been careful to select an establishment renowned for its expertise with accelerated senility, just in case his molecules did decide to drift apart.

As Nightingale anticipated, Jeff Devlin had been returned in the same arrogantly pristine condition as when he was snatched. Forty years had not mellowed her opinion of him. Two centuries ago he would have been called a "smoothie" and his like found, bourbon in hand, gracing pulp fiction. Since then, publishers had been persuaded to be more selective in the way they used paper and thankfully the acid content of so much bad literature was happily munching its way through the surviving pages.

Nightingale ascended the steps to the terrace where Devlin sat basking in the sun. He was alone apart from an attendant nurse as it was too hot for the other residents. At the sight of Nightingale, the young woman flinched and promptly left at her half nod in the direction of the door. With the keen instinct of a lecher, Devlin sensed her perfume depart. He squinted to see Nightingale silhouetted against the sun.

Her shape was unmistakable.

'Oh,' he chuckled. 'I thought paradise would have its serpent.'

Then she stepped out of the direct sunlight. The body and bearing may have been unchanged, but the hard lines age had hammered into her already intimidating features answered volumes before he could put the question. He had lost decades. Until then, Devlin believed he had only been gone long enough for a minor change in interior décor.

Nightingale was old. Not fragile or decrepit: aged like a pinnacle of granite defying the elements. Little about her expression had changed, though the explosion of crinkly hair was a little thinner and generously powdered with white.

Nightingale sat opposite Jeff Devlin. She fixed him with a needle glare.

'How long?' he eventually asked.

'Forty years. You've got some revision to do if you want to come back to Group Indigo.'

'I was never discharged.'

'If I had found any bits of you to interrogate, I would have asked what happened?'

Devlin was silent again. Whatever else might have slipped his mind, he could remember how tricky Nightingale was.

'How should I know? I don't recall anything.'

'Never discovered enough of the other two for an autopsy.' Nightingale lounged back and smiled agreeably. 'We assumed that a sudden flux caused their molecules to disassemble.'

Devlin couldn't make out what she was up to. He would have to live another forty years to be that sharp.

Nightingale looked at him with mock concern. 'I thought you were fond of Sally?'

'You know that her child was mine?'

'You mean Ben? Well he certainly wasn't her husband's. Oh, that reminds me.' She took some papers from her waistcoat. 'You'd better sign these.'

'Still using paper?'

'Nobody realised how useful it was until everything became automated.'

'What are they?'

'Authorisation the clinic needs to treat your biological genius for wiping out members of the opposite sex.'

There was no answer. Devlin had been aware he was passing on a mutated virus when he had sexual intercourse with any woman foolish enough to give him a second look. None of them could have lived into middle age. For some cynical motive of Nature, the same condition had not wiped out Devlin, but then, other powers had interfered with his ageing process.

As his eyes narrowed at the small print, Nightingale added, 'Cure anything now, you know. Except freckles, but you'll meet him later.'

Devlin signed the papers. He knew better than to ask what she was talking about.

'If I'm forty years out of date, what use am I going to be to Group Indigo?'

'Oh, nothing much has changed. Managed to have you transmitted back through the portal, but we've hardly improved on it. World Government doesn't even know I've got it working again - if they were aware we had it in the first place.'

Jeff Devlin's sweat glands were still working. 'They must have known.' He shrugged to mask his guilt.

'Oh, quite probably.' Nightingale thoughtfully scratched an eyebrow.

'Why bring me back now?'

'The aliens had this peculiar notion that you were responsible for the death of their agent. Wanted to keep you in that jar forever. Time for them runs at a different pace. Lifespans are much longer than ours. To them, forty years is a brief interlude.'

'And what can I be expected to do after forty years out of circulation?'

'You'll be my number one's assistant. He can be a quaint old-fashioned thing at times.'

Devlin felt as though he'd been tossed the bride's bouquet and would have preferred to enquire about her secretary instead. Ignorance of which way morals and manners had evolved made him think twice.

Nightingale watched Devlin going hot under the collar of his simulated satin dressing gown. She then turned her attention to the romantic remains of the old sea barrier, artificial islands swarming with squabbling birds and a shallow draught ship like a massive tea tray chugging a prototype airbeam ship from Holland. Oh, that all prototype aircraft were so benign. Not that she would fly in one. As a scientist from the old school, she had reservations about being kept aloft by sunbeams and elastic bands.

When she turned back, Nightingale thought the lecher was looking too comfortable. 'We'll have you out of here before the next North Sea surge.'

Devlin believed he was somewhere in the Mediterranean instead of what was left of East Anglia. This degree of weather control had only been a pipe dream forty years ago. 'North Sea-?' No, he wasn't going to give her the satisfaction of being amazed.

'Sea levels are still erratic during sun spot activity.

Not been able to do much about them except lock up more water in a few icebergs.'

'What else.'

Nightingale tossed a sugar cube into the calm water below the terrace. 'Nice lake. That blue agent works wonders.'

'Blue agent?'

'Doesn't harm the fish. The Mediterranean's even bluer and the Red Sea even rustier.'

'What about the Dead Sea?'

'Dried up. Salt flats now. Worked by spies World Security found lacking.'

Jeff Devlin's eyes narrowed. 'What happened to the worker robot programme?'

'Novelty wore off. Now it's either computer controlled heavy machinery or precision androids.'

'The world population recovered, then?'

'Gone down, if anything.'

'How?'

Nightingale shrugged. 'People lost interest after World Government let Security get out of hand for a few years. Lot of dissidents.'

Devlin wasn't sure whether to believe her. 'So they dig salt as well?'

'Oh no, market gardeners mainly. Growing things best suits those sort of people. Only ex-spies dig salt.'

Before she strolled from the terrace to the bridge where she had parked her vintage Amethyst, Nightingale tossed another sugar cube into the water. A mechanical cleaner trout spat it back.

CHAPTER 15

Despite the passing of forty years, Jeff Devlin felt at home. The population was even smaller and seldom interacted so the potential for intrigue had greatly increased. The security of his own time had been more obvious and obsessive. Now, surveillance had been given over to chips, tags and sophisticated grids of scanners. People, genetically predisposed to wrong-foot anyone rocking the even keel of the munificent status quo, controlled them. Transgressors had no escape. Devlin knew which side he was going to be on, whatever Nightingale might have had in mind.

Plotting the new layout of Group Indigo's listed HQ, he stood on the foyer landing and watched the tubby pink-haired man scuttling about below. Jeff Devlin had used make-up in his time, but it was like a second skin on this character. Having managed to successfully oil his way into the fabric of the secret establishment, Tim Tharby came as a shock. The outrageous character would have been re-educated in Devlin's time. Here, the ostentatious medic was under the protection of Nightingale, and her sense of protocol had grown even more bizarre over the years.

Tim Tharby was unaware that he was being observed with a mixture of disbelief and scorn by the result of Nightingale's most recent lapse in good taste, and continued to supervise the arrival of a diagnostic machine. He used his own plump body to cushion it from a buffeting as it was pushed through the front doors the Senior Controller had refused to have automated.

'Daris! Be careful! This equipment is delicate!'

'Sorry. Did I hurt you?'

'No - try again and you might crack a couple of ribs.' Sometimes Tim Tharby didn't realise just how well upholstered he was.

Devlin was bored now he had mentally worked out

the circuitous route he would take to wheedle himself back into a position of influence. All the women at Group Indigo were too worldly wise to corrupt. And there were so many women! They had always outnumbered men since the epidemics swept the planet.

Jeff Devlin turned his attention back to the middle-aged anomaly below. That aberration was his superior! His eyes narrowed dangerously at the thought. Had Tharby known what was going through that murderously amoral mind, he might have indented for a few bandages on his own behalf.

JB Sendall was no easier to fathom. Devlin's icy superior had obviously not requested an assistant, especially one with smooth-skinned, dark-haired good looks that made his appear aged and anaemic.

His new assistant may have been charming and well mannered, but JB disliked Jeff Devlin at first sight, then promptly went on to thoroughly loathe him. He wanted to back him into one of Nightingale's experiments to see if an armadillo trotted out in his place. Unable to intimidate Devlin, JB put up his frostiest front and only spoke to him when he had to.

From behind his amiable smoke screen, Jeff Devlin continued to observe; particularly the foppish tantrums of Tim Tharby. That contemptible little secretary medic, who wielded more influence than any of the other qualified beards and button pushers in Nightingale's HQ, might well prove to be the one weak strand in her intricate web.

Hazlewood and Nichols would have put Devlin's rising spite down to a few stray molecules trying to find their way home. Thwarted at not getting what mostly occupied his urges, he was becoming dangerous. Nightingale had taken everything into account, except the possibility that the man could become even more vicious.

JB Sendall noticed Jeff Devlin on the landing as he

observed Tim Tharby and realised why he didn't like his new assistant. Eventually, against his better judgement, JB pressed the button on Nightingale's office door.

Unfortunately, it immediately opened.

Nightingale was surprised to see her number one. He usually had to be summoned with veiled threats.

'What is it?'

JB took a step inside. She pushed the button that closed the door before he could change his mind.

'I'm not sure.'

'In that case you'd better sit down. It might come to you if your brain's nearer the floor.' JB obeyed. 'Your treatment going all right?'

He knew what she meant. 'I haven't had a relapse since I collapsed in the strawberries, though the sight of jam now makes me throw up.'

'Tharby's been looking after you, then?'

JB hesitated. This wasn't what he wanted to discuss. 'Never lets me out of his sight.' He pulled himself together. 'There's something else.'

'What?'

'Devlin.'

'Devlin?'

'The man's watching Tim Tharby like a cat stalking a mouse.'

Nightingale was surprised that her number one had taken so long to find something about Jeff Devlin that bothered him. She hadn't expected it to be this.

It triggered a nightmare scenario. She quickly returned it to the dungeons of her subconscious. Whatever abuse the Senior Controller heaped on the medic, she wasn't prepared to entertain the thought of him coming to grief because of her machinations.

'Go on?'

'I don't know why the man does it.'

'Well, given the way Devlin thinks, he's probably studying form.'

'For what? He's only interested in women.'

'Blackmail, I wouldn't be surprised.'

It wasn't often Nightingale made a slip like that. She would have kicked herself if her feet hadn't been on the desk. Behind those icy pale eyes, JB Sendall was calculating an answer.

'Blackmail? What could he blackmail Tim Tharby about?'

Nightingale shrugged. 'No idea. That's the sort of thing Devlin would do. You've no idea what our podgy little medic might have been up to, have you?'

After thinking about it, JB was surprised that he hadn't. Tim Tharby was too straightforward and busy to bother with Machiavellian intrigues. Group Indigo was only large enough for one Nightingale.

The Senior Controller swung her feet from the desk to face JB. 'Whatever Devlin's up to, it'll have to wait a few weeks.'

'Why?'

'I'm closing the place down for a while. Refurbishments and all that.'

Nightingale had not allowed the decorators in for thirty-five years. Any new fittings or lick of paint had been added by a tired prototype robot that should have worn out twenty years ago, and members of staff who were fed up with finding new life forms evolving in the cobwebs.

'Decorating?' The disbelief in JB's tone had its own specific gravity. 'The only paint strippers you believe in are uncontrolled explosions.'

'You need a holiday, Sendall.'

'You know I never take holidays.'

'You must be entitled to several years since your divorce. You can survive a couple of weeks without Tharby's medication. Why not go away somewhere?'

JB thought it over. 'What about Devlin?'

'He doesn't have to go with you.'

'You know what I mean.'

'Tharby is taking a holiday as well. No doubt in that tatty little beach house held down by polished pebbles.'

'Polished pebbles?'

'Yes. When he's there he stops painting his face and polishes pebbles instead. Probably gives the seals a laugh.'

'The place was filled with fans at last time I saw it.'

'The sea air started to rot the lace. Sent them to his father. Did you ever meet Chas Tharby?'

JB was suddenly aware of being lured into small talk. He shook his head before he was mesmerised. 'All right, all right! I'll take a holiday!'

'Good. Now, there is something downstairs I want you to see.'

Knowing Nightingale, it wasn't pressed flowers or tatting.

JB followed her below into the laboratory encircled by World Security's console.

As soon as JB Sendall saw the molecular transmission portal at its centre, he knew. 'It's operative! How long? Why didn't you let me know?'

Nightingale ignored him and began checking the portal's control panel.

'Has it been tested?' JB hectored.

Nightingale laughed. 'Don't worry, it works. That's why you're down here. Engage that remarkable memory of yours and watch me carefully. These instructions are only on the master computer. No one but Tim Tharby and I have the code for them. When you've seen this, we will be the only three people who know how to activate the portal.'

'Apart from the Lictana.'

Nightingale froze. He hadn't learnt that name from her. It had to be Tharby. Unhurriedly, she carried on pushing a sequence of buttons, then turned a dial until the air in the booth was buzzing with agitated particles.

'Transmission can be made in either direction.'

JB was horrified. 'My God! That means they have unrestricted access to us!'

'Not through here. When we transmit to them, molecular integrity only lasts minutes.' Nightingale smiled. 'Like to send them a message?'

Out of his depth, JB Sendall stepped back for fear of being engulfed by the ultraviolet cloud. 'How many of these transmission portals are there?'

'Half a dozen more with one-way facilities. Our way. The aliens could never gain access through them, even if they knew they existed.'

So there had been a point to Nightingale's secretive behaviour after all. 'How did you manage all this by yourself?'

'As soon one system was set up, the rest were easy to duplicate.' Nightingale illuminated a bank of keys on the panel. 'Our insurance against them doing any more body snatching. They're all activated from this control. It can only be operated with the right password sequence.' Nightingale fed a code into the panel and a small flat drawer slid from it. She took out a disk smaller than a child's fingernail. 'In here are the passwords and only record of the portal locations. If anything happens to Group Indigo, this has to go with me.' She returned it to the drawer which closed seamlessly into the panel. Satisfied that JB Sendall's orderly mind was absorbing everything; she keyed in some numbers. 'This is the code for the drawer. Remember it.' Then she cancelled it from the panel's screen before a lesser mortal could have taken in the first three digits.

'You think something could happen to you?'

'I'm held together by vitamins, folic acid and parcel tape. Without Tharby for a couple of weeks, I might start getting absent-minded.'

JB knew the Natural Living Campaign would achieve world domination before that happened.

'Start packing,' Nightingale ordered before he could

think too deeply about things. 'And don't come back until I beam you a clearance.'

'Why not?'

'The new scanner won't recognise your paw prints.'

'The old scanner didn't recognise anyone's palm prints and that's been disconnected for over ten years. What do you need a new one for?'

'The paranoia of old age.'

Her number one gave up. 'If anything went wrong, surely you could destroy the disc?'

'It is the only record.'

'Why?'

'Because there is only one safe place to keep it.'

'Here?'

'Can you think of a better location?'

JB had long since given up trying to work out the idiosyncrasies of Nightingale's behaviour. There always turned out to be a good reason for them in the end.

'I see.'

JB Sendall resentfully packed a suitcase, then spent a few hours wandering the overgrown grounds. Though he had a good many thoughts to entertain, he didn't like being alone with them for too long.

He passed the back courtyard's security mirror and jumped at the sight of himself. It came as a shock to be suddenly reminded what he looked like. Nightingale's number one realised what a strangely tasteless creature he was. Tentatively touching the reflection of the wan face, the movement of JB's doppelganger seemed to dawdle.

Was it safe to drive a car while his reflexes were in this misaligned state? How much had he taken Tim Tharby for granted? It was hardly surprising the medic went about in a state of badly suppressed hysteria most of the time. Nightingale and he must have reduced the man's reflexes to raffia.

Perhaps it was time to take a holiday for everyone's

sake. Where to, though? Only one person had ever invited JB to stay with them and that made him recall that he once had one of those old-fashioned things called a marriage.

From what he could remember, it hadn't been a bad marriage, just full of infuriating holes. For Melony, his wife, those holes grew too large. She at last had to admit that she didn't, after all, understand JB Sendall and left him for someone so sane it was like entering another plane of existence.

* * *

'Where do you get your hair done?' quipped Devlin for the third time.

Tim Tharby gave up and put down the Petri dish of mould he was counting. 'I do it myself.'

'Why not let it go naturally grey, then it'll match your freckles.'

'Some people carrying unspeakable genetic mutations should know when to keep their mouths shut. Though with the number of teeth needed to fit that smarmy grin of yours, you must find it quite a job.'

Tharby had hit a nerve.

'My condition's not genetic, it's viral, you little slug! Where did you find out about it anyway?'

'I am the medical officer for this establishment. I do have access to your records.'

'You know where you can shove them.'

'The next stop from where you keep your "viral" mutation, no doubt.'

Devlin suddenly smiled in a disconcertingly boyish way. 'How old are you, Tharby?'

Tharby refused to be intimidated. 'If we're going to discuss longevity I might end up giving you a molecule count.'

'At least I was never short-changed. How many of you were there originally, Tharby? Was that shape

138

the result of one of Nightingale's experiments?'

'The only molecular experiment she ever carried out was with a lower life form, and you were it Devlin. Just because there's no woman here who will give you a second look, I'm sure you could find a better way of using your free time instead of pestering me.'

'So, how do you know I haven't been able to pull any talent?'

Tim Tharby gave him a withering glare. 'Naturally I warned all of them about your viral problem.'

Devlin was silent for a moment. In its surprise, his face looked blandly handsome. Then the eyes narrowed. 'You treacherous lizard. I'll make you suffer for that. I'll see this little piggy die squealing.' He plucked Tharby's hair viciously.

'Look, you oily sliver of rat dropping ...' Tharby was about to start in earnest, but the door slid open and Nightingale's presence bought a few seconds silence.

'Did you hear that, Boss?' Jeff Devlin exclaimed.

'I'm afraid I'm a little deaf. Getting past seventy now you know. What did he say?'

Devlin almost repeated Tharby's observation before realising she was mocking him. Flustered, he made for the door.

'I have to check the solar pressure.' And he bolted from the room.

'Solar pressure?' scoffed Tharby. 'What's he on about?'

'It used to be his way of excusing himself when his venereal condition demanded relief. I've no doubt your little tantrum had the same effect on him.'

'Well I'd certainly never get that close to him, even to pass on a mutated venereal virus if I had it. It's a wonder any malignancy would want to use him as a host.'

'He picked it up when he was in Space Security. There was a rumour he secretly made first contact and screwed around with the aliens.'

Tharby glowered at her. 'You no doubt started it as one of your perverted jokes. Don't you dare tell me now that everything that came into contact with the man has to go into Alpha Level sterilisation? I'll throw such a tantrum that even your precious Lictana will hear it.' Tharby's eyes suddenly widened in horror. 'It wasn't the Lictana? Was it?'

Nightingale gave it some thought. 'Well, even something with four legs would do if he became desperate enough.'

'Oh shut up, for pity's sake! Tell me where he contracted the bloody mutation?'

'When antibiotics became ineffective, there were thousands of dangerous viruses floating about. The mutation Devlin picked up knew a good chance when it saw it.'

'Pity you didn't put the turd out of everyone else's misery when you had the chance.'

'Snappy little soul today, aren't we?'

'He is the most obnoxious ...'

Nightingale raised her hand. 'I know. But I don't want him provoked.'

Tharby was puzzled. Nightingale could be secretly protective over worthwhile people. Defending a waste of space like Jeff Devlin was totally out of character, even for someone as devious as her. 'What could I do to him?'

'He's lacking enough imagination to be very dangerous.'

So she was really protecting her medic. Reluctant to say anything that would change her mind, Tim Tharby let the matter drop. 'Where's JB?' he asked.

'Taking a walk. He's agreeing with himself to have a holiday.'

'Oh.'

Nightingale had expected more reaction from Tharby. 'He'll be all right won't he?'

'There are enough chemicals swilling about in his

system to take him to Mars and back. If I give him any more, it'll probably iron out his cerebral cortex and kill him.'

'All right.' She paused, as though unsure about something for the first time in her life. 'I've told him about the transmission portals and their location disc. Now nothing can stop him thinking things out for himself. When he does, I want him to be a long way from here - especially you. After all the time I've invested in Sendall, I don't want to end up having to kill him.'

Tharby shuddered at the thought. Whether she meant it or not, she was certainly capable. 'He won't recall everything immediately. He'd need a pretty powerful catalyst.'

'I hope you're right, but I think he's beginning to remember.'

'Remember what?'

'Unless it was you who gave him the name of the Lictana?'

Tharby closed his eyes and swayed. 'Oh hell! Oh hell and damn!'

CHAPTER 16

Hazlewood was bored with collating intelligence on everything from the movement of ancient satellites to the colour of the World President's beach sandals. 'Surely we can ditch those links with the South Pole? They haven't sent us one message worth looking at.'

Nichols was more interested in checking out Nightingale's other transmission portal installed in their parasitic blister on the jugular of world-wide communication. 'The collators might come up with something.'

'We only ever hear about penguin communication experiments and seasonal ice density. What are they doing down there, teaching the birds to mix cocktails?'

'They may see a UFO. If Nightingale did not hear about it first she would be suspicious.' Nichols paused. 'Apart from that ...'

Hazlewood groaned. 'Oh no, you cannot believe she has managed to set up other transmission portals without us knowing, can you?'

'It is possible, and one could well be at the South Pole.'

'So could Santa Claus.'

'That is the North Pole.'

'He might have fusion-powered reindeer.'

'The portal equipment could be put in a crate with an intelligent android to assemble it.'

'In Antarctica? Part of it still freezes solid four months of the year.'

'Or in the middle of some conservation park. They cover at least fifty percent of the temperate zones and eighty percent of the rest. Not all of them are visited.'

'Look, I do not trust Nightingale either, but this is taking speculation too far.'

'Since she developed her own transmission system, the woman is capable of anything.'

'Even if it is true, she is hardly going to tell World

Security.'

Nichols was growing irritated with her assistant. 'They managed to pick up Sendall. No doubt gave him a brain probe. Nightingale could have taken the man into her confidence.'

'Probably froze their instruments.'

'And she shrugs the abduction off as though it was just another of his turns.'

'All Group Indigo seniors are given implants to stop their memory being probed. If anything touches their cerebral cortex they go into a coma.'

Nichols hummed. She'd forgotten about that. 'But they did manage to wipe part of his short term memory.' She paused. 'We will have to tell Nightingale.'

'Tell her what?'

'About the boy.'

Hazlewood pushed her eyebrows up. 'Oh dear. He has been very useful to the Lictana.'

'Dey and Hysle think Ben is slipping away. He met some Trocan captain who insisted on giving him good advice.'

'All the same, be careful.'

* * *

Nightingale viewed the enormous cavity in the ground where a green dome had once towered. A salvage squad was pottering around inside it like baffled ants. It was obvious that Landscaping Control didn't know what to do with it. Too many arterial services ran through the road at its bottom, so it couldn't be turned into a lake and that formerly docile monster, public opinion, was becoming more and more influenced by the Natural Living Campaign. It would never allow them to rebuild it.

Nightingale smiled wryly to herself. Of all the monsters she had ever had to contend with, public opinion had so far not bothered her.

Gradually, other onlookers started to find her presence more interesting than the huge void below them. Nightingale tried to smile politely at the stony hostility human expressions assume when confronted by something they don't understand then sauntered off. Once out of sight, she darted into a lift lobby.

The lift was not used to receiving requests for the level she needed. It spat her card out three times before humming its way down. Still not accepting that it was able to stop at any level other than those on its indicator, it would only let the Senior Controller out two floors above. Nichols and Hazlewood must have sabotaged it. Irritated, Nightingale wended her way down several passages and stairs, through three security doors and eventually into their control.

Hazlewood was hardly elated by her arrival. 'Close the door please.'

'What?' Nightingale noticed that she had to retrieve her security pass from the slot which had pushed the card through to the inside wall. 'When did you install that?'

'Couple of weeks ago. I was bored.'

'Useless piece of apparatus. The rats down here can't be that ambitious.'

'Nichols is in the transmission portal.'

'Something wrong?'

'No. Just a check. These two-way portals need more maintenance.'

'More maintenance than what?'

'One-way portals of course.'

Nightingale glowered. 'There are no-one way portals. We agreed on that.'

'Of course.' Hazlewood changed the subject. 'How is yours doing?'

'It's fully operational. I've done a test with the Lictana. They're satisfied.'

'Oh good.' Hazlewood beamed. There was rebellion behind the bovine expression. 'We will have to see it some time.'

'Whenever you like.' Nightingale rummaged in coat pocket. 'I brought your passes.'

'How thoughtful of you.'

'Try to look reasonably human when you decide to come, the squirrels are easily panicked.'

Hearing her assistant beginning to founder on the rocks Nightingale was dropping, Nichols joined them.

The Senior Controller gave her a long hard look as though she had just descended from a cobweb. 'All right, what is it you want to tell me?'

Nichols pressed the switch that brought down lead shutters to block out any electromagnetic radiation.

'Must be serious?'

Now totally sealed, Nichols altered the atmosphere gauge to reduce the air pressure.

'I know you two would like to float about, but if I get a headache I'll blow out a wall,' Nightingale warned.

Nichols knew she was probably carrying a weapon capable of doing it. She smiled and re-adjusted the control. 'You remember the child your operative Sally had?'

Nightingale shrugged dismissively. 'I only glimpsed him once.'

'I meant, you know that she had a child by Jeff Devlin?'

'Well, of course. Her husband absconded with the boy before I could find him a decent home. Took me years to trace the man.'

Nichols hesitated. 'You managed to find them?'

'Oh yes.' Nightingale slumped into a chair. 'By then the boy's brain had been damaged by a mutated virus inherited from Jeff Devlin. Had to be put into an institution - poor kid!'

'What about the other father?' asked Hazlewood.

'Who? Dr. Harold? He had an accident.'

'Really?'

'Yes, mountains on that side of the continent tend to

be very high. Long way to fall. Not that he felt anything at the time.'

'Why not?'

'I anaesthetised him with a bullet through the brain. You remember bullets, don't you?'

Nightingale relished the surprised silence of her two spies, then demanded, 'Well, what is this astounding information you have for me?' she demanded.

Nichols took a deep breath. 'That boy.'

'Ben.'

'He apparently found the transmission key his mother lost.'

'Really?' Nightingale tried to appear surprised, but looked more like an enquiring hawk. 'Go on.'

'He was trying to return it when his mother and the Lictanan agent were blown up. No one knows how, but the boy's metabolism was able to operate it. The key gave him the ability to forge a mental link with the Lictana. It was so effective, he managed to project his appearance and converse without a translator.'

'And now?'

'He still is.'

'Oh?'

'He has been passing on information to them.'

Nightingale was silent for so long, the other two heard ticking.

'What?'

Nichols relished her role as much as she dared. 'The boy may have been intellectually damaged, but he proved to be an effective spy.'

Nightingale suddenly relaxed. 'How could he have known anything of interest to the Lictana?'

'We have no idea. Just take it from me, he does.'

'How can they be so sure it's not the invention of an unstable mind?'

'Everything he told them checks out.'

Nightingale's brow furrowed. 'You mean, it ties in with Group Indigo's intelligence?'

'Too tightly to be dismissed. The Lictana believe that the damage to the boy's brain enables him to divorce his consciousness from his body.'

'It's called astral travelling.' Nightingale's tone was flat.

'Well, however he does it.'

'All right then, let's say I take your word for it.'

'You had better hear his latest intelligence.'

'What is it?'

'He told them about an underground weapons testing complex.'

'What sort of weapons?'

'Missiles with enough implosive potential to cause atomic disruption.'

Nightingale's eyebrows rose in disbelief.

Nichols went on. 'A high-altitude aircraft tested the missiles above the atmosphere. They accidentally wiped out twenty satellites. It would take no more than three of them to lay waste to a planet.'

'Total molecular disintegration,' added Hazlewood.

Nightingale seemed to have difficulty taking it in. 'Has the boy told them any more?'

'They must be for use against the Lictana,' Nichols went on. 'There are no conflicts on Earth that could justify weapons like that. If one of those things were fired through a transmission portal ...'

Nightingale didn't feel too outraged. 'Fancy a young child being able to astral travel like that.' She changed the subject without warning. 'You know about Devlin?'

The momentum of Nichols' revelation lurched to a sudden halt. 'What?'

'He's working at Group Indigo's HQ now.'

Hazlewood had guessed at much. 'We wondered what you wanted him for.'

Nightingale changed tack again. 'Of course, if World Security does have a strike capability, how do we know that the Lictana don't have the same?'

Nichols cut in before Hazlewood started to discuss

the possibility of a penguin operating a portal. 'You do not. There are at least two more Earth years for either side to obliterate the other without warning.'

Hazlewood felt obliged to rationalise Nichols' nightmare scenario. 'The Lictana have not shown aggression over the past two centuries. Things only became dangerous when Nightingale brought a two-way system on line.'

Nightingale gave a hard smile. 'I'll never know for sure what the Lictana were up to before then. I've a lot of data to say it wasn't all good. We were just of experimental interest. Knowing that the portal could be made two-way was the only thing that stopped their little forays.'

'You have no proof of that.'

'The number of suspicious sightings fell off wonderfully. And, given that the Lictanan life span is five times ours, it's unlikely that their curiosity just petered out.'

'All right,' conceded Nichols. 'Say this is true, it still does not square with what World Security is up to.'

'Wait until that boy tells them more. He might come up with something to persuade the Lictana to think twice about over-reacting.'

Nichols hesitated. 'If you know who he is, aren't you going to have him picked up?'

'He disappeared without trace years ago. Given the condition he inherited from his father, everyone believed he was dead.'

'Come on, nobody on this planet disappears that easily.'

'Dr. Harold was an informer for World Security. They would have allowed him to slice the boy up and scatter the pieces. They probably gave Ben another identity as soon as his father became bald eagle fodder.' Nightingale rose. 'All right, I'll get Tharby to dig out his mother's DNA map. You've already got Devlin's, of course. If we ever find the boy, we'll have to keep this from him. Being raised by one scumbag is enough for any child; he doesn't need to know half his genes came from a sewer rat.'

'Well, Devlin is not likely to find out. His IQ did not appear to be that wonderful.'

Nightingale saw no point in correcting their misapprehension. 'Oh, that man works by instinct. His olfactory senses pick up secrets like a dog can smell a bitch in heat. Mind you, he's a bit like that as well.' Nightingale strode to the shutters, then turned before she reached them. 'Of course, if the boy can astral travel, the only way he can be silenced is with a bullet, and that seems a bit hard, don't you think.'

Nichols opened the shutters and Nightingale left.

Nichols and Hazlewood waited until she was above ground before saying anything.

Hazlewood watched Nightingale striding across the neighbouring disaster area on the surveillance monitor. 'The lead shutters were a little melodramatic.'

'Stopped her walking out in a hurry.'

'What do you think?'

'She is lying about something. I am not sure what.'

'I am more worried about the risk she is running with Devlin. If everything Ben said was true, World Security will have to make their move soon, or not at all.'

'The planets will never come into contact again. Why should World Security destroy Lictan? But then, she was right about the things they got up to before she opened her two-way portal.'

'We will have to hope she never finds out what they were.'

CHAPTER 17

Encouraged by the way he had eased himself back into Group Indigo, Jeff Devlin's next aspiration was to get access to the restricted files. As usual, Nightingale was tight-lipped about the very matters an ambitious rat like him needed to know if he was going to be king of the sewer.

Devlin had made the odd foray outside, into the bland clinically restored ecosystem. It was disconcerting. Not a uniform in sight, just an unsettling awareness of being scanned and filed according to height, age and any political, sexual, religious, or disruptive inclination. It was enough to put many nature lovers off the scenery.

Social interaction also had its pitfalls. Devlin spent most of his time in Nightingale's HQ and believed its resident eccentrics represented normal behaviour. Beyond its boundaries, there was no point in being rude or patronising. Others simply put it down to social inadequacy and offered him the card of a councillor. What sort of world was it where a well-turned insult was transformed into educational deficiency?

Tim Tharby's reaction at being baited gave Jeff Devlin more satisfaction than trying to interact with the homogenised population outside. It was no good, he had to pay the medic another visit. This time it wasn't only to exercise his spite. He needed something.

Tim Tharby was in the middle of some delicate research.

'Go away, can't you?' he snapped. 'Haven't you got anything better to do?'

Devlin chuckled. 'Now JB is on holiday, there's no one else to play with.'

The medic was sharper than his tormentor had taken into account. 'I know you're only carrying on

like this because Nightingale wouldn't trust you with
the master computer code.'

This made Devlin hesitate. 'Now why should that
bother me?' He smiled innocently. He could think of a
far better reason to persecute Tharby. 'I hardly
expected to be taken to everyone's bosom as soon as I
arrived.'

'I doubt if a sex-starved baboon would want to take
you to her bosom.'

Tharby's off-hand remark struck Devlin square in
the ego and he was quiet for a few seconds, vindictively
calculating.

'Why didn't Nightingale want Sendall to know
where I really came from?'

'She already had her work cut out trying to persuade
him to put up with you. You do have the inclinations
of a raddled tomcat and charisma of a rattlesnake, you
know.'

Bull's-eye again. Without knowing it, Tharby was
becoming quite a marksman. As the medic revealed
the edge he had inherited from his test pilot mother
and conjuror father, Jeff Devlin was almost persuaded
to leave the prickly pink hedgehog alone. No longer an
object of contempt, the medic was becoming too much
of a challenge.

Tim Tharby might have swallowed his venom had
he been able to hear him mentally break every bone in
his body. Humane poisoning was a better fate than
the one Devlin had in mind.

The medic needed to concentrate on his work and
his presence was becoming intolerable. 'What is the
matter with you? You should have calmed down by
now.'

'Calmed down?' Devlin was puzzled. 'What do you
mean? Calmed down?'

'Well, if you don't know by now, you must be leading
a celibate life.'

'How did you know Nightingale tricked me into

signing that authorisation form?' Devlin snarled so viciously Tharby could feel his ends split.

'What authorisation form?' he asked ingenuously.

'Of course.' The truth slowly dawned on the Lothario. 'You must have been the one who supplied the clinic with the details.'

Tharby shrugged. 'You'd better take it up with Nightingale.'

'You knew all along that operation would make me impotent.'

'You could always learn how to shake hands.'

Devlin was ominously quiet for some while.

Tim Tharby went back to pipetting samples into phials.

Devlin's arm suddenly shot out and obscured them. His pupils were dilated like a cat's about to pounce.

'Now what game are we playing?' the medic asked with an air of tedium.

'I know you've been drugging Sendall.'

Tharby hesitated. 'Well of course I have to give JB drugs.'

'Not these.'

'What are you talking about?'

'I don't know why you do it. Perhaps you think it keeps him quiet.' Devlin's voice dropped to a whispering hiss. 'I've been watching you. You've been pumping mind-altering drugs into Nightingale's number one.'

'I'd no idea you knew so much about medicine.'

'Is she aware of what you're doing?'

Tharby said nothing.

A cruel smile crossed Devlin's face. 'Well, well. Now what would the Senior Controller do if she found out? What are you up to, Tharby? Trying to convince him of things his better sense would avoid? I can see the possibilities in that.'

Tharby suddenly caved in. 'All right! What do you want?'

Devlin feigned indifference. 'Me? I thought I'd just warn you in case Nightingale found out. I've no doubt you would have a simple enough explanation if she asked.'

'If she finds out?'

'Why should she?'

'Because you will tell her if I don't give you something that you haven't been allowed to get your grubby paws on.'

'Something like that.'

'What is it?'

'The code to access the master computer.'

Tharby fell silent. Devlin reached out to ruffle the medic's immaculate hairdo. Tharby struck his hand away. After a difficult pause, he put the pipette down and wrote the code on a pad. Devlin tore the page off and blew him a kiss as he sped out of the room.

As soon as he had gone Tharby turned to his intercom. 'How was that then?'

Nightingale had breathed in too much dust from the major accident site and sounded huskier than usual. 'Very convincing. You should have gone on the stage.'

'What, with all those lights and weird people? I get enough of them around here.'

'Careful Tharby, you weren't that good.'

'Well, what about all those mind-bending drugs I've been giving JB then?'

'How long will they stay in his system?'

He sighed. 'I told you, for long enough.' The medic hesitated. 'You did mean it when you said I wouldn't have to give him any more after this?'

'I meant it. As long as he obeys orders and doesn't return here.'

Tim Tharby apprehensively recalled the inference she had made about having to kill JB. 'He usually does as he's told, doesn't he? Nothing will go wrong. What could trigger total recall during the next couple of days? Highland cattle don't make conversation that stimulating.'

'All right, now get back to work. You still have to duplicate all the records in the south basement. Have them ready by this evening. You can smuggle them out when they change the surveillance disc.'

'When am I allowed to get some rest?'

'You don't need any. You left it too late for beauty sleep.'

'You sound like bloody Devlin!'

'And keep well clear of that man from now on! I think castration has persuaded him to change his diet.'

'What? You think he'll start ring-barking the trees then? He's certainly got the teeth for it.'

'Don't mistake him for a squirrel, Tharby. The only pudding he wants to sink his teeth into has pink icing.'

'He doesn't scare me.'

Nightingale coughed with dust and annoyance. 'Look, you obtuse little wombat, just do as I tell you!'

'Why?'

'I want those records out tonight.'

'Why the rush?'

'Don't argue. Do it!' Nightingale clicked off her intercom.

Tharby had the uneasy feeling that Nightingale hadn't told him everything. A sensation that came over him quite often. JB Sendall may have obeyed orders without question, but Tharby had the dominant gene for curiosity.

* * *

Gita Medlock's travel planner had not forecast this downpour. It seemed some deity had decided to wreak vengeance on World Government for altering the water table by a few inches. Barely able to see the road through the torrential rain, the senior official recalled Alison Spudely's foreboding that the climate of the Northern Hemisphere was on the verge of catastrophic change. If something was on the blink at Climate

Control, the Natural Living Campaigners must have been dancing in the mud.

At last, the gates of Group Indigo's listed HQ came into view. Being keener on neatly cultivated gardens, Gita Medlock steeled herself to enter a rampant jungle occupied by hungry failed experiments.

Branches bowed down under the weight of water and gangling weeds straddled the already slippery road surface. What was wrong with Nightingale? No one else would have been allowed to let the flora take over like this. Unfortunately, despite all her eccentricities, the planet's survival lay in that delinquent geriatric's hands.

The outline of the historic house loomed against the leaden sky. It was not until Gita Medlock had driven into the brightly-lit reception porch that she stopped thinking about dangerous wildlife and visitors from the grave. An encounter with Nightingale was daunting enough.

Short, ostentatious and friendly, Medlock was hardly the sort of person most people would take for a senior official of World Government.

A guard in a uniform more like casual wear strolled from an antechamber to greet her. She lifted her ID to his scanner before he could ask for it.

Gita Medlock's credentials confirmed, he replied with a lazy smile and touch of the forehead before returning the scanner to his inside pocket. The badge under his body warmer was revealed. She gave it a cursory glance and made a mental note of his name for future reference. "Mature, dependable, probably loyal. Keep outside sensitive areas."

'Thank you, Mr Shultz.'

'I shall call someone down, Marm.' Shultz pulled a phone from another pocket, pushed a button on it once, then returned it.

Gita Medlock would have received an effusive welcome anywhere else given her status. The intense novice physicist sent down to collect her refused to be impressed.

With casual deference, the young bearded man showed her the lift to Nightingale's office. 'Can't come up with you I'm afraid. Nightingale only lets beards have "B" passes.'

With a jolt, the lift hurtled Gita Medlock upwards. She realised too late that most people at Group Indigo used the stairs. Malfunctioning lifts were Nightingale's way of compelling her staff to take exercise.

As clear-walled levels flashed by, she wanted to stop and take a look at the high-tech machines rubbing explosive proof casing with medieval flasks. She had long been convinced that dimensionally unstable molecules and machines didn't mix. In any other facility they would have been kept well apart. Had World Government known forty years ago that the one exception they made to that policy would leave them at the mercy of a Machiavellian senior citizen, the planet would have been organised a little differently - mainly with escape hatches in the form of an effective space programme. During that time they could have been using their resources to set up colonies on Mars, mining the asteroid belt and seeding Venus's atmosphere to make it habitable, not playing tag with aliens they couldn't see.

The lift stopped with a jolt. As Gita Medlock stumbled out, Nightingale was waiting, sphinx-like, to meet her.

The visitor rearranged the frills on her blouse. 'Why aren't beards allowed an "A" pass?'

'They get singed in the sort of research we carry out up here.'

'What about the research you carry out downstairs?'

Nightingale paused to gaze down at the senior official. Gita Medlock came from a prestigious hierarchy. No social committee or government directive would have dared tell her how to dress and she took full advantage of that privilege. Good taste to Nightingale was anything black, zipped and functional. To Medlock, everything frilly, fussy and fringed. Nightingale was grateful that Tim Tharby would never get permission to totally disregard the dress code. He must have been the one to talk JB Sendall into wearing silver edging on his otherwise anonymous light grey jackets.

'Come inside.' Nightingale ushered Gita Medlock into her office and closed the door. 'I suppose you want a progress report?'

The visitor glanced about the office for the odd alien or failed experiment before sitting down. 'That's not why I came.'

'Really?'

'Don't feign innocence, Nightingale. You'll never be as good an actor as Tharby.'

'Tharby can convince himself he's telling the truth.'

'Weird little creature. Where did you find him?'

'Sitting on the toadstool one of our biochemists grew to process hallucinating drugs from. We've been wondering who's hallucinating about whom ever since.'

'You were probably the one to stunt his growth so he could spy on the fairies living in that jungle out there?'

'No need. I am a fairy from that jungle out there. But that's not what you came to talk about either.'

Recovering from the bizarre mental image of Nightingale sprouting wings and giving up her zipped black for gossamer, Gita Medlock said, 'You've been looking for a child who disappeared forty years ago.' Nightingale remained silent. 'This boy was the offspring of Jeff Devlin and the molecular biologist killed about that time.'

'So?'

'Oh, Nightingale, don't be obtuse. This is Gita Medlock, not some misdirected poultry analyst.'

'You'd be surprised at the number of eggs that get

scrambled in this place.' Nightingale wandered away to think for a moment.

Medlock persisted. 'I would never have received this information if you hadn't wanted me to.'

'All right. But strictly between ourselves.'

'I take it there is a condition?'

'No harm must come to the boy.'

'That's your condition?' The senior official had expected something more cosmic. Perhaps Nightingale was going soft in her old age after all.

'It is.'

'He must have been up to something dramatic?'

'You won't like it, but it's safer you know.'

'Go on.'

Nightingale sat and faced her. 'This boy found his mother's missing transmitter key and was able to "plug in" to the aliens.'

Gita Medlock's tone became leaden. 'How?'

'He was somehow able to communicate with the aliens. Over the years, he has kept them briefed with knowledge no ordinary agent could have had access to.'

'What knowledge?'

The scientist leaned across her desk and looked Gita Medlock in the bindi mark. 'How should I know? I only have ordinary agents.' Despite the amiable expression, Nightingale could tell that the official was cursing her. She relaxed back in her chair. 'So, if World Security is up to something dangerous ...'

'Why should they be? According to your calculations, we'll only be in full contact with them for another two years.'

Nightingale shrugged. 'Well, there you have it.'

'How did you find out about the boy?'

Nightingale smiled enigmatically. 'Does it matter?'

'His whereabouts will have to be established of course.'

'It was one of your departments that allowed Dr. Harold to disappear with the child. Check the records.'

Gita Medlock didn't like her connection with World Security being trivialised. 'You've nothing else to tell us?'

'I think Tim Tharby is about to murder your agent.'

'Oh, I'd double his pension if he managed to reach up and do it. Obnoxious man, Devlin. I don't know why you let me talk you into having him back?'

'We needed something living to test the new transmission portal on. With a bit of luck he might start to break up soon.'

'Oh yes,' Medlock remembered, 'he also dug out some records of alien sightings from your computer.'

'I didn't expect him to be that interested. I thought he was only into blackmail and any wild oats he could sow.'

'They confirm what we've always believed about these creatures snatching people.'

Nightingale shrugged. 'Just clumsy information gathering.'

'You know quite well what used to happen to anyone taken through their transmission portals. The aliens' interest was a little more than clumsy. Before you opened your two-way portal, it was experimental butchery.' Medlock gave the Senior Controller a sharp look. 'Just you remember that in your cosy little dealings with them, Nightingale.'

'All right. Point taken.' Nightingale rose. 'Now, I don't wish to appear rude, but I have to give World Security's command console its monthly check. Perhaps you would like to join me?'

Medlock looked at the timepiece on her chiffon cuff. 'Oh dear, I'd love to but I did promise to check in by four. My

secretary can get very agitated if I go off the air for more than a few minutes. Claims voiceprint can be counterfeited over phones.'

'Lucky he doesn't get many calls from the Queen to put through.'

'Oh her - not many now. Jemima's family at last seems to be taking the loss of their estates with good grace. Though why they have to keep blaming World Government instead of the conservationists baffles me.'

'They were pretty good conservationists themselves, and kept the regalia well polished.'

'That and a couple of palaces are about all they own. A retired robot engineer is allocated more acres, though the family has proved no end of a boon to the diplomatic corps - except Prince Alec of course.'

'Whatever happened to him?'

'Got four years re-education for pimping.'

'Only re-education?'

'He apparently wasn't very good at it. His mother was a farm worker, so it couldn't have been inbreeding.'

'Whatever happened to his father?'

'Died of a certain sexually transmitted plague like many of his recent ancestors. The resulting cult of celibacy and lack of a vaccine has certainly left some wide open spaces for robot engineers to retire to.' Gita Medlock noticed that Nightingale was smiling enigmatically. 'Oh, I forgot! You're a Nature fairy, aren't you? Probably believe it's her way of keeping us under control.' An eerie thought crossed the senior official's mind. 'Do you know anything about sexually transmitted diseases?'

'Only one thing and he's unique.'

Medlock checked her timepiece again. 'Well, I must be going.'

'Of course. The rain's stopped so it should be an easier drive out.'

On her way down the stairs, Gita Medlock wondered how Nightingale could tell it had stopped raining in her windowless office. It bothered her all the way back to headquarters.

CHAPTER 18

Three hundred miles north of Group Indigo the tidy deciduous woodland was turning to red and gold. Autumn's medley of glowing hues made the air feel warmer and Nature's perfume filled JB Sendall with a delicious dreaminess. It was not the drowsiness he experienced when gazing up at the ceiling in his bedroom at HQ. The hexagons that patterned its surface seemed to wink at him as he dozed. The next thing he knew, he had lost several hours to some deep dreamless well and woken with a splitting headache. He had mentioned it to Nightingale. She told him to see Tharby. The prospect of having the medic listen like a condescending owl to his delusion of a ceiling winking at him had persuaded him to forget it.

JB dismissed the misgivings he had about the sinister ceiling and left the comfort of his car. He picked his way down into a dell where the hard sparkle of a stream cut through a blanket of fallen leaves.

He sat and watched a peaceful world only disturbed by the thrumming of a sweeper scooping leaves from the road and shredding them for compost. In the distance, there was the faint whine of a super-conductive train flying its way to the outer islands on unobtrusive steel viaducts and, nearby, the rustling of red squirrels chasing through the hazel and larch.

A pine forest clad the misty horizon of the distant hills like gauzy green cloth trimmed with pinking shears. It reminded JB that he should have brought a thermal suit. At any moment Climate Control might decide to have a snap blizzard to remind the residents that it was time to fatten up for winter. As the beavers and bears had no terminals to access weather forecasts, they were often caught out if autumn lasted too long. Not that winters were harsh enough to justify hibernation. Now technology had taken over, Nature was curbed from venting her full spite.

161

As he sat in the middle of the land reclamation scheme, JB Sendall realised that this was the nearest he had ever come to Nature. He may have been closer at one time, but most of his youth was still a blank. The condition that had robbed him of his long-term memories might have engulfed the rest of his brain if it weren't for Tim Tharby's drugs. For years, his mind would shut off from everyone else's reality to go he knew not where without treatment. Now he had successfully survived five days with nothing more than a mild stimulant. The only withdrawal symptom was a growing awareness of his surroundings. JB couldn't remember ever hearing squirrels squabble. Now he noticed what was on the horizon. He didn't even need a pair of glasses like the ones Tim Tharby kept hidden in his breast pocket. It was just as well that contact lenses had been phased out. The medic would have probably worn a pair to match his pink perm. It was surprising that Tim Tharby hadn't put in for the operation to correct his long sight. JB chuckled to himself. Perhaps he was hoping that Nightingale would eventually fade from view.

Something on the ridge above suddenly bellowed. JB leapt up and momentarily thought he was facing the devil incarnate. It was only a bull from a herd of highland cattle. Looking like a heap of badly knotted macramé hanging from wickedly sharp, wide horns, its dilated pupils glowered down at him through the flame red beech.

JB hastily swallowed a tranquilliser to stop himself shaking. Fancy a grown man being so alarmed at cattle. It wasn't surprising his marriage broke up. One minute he was like an icicle, the next climbing the wall because he'd heard or smelt something from the pit of lost memories. The dragon that lived down there would always control him until he found a way in to slay it.

How had Nightingale's number one found a slot for

romance anyway? It must have started on a day like this, when a beautiful woman cast a second look at his clean-cut suit. Could it have been the blond hair and ice blue eyes that attracted Melony? Even butterflies would avoid buddleia if he was standing next to it. JB Sendall spent so much time wondering why she loved him, he never realised how much he had loved her. Of course, Nightingale warned her that his soul belonged to Group Indigo and she might find what was left pretty insipid. Melony had been prepared to accept those terms. Most marriages were based on being apart - everyone was now entitled to their own space - so what had gone wrong? It was that genetic counsellor who had advised against children. She was the one who had introduced Melony to Dr. Jervis; witty, good-looking Dr. Jervis. Not having much wit, and milkshake looks, JB hadn't stood a chance.

That was years ago, and it still hurt. Despite Melony's insistence he should visit them and Dr. Jervis' guilty concern for his welfare, JB had never before found the courage. The adoration for Melony faded over the years and been replaced by the need for her friendship. At last JB understood why she left and no longer resented the partner who replaced him. Dr. Jervis was probably the best thing that had ever happened to her.

The tranquilliser had taken effect. His resolution restored, he went back to the car.

JB drove through a sports village where the underground heating on a golf course was being serviced and synthetic summer snow cleared from the ski runs in preparation for the real thing. With a bit of luck, some golfing novice would land a few balls amongst the herd of that highland bull.

The road disappeared into a dense wood. Last year's pine cones were still piled on the verges, bat boxes strung under the shadow of branches and "beware of the bears" signs glowed every few hundred metres. As it became darker, the car's automatic headlights snapped on. JB started to feel uneasy again, but was determined not to turn back, especially on that narrow road.

At last crisp sunlight reappeared through the trees.

Melony's home stood in a clearing of heather, screened from the other residences by tall conifers. The main living quarters and outhouses were dome-shaped in keeping with the region's heat conservation legislation - huge black puffballs with jewel like windows catching the late sun. Their property was Grade 1 Professional Allocation Class. The garden, filled with Melony's favourite plants, had matured over many years. The deep green of the rhododendrons gleamed against the flaming fringes of acer, and splashes of chrysanthemum that lined the access road.

JB's light blue car slowly wound its way up the drive of pink marble chippings. Melony was out of the house before he could switch on the vehicle's recharger. She looked the same as he remembered her, golden skinned and slender, though her black hair was now shot with white.

Then the irony of what he was doing struck JB Sendall. After having made so many token attempts in the past, it seemed unreal to be here now. What scatter-brained fancy had hauled him by his silver braided collar over three hundred miles? Was it just to make a fool of himself?

Melony waited expectantly a short distance from the car. She knew from old that it wasn't wise to make sudden moves where her ex-husband was concerned. As though caught out in some sentimental act, JB quickly left the vehicle. The door whirred politely shut after him, cutting off retreat and keeping in the air-conditioning. One gulp of the northern autumn air told him he should have opened a window instead. It was so bracing he didn't notice the large red setter until it had nearly bowled him over.

'Off, Jericho!' ordered Melony.

The dog galloped away to bounce in the dahlias instead.

JB took his next breath more warily, as though anticipating a stampede of highland cattle.

'You look well.' Melony smiled.

It was true. JB felt better than he had been for years.

'How's your ...' She stopped, not sure how familiar she should be with an ex-husband.

'Brain?' He smiled wryly. 'Medic who treats me behaves as though I'm cured. He'll probably never let me know. Prefer me to find out for myself. Mind you, even if he discovered a name for the condition, he wouldn't tell me that either.'

'What a strange bunch of humans you are.'

'I wouldn't guarantee that everyone at Group Indigo is human.'

Melony laughed. JB Sendall seldom made wise cracks. She had no way of knowing it might be the truth.

'You've put on weight - It suits you,' she added in case she'd said the wrong thing. 'You were always so thin, you could have made a living renovating old chimney stacks from the inside.'

'They weren't in fashion twenty years ago.'

'Just a joke, sweetie, just a silly joke.'

Of course it was. He gave a wry smile.

Now it was time for the really difficult bit - meeting Dr. Jervis.

JB no longer hated the doctor. He was more worried about what her partner would think of him. All the suspicions about the strange nature of Melony's ex-husband might be confirmed. So far away from the madhouse that was Group Indigo, JB realised how peculiar he must seem to people who revelled in their humdrum lives.

Melony took JB's hand and led him inside. They

walked through the hall to the large open-plan house on three levels. The kitchen, library, lounge, and bedrooms were all lit from above by the triple glazed roof. There were at least four work terminals dotted about, with two more in the second balcony bedrooms. Dr. Jervis was in demand as a consultant and Melony's image bank supplied clients across the world.

She pointed to a small thermostatic unit. 'In midwinter we sometimes supplement the solar heating with power from the Icelandic grid.'

'Of course,' remembered JB. 'Scotland voted to keep winter, didn't it?'

Melony took him to a sunken table surrounded by a well of soft seating. 'You still drink coffee?'

'Can you get it up here?'

There was a voice from above. 'Only decaffeinated I hope.'

JB looked up to see Dr. Jervis in the library on the mezzanine floor.

'Of course.' He was too uncomfortable to say anything else.

'May I join you?'

'Why not?'

Melony sensed JB freeze. She clutched his hand in case he decided to sprint for the door.

The tall doctor came down. JB found the strength to briefly clasp the extended hand. Dr. Jervis sat down opposite him.

'Fran has been given a government research project,' Melony told him.

'Fran ...' JB started, then realised he had never known the first name of the woman who had stolen his wife.

'It's very secret and she won't discuss it with me.'

'Oh.'

Dr. Jervis chuckled. 'I imagine your work is more secret than mine?'

For some reason, looking at the person who had

broken up his marriage concentrated JB's mind. Having made the huge step of meeting her, it was a strangely cleansing experience. A logjam of irrelevant thoughts dispersed and some of the puzzling things Nightingale had done started to make sense. JB shuddered. He didn't want them to. If there was method in her apparent madness, there could be terrible consequences.

'Are you all right?' he heard Dr. Jervis asking. 'You look as though you could do with something stronger than a coffee.'

'And you looked so well a moment ago, sweetie,' complained Melony. She sounded quite aggrieved.

'I'm all right,' JB managed to apologise. 'Not allowed alcohol anyway.'

Melony was suspicious. 'They still give you drugs? I thought you were cured?'

'I've just been off them for longer than usual.'

Without asking permission, Dr. Jervis reached out for JB's wrist. She took his pulse then pulled down his eyelid. The doctor was puzzled. 'What medication have they been giving you?'

JB shook his head. 'A variety of things. I never get a straight answer when I ask. I only know they've kept me upright. Nightingale wouldn't allow anyone to freak out on the job unless they were on the receiving end of some experiment which went wrong.'

'You experiment on each other?'

'Oh no, we do get a few singed beards. Just minor stuff. The boffins never needed to indent for vegetable guinea pigs.'

Dr. Jervis was momentarily defensive. 'At least turnips don't have beards.'

'Ever used them?'

'Of course.'

'Any good?'

'If you want to find the cure for turnip TB.'

'What about human headaches?'

'Aren't you interested in your own medicine?' Dr. Jervis evaded. 'Most patients now insist on an atomic breakdown of every grain that goes into a capsule.'

'I suppose I should be. I could happily wring Tim Tharby's neck over many things, but he's been treating me for over twenty years and I trust him not to dose me with anything harmful.'

'Tim Tharby?' laughed Melony. 'Didn't I meet him once?'

'You must remember? Hardly five foot, tubby, like an irritated owl, usually wears carmine or orange suits, and has pink hair.'

'Age hasn't mellowed him then?'

'That's why I've never mentioned him before.'

Dr. Jervis raised a knowing eyebrow. 'I think you're fond of him and don't like to admit it?'

'Of that little gargoyle? I sometimes think nature invented him to persecute me.'

'You've no reason to distrust him, though?'

'No.'

Melony didn't understand what her partner was driving at. 'What's the matter, Fran?'

'I'm not sure.' The doctor turned to JB. 'How often are you examined by someone other than a Group Indigo medic?'

'No one else is allowed to. My brain has this security implant, you see-' JB realised he had said too much.

'Would they let me take a sample of your blood?'

'Fran ...' Melony complained gently.

'I think Tharby had most of it. I don't see why you shouldn't take what's left.'

'Oh Fran, we should let Jonathan rest. He's not as well as he's making out.'

'You can put him to bed as soon as I've filled a syringe.'

* * *

168

The setting sun's rays were still playing through the curtains when a JB Sendall plunged into the deepest sleep he had known for years. There were no bizarre nightmares, buzzing sounds or sinking sensations this time, probably because the hexagon ceiling in his HQ bedroom was not glowering down; just a gentle drifting in and out of dreams on a cushion of warm autumn air. He was briefly nuzzled by the large red setter until Melony pulled it away. He slept until the morning.

JB woke with the rising sun. Dr Jervis was in a dressing gown, examining a batch of samples on a microscope screen. The doctor blew them up to view their molecular structure, and he could see that she was puzzled by their composition. Then JB had the inexplicable sensation of sinking through to another planet. He closed his eyes again. Long suppressed memories rushed out like bats escaping a dungeon.

His eyes opened in horror.

The torrent grew into a tsunami as recollections surged through his mind.

World Security had designed missiles to destroy the Lictana! All they needed were the locations of Nightingale's one-way transmission portals.

JB covered his mouth to stop a startled cry escaping.

The terrible pieces of the jigsaw inexorably slotted together. What game had Nightingale been playing? She must have known what World Security was planning. So why hadn't she told him? As if that wasn't enough, he was suddenly aware of Dr. Jervis leaning over him like a benevolent giraffe contemplating whether to spare an acacia branch.

The doctor had decided that her partner's ex husband wasn't so prickly after all. 'We mustn't wake Melony. She'd be upset if she overheard what I have to tell you. Are you feeling any better?'

JB sensed that he was about to learn something that would soon alter that arrangement. 'Yes.'

'Did you tell your HQ where you were going before

you left?'

'Not about coming here. I was just instructed not to return until notified.'

'So they had no idea you were going to meet a doctor?'

JB Sendall's pale skin paled even more and fine blue veins wrote extreme apprehension in his cheeks. 'No. They wouldn't expect me to. They know I have an aversion to them. Tim Tharby has always carried out my treatment.'

'I see.'

'Tell me what's wrong?'

Dr. Jervis hesitated. 'I did several tests on your blood.'

JB tried to parry the truth with irony. 'I'm the carrier for some new incurable plague?'

'No. There are traces of viral damage, but the condition has been totally cured. You seem healthy enough to me, apart from ...'

'Go on.'

'There were other elements I couldn't account for.'

'What elements?'

'Manipulative drugs.'

JB pushed himself upright. 'What?'

'I can only guess why.'

'Go ahead.'

'As you have an implant in your cerebral cortex, they may have been used to control you.'

'Control me?'

'Make you sleep at certain times, wake you up - possibly hallucinate.'

JB slumped back. He didn't know whether to fly into a rage or burst into tears.

'I'm sorry,' said Dr. Jervis. 'Had we been on better terms when we first met, I might have discovered it then.'

'You believe I was being given manipulative drugs that far back?'

'Your system has had time to build up the ability to cope with them.'

'Twenty years?'

'Perhaps longer.'

'It's not possible,' groaned JB. 'Tharby wouldn't have done such a thing. He's a hysterical package half the time, but he wouldn't do anything to harm me.'

'He is very good at his job. You would have been killed in less capable hands,' was all the consolation Dr. Jervis could offer.

'The little monster!'

'You said he resembled an owl. Perhaps there was some reason for him breaking his Hippocratic Oath.'

'I'll ask him after I've plucked all his feathers.'

'Don't be hasty.'

'I have to get back!'

Jervis grasped his arms tightly. 'No. Don't do anything to make Melony suspicious. She was so guilty at leaving you she was upset for months. If she suddenly found out that you weren't responsible for your condition, it would bring everything back.'

'What the devil made her want to marry me in the first place?'

'What can you remember of your childhood?'

'Nothing.'

'That's very odd. Memories are rarely suppressed so long in a healthy mind.'

JB realised what the Doctor was driving at. 'You believe that has something to do with Tim Tharby as well?'

'Only you know if there's some reason he didn't want you to remember your childhood.'

'That's a catch-all.'

'Do you want to remember?'

JB was silent. Then he sighed heavily. 'I daren't!'

'I think you must.'

He looked at Dr. Jervis carefully and realised she was right.

'Let's take an early walk. It will help you think things over.'

'I'm going to kill Tharby,' JB swore.

'You probably will if I let you go now.'

Dr. Jervis and JB took their long walk with the large red setter.

By the time they returned, JB Sendall understood the benefits of living in ignorance.

CHAPTER 19

Tim Tharby paced the deserted autumn sands outside his small beach chalet. His suspicions about Nightingale had even stopped him thinking about food. There was nothing unusual about her insisting he take his leave when JB did, but being rapidly ushered away like a rodent with rabies after he had duplicated the HQ files made him apprehensive. Now that was boiling over into paranoia.

A seal barked from a distant sandbank. Even though the territorial male was only a blur on the horizon, Tharby mouthed abuse at it.

There was no one else about now summer was over. The tourists had gone overseas. Perhaps he should have taken a couple of weeks in Antarctica which was now temperature six months of the year. Who was he kidding? Probably only be penguins to talk to down there.

Beachcombing was a waste of time. Nobody ever lost valuables worth finding and nothing interesting was washed over the sides of ships. They were so comfortable, the crews hardly needed to go up onto deck. There were plenty of shells, but only slipper limpets, cockles and whelks. Tim Tharby had already collected and polished all the interesting pebbles. There were so many in the chalet it would have taken a tornado to lift it.

The only reason the medic had bought the remote beach house was because he occasionally needed a place where he didn't have to bother about make-up or letting his grey roots show - not that Nightingale would have allowed him time off for his hair to grow long enough.

He sat on the chalet steps, wondering what the Senior Controller was up to. If she was riding with the Devil, everybody in Group Indigo would need a getaway broomstick. He only had a lavender dustpan and brush.

Tim Tharby became aware of another presence. He must have been standing there for some while. The thought that he might be alien crossed the medic's mind and his blood ran cold. Fearfully he turned, only to see the silver-edged suit.

'JB! You scared the life out of me!'

His superior remained motionless. He stared down, malice burning in his eyes.

Tharby didn't understand and began to wish he did have a getaway broom.

'What's the matter? What are you doing here?'

'A doctor gave me a blood test,' JB eventually announced. 'And told me the results!'

Tharby slowly rose. JB could see the colour drain from behind his freckles.

'I didn't think he was lying.'

'I had to-' Tharby was stopped in mid-excuse by JB's fist colliding with his jaw. He was sent spinning into the shingle. This rallied the medic's disorganised thoughts. He leapt to his feet. 'You imbecile! Of course you had to be drugged. Neither half of your brain would have recognised the other if you hadn't been!'

'You little fiend!'

Too hurt and guilty to burst into tears, Tim Tharby engaged in his next best defence, and became hysterical. 'You stiff-necked moron! There's not a synapse in your brain that would fire without some drug to give it a kick! When Nightingale discovered you, you had less intellect than a bowl of macaroni! You're mad JB Sendall! You always have been and never knew it!'

'You liar!' JB struck Tharby. He made another dent in the shingle. 'I'm going to get the truth out of you!'

'Don't hit me again!' Tharby had the sense to dodge JB's fist this time. 'I can't tell you.'

'You can't say because there was no reason. You fed

me that poison just to have control over me.' JB seized the medic and shook him violently.

'No ...' Tharby eventually sobbed. 'I can't tell you why.'

'And Nightingale thought you were bothered about me.'

'It was Nightingale ...'

JB was reluctant to believe that, even though it would have made better sense. 'Why would she want me drugged?'

'I can't tell you.'

Realising the futility of his onslaught, JB released the medic. What if Nightingale was responsible? Perhaps he hadn't allowed that to occur to him because it was far easier to beat up Tim Tharby.

Without a word, JB strode off through the sea thrift and mallow to the breakwater where his car was parked. He paused before opening the door and gazed at the swell spilling over the breakers. His thoughts were clearer than they had ever been before. He knew what he had to do next. It wouldn't be easy.

Checking that his car was fully charged, JB climbed in and drove away.

Sore and numb, Tharby went inside his chalet to hide from the inquisitive gaze of the seals whose heads were bobbing a short distance from the shore. He didn't know who to hate more, Nightingale or himself. So he smashed some plates, threw a few cushions and drank a sedative. There was nothing else for it. He would have to follow JB and try to break the truth gently in the hope he didn't break his back first.

* * *

JB Sendall wondered if his outburst hadn't triggered a mild hallucination as he drove through the grounds to Group Indigo's HQ. Most of Nightingale's jungle had been pruned back and tidied up. Enough light now spilled through it to make the Catseyes obsolete. This couldn't have been her doing. The rampant vegetation had put off casual callers and given the wildlife a rare battleground.

JB drew up inside the porch and warily entered. There was no Shultz reading the latest sports news in his cubicle, and no one else tried to stop him. The inside of the listed building was also unnervingly tidy. Strangers, some of them in imitation brown leather uniforms, were milling about. There wasn't a beard in sight. No one so much as glanced in his direction. These were bloody funny decorators, even for Nightingale.

Something moved above JB's head. He was being watched by a camera that had been out of commission for the past two years. They inner security doors emitted a businesslike beep instead of the usual tired whine when his pass allowed him through. For some ominous reason, efficiency had struck Group Indigo one almighty blow. These precautions were not Nightingale's idea of security. Prickles of apprehension lifted the roots of JB's white hair. Having come so far into the mysterious web, he could hardly walk out again without introducing himself to the spider.

It crossed his mind that he and Tim Tharby had been sent packing while Nightingale engaged in some experiment they were bound to disapprove of. That was even more unlikely than her keeping him drugged for over twenty years. She wouldn't have cared what they thought. Something more than one of her anarchic whims going on here.

JB tried to look businesslike, summoned the lift, and went down to her basement lab.

No one intercepted the interloper as he stepped into the chamber that housed World Security's command console, Nightingale's lab and the transmission portal. Everything was in half-light. JB knew that things lurked in the shadows so he put on the best performance of his life.

He knew where the surveillance cameras were and ensured they couldn't see every movement as he checked the transmission portal systems. He surreptitiously keyed in the code to open the small drawer containing the disc with the locations of the one-way portals. With magic deftness, learnt by watching Tim Tharby perform the conjuring tricks his father had taught him, JB picked out the tiny disc and palmed it.

Seemingly satisfied that everything was functioning, he slyly pinched the disc under the Group Indigo insignia on his collar. Then he made his way up to World Security's console and strolled around the balcony until he came to the command chair. It swung round to face him.

'Good afternoon.' The dark woman dressed in pale pink flounces and gold two-piece smiled. 'Do you remember me?'

For one cold, clammy moment, JB Sendall thought that she was a friend of Tim Tharby's.

Of indeterminate age, she had a decorative pink bindi mark between large Indian eyes and earrings like a cluster of gold larch cones that should have stretched her earlobes to the same length as Buddha's. No, not even Tharby had that sort of dress sense. Anyone able to get away with it had to be important.

'Of course. World Government. Gita Medlock, isn't it?'

She clasped her lace-gloved hands together in delight. 'Excellent recall. Nightingale always insisted it was quite remarkable. What a shame you're not on our side.'

'Also doubles up for World Security.'

'Better still.'

'Where is Nightingale?'

'Taking a short holiday, as you should be doing.'

'I got bored with watching leaves fall and trying to

hold conversations with prehistoric cattle.'

Gita Medlock sighed. 'I hope Nightingale has discovered something more elevating to occupy her.'

'Why?'

'She sailed out of here with two shoulder weapons and Lord knows how much explosive. Threatened to come back and blow us all sky high. No one dared stop her of course.'

JB took a deep breath. 'You'd better believe that she means it.'

'Oh, we'd have done what we need to do by the time she comes back.'

'So, am I supposed to enquire what it is?'

'I'd rather you didn't. I wouldn't be able to let you leave with an honest answer, and you do seem such a nice man under all that frost and silver braid.'

'Clean underwear as well.'

'I've no doubt.'

'Tendency to wake up in hospital.'

'Tim Tharby must be overworked.'

JB scowled. 'He's overwrought at the moment. I don't suppose he's part of this little caper, is he?'

'Goodness no. He'd clash with my blouse.'

'Then I must assume you know how to operate everything in here?' JB caught sight of Jeff Devlin arrogantly sauntering round the console. 'Yes, of course. You employ educated rats, don't you?'

'Endangered species. You have to admit that there aren't many left since we introduced moral responsibility clearances for children who wanted to grow up.' Gita Medlock peeled off her lace gloves. 'We never did have much success with capital punishment. It was usually men, and they are in such short supply.'

JB tried not to sound puzzled. 'What do you mean?'

Medlock smiled sweetly. 'You don't really believe that plants are a good substitute for human tissue when it comes to medical research, do you? As the plague viruses grew more and more devious, synthetic cultures became useless. No other animals were compatible. Medical research had to take a somewhat radical turn if we weren't to be totally wiped out by the odd rogue infection carried by the carrot fly or marmot flea.'

'Rogue carrot fly virus?' scoffed JB.

'And stranger viruses than that. Nature has really done her best to get rid of us, you know. How do you think World Government was able to produce the cures for everything from AIDS to ingrowing toenails? Or perhaps it was something you never needed to think about too much?' She anticipated JB before he could protest, 'Only the most obnoxious criminals I assure you.'

JB Sendall could see Jeff Devlin enjoying his discomfort. That rat would be in his natural element, scurrying about the sewers of World Government's "improvement" schemes.

For some reason, JB suddenly noticed a terrible familiarity about Devlin's features.

'Are you all right?' asked Gita Medlock. She well aware of the number of blackouts listed on JB's medical record.

'The consequences of you curing human nature altogether have just occurred to me.'

'But World Government represents human nature more democratically than any political experiment. We merely carry out the wishes of the human race. It's surprising how few questions people ask when so many benefits could be lost as a consequence.' She beamed a smile. 'Hypocrites, my dear. The human race are all hypocrites.' She patted the back of his hand. 'But don't worry about it; I'm sure you must have other things on your mind.' Medlock lowered her voice. 'Now you run along like a good boy.'

'No, wait boss!' Devlin suddenly burst out.

The senior official shot a dangerous glance at her minion. 'There's nothing he can do to interfere with us.'

'We've already let Nightingale go.'

'I noticed you didn't try and stop her.'

'She would have shot me.'

'Well in that case, stop picking on people who aren't armed.' Gita Medlock turned to JB. 'You had better go before the rodent really starts to get out of hand.'

JB said nothing. By Devlin's expression, he could tell that his life wouldn't be worth much out of her influence. He had what he needed. They couldn't attack the aliens without the one-way portal locations, however sophisticated their missiles.

He quickly left Group Indigo HQ before it occurred to someone that his visit had been anything other than bad timing. World Security could afford to be overconfident. It wouldn't have crossed their minds that any civilian, apart from Nightingale, could be as devious as they were. JB drove off before they found out how wrong they were. He had to find some place to hide. That was going to be difficult given the web World Security had enmeshed the planet in.

JB Sendall drove through the thinned out estate grounds and past the main entrance sensors.

Inside, Devlin continued to search the console. 'I still can't find the coder.'

'Well look on the transmission portal's controls, dear boy,' chided Medlock. 'I don't have to call up a boffin to help, do I?'

'How am I expected to know where she put it? That woman's too devious to hide it in the usual places. I had enough trouble lifting the combination.'

Medlock sighed. 'Oh you really are chock full of old-fashioned incompetence, aren't you? We could have four-legged aliens stampeding all over us by the time you get your act together. After being held captive by them for forty years, you don't even know what end they defecate.'

'If I'd been conscious, that wouldn't have been my

main priority.'

Gita Medlock muttered under her breath. 'Really? That's not what I heard.'

At last, Devlin discovered the inconspicuous coder to the small seamless drawer in the portal's panel. 'Got it!' he whooped.

'Well open it then.'

Swiftly he keyed in the sequence he had hacked from the master computer.

An angry silence followed.

'Now what's wrong?' sighed Medlock.

'Damn!' he exploded. 'Sendall must have taken it!'

'We were watching him - weren't you?'

'Well who else could have it? Nightingale wasn't given the chance to come in here and Tharby's miles away.'

'This is very inconvenient. Are you sure there isn't another disc?'

Devlin was thinking unusually deeply for him. Gita Medlock had to admit that it was disconcerting.

'I don't want any harm to come to Sendall,' she warned. 'The planet needs competent people, whatever side they're on. They are worth more than all the idiots who claim they can help you.'

Devlin smiled innocently. 'Of course I won't harm him, boss. We could have him picked up, though?'

'All right,' she agreed.

* * *

JB Sendall dare not risk being on the road as the sun set. He had come across some pretty remote nooks and crannies in his travels to investigate UFO sightings and drove to an outcrop of newly eroded coastal rock where he hid his car. At night it would be invisible from the nearest road and its pale blue shell would only be spotted from the air when the sun rose. JB didn't know the area well enough to risk searching for a better spot in the dark and needed to rest. He pulled out a rug and cushion to find a safe nook to sleep in.

The fugitive was exhausted. Every gully and cave looked like a corner of Triton's graveyard in the light of his torch. He wandered on. Just as he thought he was a safe enough distance from the car, the ground slipped away from under him. As he fell, JB Sendall was aware that he had just become a minute part of erosion's plan.

CHAPTER 20

From their round observation tower, Hysle and Ben watched Dey dart backwards and forwards between two domed buildings. Having four legs, she moved fast. Other Lictana parted like confused waves as though making way for some enraged tyrant. It was a novelty to see the self-possessed species behaving with such agitation.

'What's going on?' Ben asked.

Hysle fidgeted with a fringe on his overalls. 'No one in the Main Counsel believed us when we told them how efficient you are, little minnow.'

'Is that where Tamble and Datch are?'

'No. Why do you keep worrying about them?'

Ben wondered why Hysle was so irritated. It wasn't like him. 'I haven't seen them for such a while.'

'Well, they are doing other things. You should have forgotten about them by now.'

'I never met them that long ago, did I?'

'You don't know?'

Ben felt uncomfortable, as though suddenly discovering that he was flying an aircraft with unfamiliar controls. He had always taken the companionship of the Lictana for granted. Now he began to wonder what he was doing there: the child had nothing more to tell them. The ambivalence of his situation enabled long suppressed thoughts to scratch at the walls of Ben's infant memory. Suddenly he was no longer a child, and could view everything with an adult's perception. The Lictanan dimension seemed to revolve like stage; one moment glittering and friendly, the next dangerous and sinister.

Ben almost let out an exclamation of alarm but stopped himself in time. It was imperative to retain his childish manner, otherwise the Lictana would instantly be suspicious.

For fear of Hysle detecting the sudden change, Ben

diverted his attention with a typical inanity and pointed to a sparkling tower on one of the domes. 'Is that where they keep the cones of Soolain?'

Hysle was taken aback. 'The what? Goodness no.' He forced a laugh. 'What makes you think that?'

'It glitters so much.'

'That is one of our government buildings. The cones of life are kept everywhere.'

'Everywhere? How can they be kept everywhere?'

'The energy that creates them comes from this planet. Only guardians can harness the power for them.'

'What do they keep it in then? A cone?'

'Is it important, little minnow?'

Ben persisted. 'How many cones have they managed to fill?'

'I cannot remember the last time a cone was used.'

'Why not?'

'The reason has to be extremely important.'

To Hysle's relief, Dey joined them.

She was exhausted. Her multi-faceted eyes fixed Ben with an intense gaze. 'You must come with me, Ben.'

'Why?'

'You are sure about those one-way portals put in place by that tall purple woman, aren't you?'

'Yes,' insisted Ben. 'I told you. There are six of them.'

'Very well. Are you ready to come now?'

Ben looked to Hysle. The Lictanan's expression was not reassuring.

'I will go as well if you want.' Hysle didn't seem enthusiastic.

Ben accepted his reluctant offer before he could change his mind.

Flanked by the two Lictana, the child was led down a long avenue overhung by a crystal lattice of interlocking branches. Beneath the sparkling bower groups of Lictana silently watched them pass. Dey and Hysle's footsteps made no sound as though they were walking on velvet.

A wide approach led up to a towering beehive-shaped building rippling with tangled strands of silver.

At last it dawned on Ben why he had never seen any Lictanan children or Dey and Hysle's superiors. Until then, he had believed that there was only one type of Lictanan. Were the others, the guardians, living out of sight in these huge domes? And why were his escorts looking so worried? Their rulers should have been grateful for the news he had brought them. Then again - perhaps not.

Ben hesitated at the shimmering curtain inside the entrance of the hive. There was no going back. Dey and Hysle took him through the curtain and into a tunnel leading to the inner mysteries of a society he had always taken for granted.

They reached a huge chamber filled with intense light. Dey and Hysle remained outside.

Ben entered.

Serpentine silhouettes floated above the child. The creatures didn't have four legs. In fact, they had no legs at all. They had tails that slowly coiled and uncoiled. These aliens had evolved past the need for useful bodies. Ben knew that he was confronting the true Lictana, the entities who had created four-legged creatures as tools to deal with the rest of the Cosmos. The entities above Ben were more alien and intimidating than anything a child's imagination could conjure up. Just what had he been dealing with all these years?

Ben was grateful that the shield of light prevented him from seeing the terrifying aspect of the serpent like guardians. Given the opportunity, he still preferred to be a coward.

'You were telling the truth, weren't you, Ben?' The disembodied tones were meant to be reassuring, but their eerie resonance made the child's spine tingle. Even in translation, they rang like an alarm in Ben's adult thoughts.

'Act!' he told himself. 'Don't let go - they'd know in an instant.'

'Of course.'

'Good, Ben.'

'Why is it so important?'

'Your information about the missiles means we will have to do something which will put all of us in danger.'

'What's that?'

'Our transmission portals must be dissolved. We can only do this by vibrating the molecular composition of Lictan.'

The voice paused to give Ben time to make sense of the revelation.

'What will happen?'

'Our planets will be wrenched away from each other. They are due to part naturally in a short time. That is not soon enough for your species, though.'

'Why not let our worlds part naturally?'

'Your planet is going to use those six one-way transmission portals you told us about to attack us.'

'What with?'

'With the missiles you also told us about, Ben.'

Ben couldn't believe he had given the aliens so much information. He compelled himself to give a childish laugh. 'But that's silly. Why would they want to do that? You aren't doing any harm.'

'They are afraid we might. We mutually agreed not to construct any one-way portals. We thought your planet was keeping to the agreement until you told us otherwise.'

Ben couldn't stave off the nightmare of what he had done. 'Perhaps I shouldn't have told you anything?'

'If you hadn't, the atoms of everyone here would soon be spread through space like cosmic dust.'

'How awful! Does that mean I can't come and see Dey and Hysle any more?'

'Our dimensions shall cease to overlap. You will never be able to find us again in the atomic junkyard of any universe. Neither of us will be able to distinguish each other from a faint, busy cloud of photons and electrons.'

Ben was losing the ability to prattle as his terror increased. Hoping his appearance hadn't started to age as well, he manufactured his most innocent expression. 'Can I take one more look around?'

'Dey and Hysle will be busy.'

'Oh, that's all right, I won't do anything I shouldn't.'

It worked. For all the valuable intelligence he had passed on, the mysterious Lictana would have probably granted him much more.

Ben suddenly discovered himself outside the hive with Dey and Hysle. They were even more anxious.

'What happened?' asked Hysle.

'Nothing. They just said I could have one last look around before our planets part.'

'By yourself?'

'Yes. You don't mind. Do you?'

The two Lictana were obviously unhappy about it, yet could hardly flout the decision of their creators. 'Very well then.'

'I have to organise the engineers. Goodbye Ben.' Dey dashed off.

Ben rubbed his eyes.

Hysle looked concerned. 'What is the matter, little minnow?'

'It's all right.' Ben faded for a moment. 'I just keep getting this strange feeling.'

'Do not do that. It worries me.'

'All right. I'll try not to wake up.'

Hysle felt guilty. 'Are you sure you want to wander about on your own?'

'I know you can't take me. It's all right, really. It's

not as if anything terrible can happen, is it?'

'I know, little minnow, but ...'

'You have far more important things to do than take me sightseeing.'

Hysle gave in. 'Be careful then. Only go to those places we have been to before.'

'Oh, I can easily wake up if I get into trouble.'

'I know, little minnow.'

'Do we have to say goodbye now, Hysle?'

Hysle wanted to give Ben a hug, but their molecules wouldn't oblige. So he dashed off.

When the alien was out of sight, Ben gave a rather cynical smile for an eight-year-old.

No other Lictanan paid attention to the human child. They were scurrying about in mortal terror, preparing for the vibration that would shake their planets apart.

Ben stopped by the massive Omcrom whose scales he had once mistaken for a tree. It had come back to graze at the foot of the first transmission portal his dream self had accidentally blundered into. Huge stacks of equipment surrounded it. A small technician was trying to persuade the Omcrom to move by enticing it with weird warbling tunes. Ben looked inside the spherical room to make sure Datch and Tamble weren't there. Then he darted on his way.

With no Dey or Hysle to stop him the child could give his adult suspicions full rein. With no idea what he was looking for, he was aware of chillingly familiar resonances. Ben still wanted to trust the Lictana, even though they hadn't been honest with him but was driven on by the horror of how much he had told them since they first met.

No longer inhibited by childhood cowardice, the cutting breeze of adult judgement told Ben to be practical. He had to find out the truth, even if he was unable to undo the damage he had caused.

He flitted through the bottle-shaped structures in

the forbidden zone. Sudden pulses of bright light lit the bleak and deserted scenery with surreal desperation.

Was this where the guardians in the hive had created the Lictana? Dey and Hysle would hardly have admitted that they were artificial, let alone that they originated from this dismal place. Ben had only seen what they wanted him to; the beautiful and the benign. No one builds slums on the approach road to paradise.

Something was wending its way awkwardly about the bottle buildings. Apparently unaware of its surroundings, all its concentration was on moving its grotesquely distorted legs. This was an odd place for an alien spacer to be. Ben moved closer. The creature was an old, two-legged Lictanan. Ben recoiled in horror. It was like seeing a four legged human.

The mutant made its laboured way, dead-eyed, to an entrance in a bottle building. Ben knew that if he looked inside he would see the results of more disastrous experiments. Instead, he pressed on.

Ahead was a cluster of toadstool shapes, much larger than the transmission portals. They were a pulsating pink, the colour the Lictana used as a warning.

Ben floated up to the first toadstool. As a matter of courtesy, he had never darted through walls. Now he was spying, there seemed little point in trying to find an entrance in the seamless surface and he passed through it.

The inside of the dome was full of large clear tubes suspended from the spherical walls. They overhung each other as though in some surreal supermarket. Gravity evidently didn't apply here.

Ben examined their contents. The tubes contained a buzzing mist of tiny particles. Curiosity satisfied, he went on to the next toadstool.

This interior was gloomier, again stacked with large

tubes. Ben peered into each one. This time, he could make out structure in the particles. Some solid substance had been dissolved into busy, hardly formed shapes.

That eerie familiarity surged through Ben once again. It pricked his resolve like a dart. He knew he would find out what he needed to know in the third toadstool.

Fearfully, Ben approached the building. He floated inside. Again the tubes. This time the contents of the tubes were recognisable. Inside them were the most recent Lictanan experiments. They had managed to stabilise the molecules of living creatures. By the grotesque shapes they had been contorted into, none of these specimens had come willingly. Some had died in mid protest, others disbelief. Some were partially transformed into different species. All of them had been human at one time.

If any Lictanan in the vicinity had heard Ben scream, the child had gone by the time they reached the storeroom.

CHAPTER 21

Dr. Phoebe Shadbolt looked up from the sauropod fossil she was carefully chipping out of the Cretaceous rock. She pulled the headscarf off her ears and listened. Did somebody just groan? There was nothing but the sound of seagulls and waves slurping over the newly eroded seam. The palaeontologist removed her headscarf and pinned it under a pebble near the fossil so it was easy to find again. She pushed her ample proportions up and picked her way carefully along the beach, instinctively scanning the pebbles and rock face as she went. On the verge of believing that isolation was making her hear things, a glint of silver caught her eye. The high tide was lapping at a body clutching a blanket and cushion.

'What a strange place to go to sleep,' she muttered.

JB Sendall had not intended to slumber on the high tide mark. His fall onto the rocks the evening before had sedated him more effectively than anything Tim Tharby ever administered.

'Oh dear! Oh dear!' Dr. Shadbolt puffed as she jogged to the spot as fast as her outsize waders would allow. 'It can't be a coelacanth, I'm sure.' She carefully turned JB Sendall over. 'No, it's not an ichthyosaur either. It must be a man.' She felt his jugular veins. 'Hmm ... alive.' His eyelids flickered. She sat him up before another wave bubbled over his face.

The first thing JB Sendall saw was the cliff looming above. Only three metres or so, but a long way to fall if you're going to land headfirst on large pebbles. Then he saw an extraordinary woman, or was she an amiable lambeosaurus whose thigh-length waders were visible through a heavy tweed skirt quite sodden about the hem. No, inside the ancient tartan coat, was a large friendly woman looking very puzzled.

'You haven't come down here for the new fossil bed

have you?' She sounded quite serious.

'No,' moaned the JB. 'I fell off the cliff.'

'Shame. I do wish they would send me an assistant. These sauropods and iguanodon are more than one power chisel can handle. Have to leave them I suppose and concentrate on the saltopus. They may be deeper, but at least there's a better chance of getting one out intact.' JB's expression was glazed. She looked at him thoughtfully. 'Do you know anything about fossils?'

'They don't feel anything when they get their bones broken.'

'You haven't, have you?'

He carefully moved each limb in turn. 'No, I just ache a lot. I must have been here all night.' Then he remembered. 'Hell! The car!'

It was obvious that technology was low on the list of the palaeontologist's priorities. 'Oh, that blue thing?'

'Yes.'

'They took it away an hour ago. I didn't know that you were attached to it.' She suddenly beamed at her discovery. 'So you're the dangerous, escaped multi-murderer, are you?'

'What?' JB then realised. 'Oh yes, they would have had to say something like that.'

'What have you been up to then?' If the palaeontologist believed she had just stumbled onto a real live dinonychus, she didn't seem very intimidated by the fact.

JB pulled his crumpled identification from a pocket.

She examined it carefully. 'Jonathan Benjamin Sendall.' She was used to handling IDs. As a palaeontologist, producing permissions and identifying other people was all part of the game. 'So you're a secret agent of some sort?' She didn't seem unduly bothered by that either.

'Something like that.'

'Who were that security patrol looking for you then? They weren't local.'

'Probably secret agents of some sort.' He grasped her wrist. 'You aren't going to give me away, are you?'

Dr. Shadbolt pondered for a few moments. 'Well your ID is real enough.' She pulled her own battered ID card from an inner pocket. Barely readable, it was in no condition to activate a car or open security doors.

JB wasn't too bothered about the woman's credentials. World Security wouldn't have had the imagination to set up one of their own as a palaeontologist, especially one this eccentric. He handed her ID back.

'Well,' she said, 'come and tell me how you managed to end up amongst my fossils, and we'll see what we can do about you.'

'You'll have to help me up, Dr Shadbolt.'

She rolled up his sodden cushion in the blanket then half walked and half carried JB to a large prefabricated shack leaning against the cliff face. Just out of reach of the water line, its interior was crammed with fossils. Some were piled in boxes, some wrapped in cotton wool and others in the process of being wired together. It was obvious why the palaeontologist needed an assistant.

'Never thought I'd grow tired of the sight of prehistoric folk myself.' She sighed. 'There are just too many for one person to cope with here.'

'Why are you in such a hurry?'

'The district's going to be designated a Grade 1 Conservation Area. You know, everything allowed to crumble away as nature intended. They just won't allow the funds for palaeontology any more. They think they know it all.'

'Don't they?' JB rubbed his skull and felt a large lump on the back of his head.

Dr. Shadbolt applied some ointment to it.

'Of course they don't. You'll never guess what I found out here?'

JB was more familiar with alien life forms that

couldn't hold their molecules together long enough to decompose, let alone become fossils. 'What?'

'The thigh bone of a hominid.'

JB glanced at the partly assembled skeletons of small dinosaurs. He knew enough about prehistory to mentally flesh out some of the creatures. 'All this stuff must be Jurassic and Cretaceous, well over sixty million years old?'

Phoebe Shadbolt shrugged. 'So you tell me what it's doing here.'

'It's not possible. No hominid would have stood a chance with the owners of all those teeth lumbering about. Are you sure it's a hominid bone?'

She carefully took the treasure from a box and unwound the foam protecting it. 'Whoever owned this walked upright.'

JB had to agree. His forensic knowledge was pretty comprehensive. By the position of the femur head it couldn't have belonged to anything else.

'How extraordinary. Could it have fallen from a later layer?'

'Chipped it out myself.'

'That might mean that we're not the first intelligent life on this planet.'

'My dear boy, I doubt if humans came from this planet.'

'What then?'

She held the fossil up. 'I think this belonged to a hominid evolved from an archosaur. Probably more intelligent than we are. Most of them already walked upright, but not like this.'

'Never!'

'Why not? They had far more time to evolve than we did. We came up too rapidly to be indigenous.'

JB suddenly realised he was soaking wet and shuddered.

'Oh dear boy, you must be freezing. Remove those wet clothes.'

'I'd rather not, Dr. Shadbolt.' He was thinking more of the security agents' sudden return than modesty.

'I can soon dry everything off.' The palaeontologist switched on a fan heater driven by a windmill and solar panel on the roof. 'I'm always getting sodden myself. I've got plenty of things for you to put on.'

JB reluctantly agreed. He was far too uncomfortable to argue and it was difficult to believe his host was interested in anyone's anatomy unless they had been dead for over fifty million years.

Wrapped in a dressing gown and blanket, he watched Dr Shadbolt steam his suit clean and place it on a rack to dry. As she did so, she was aware of something in a trouser pocket.

'Hello? I could have sworn that wasn't in there a moment ago. I thought you'd taken everything out?'

JB hadn't of course - he had left the disc clipped under the insignia on his collar. He didn't have anything else of importance.

'Well I never!' Phoebe Shadbolt drew out a small multi-faceted crystal. It was winking. 'I've been through quite a few seams, but never dug out a stone which looked like that.' She held it up. It was iridescent, like transparent mother-of-pearl. 'Where did you get it from, Jonathan?'

Where did he get it? JB racked his brain. How could he have forgotten something like that? The bump on his head must have scrambled his memory. She handed the crystal to him. It rolled from hand to hand of its own accord, like a novelty toy. 'I've no idea.'

'Hmm,' mused Dr. Shadbolt. 'You're in a worse state than I thought. Why not try to get some sleep?'

JB suddenly started. 'No!'

'What is the matter with you, dear boy?'

'I daren't sleep.'

'I won't let anyone in. They've already searched the beach, so it's not likely they'll come back.'

'It's not that, Doctor.'

'Well every fossil in here, bar me, is quite dead. I've not collected enough teeth to identify tyrannosaurus, so there's no need to worry about his table manners.' She watched him gaze at the collection of bones about him. 'Well, see anyone you recognise?'

For one hot, clammy second, Phoebe Shadbolt's last remark struck a chord deep in JB's subconscious. Not all monsters were safely extinct.

'Have you found that it's much easier to sleep if you can remember the nightmare that woke you up?' he asked her.

'Well, yes, but it depends on the nightmare. I don't usually dream about being chased by tyrannosaurus. Any pterodactyl that tried to carry me off would definitely bend its beak. My dreams are usually pretty mundane, about dropping stitches or losing teeth - of fossils that is. I reckon you must go in for the heavier stuff.'

'You're probably right. I can never remember.'

'Why not tell me why you're really out here and everything might come back. Judging by the state of you, it must be pretty dramatic.'

'Dramatic?' he echoed.

'Well, who are you then, Jonathan?'

'Call me JB.'

'All right, JB. You've already got to be up to your pectorals in trouble for World Security to be after you. Telling me is hardly going to make matters worse.'

'Doesn't it bother you?'

'Of course, dear boy. Even without uniforms, World Security all have this presence peculiar to the species. Eyes like troodon, shoulders of triceratops and brain of brontosaurus. No time for the creatures myself. Wouldn't even dig them up if they were fossils.'

'So because you don't trust them, I must be all right?'

'I know the ways of these people. I've been on digs everywhere from Mongolia to the shores of the Rift

Valley Sea. They're all the same. Not sure what they're doing or why, just doing it with the same unremitting efficiency. Believe me, I also know a dangerous psychopath when I meet one.' She pulled a small, powerful hand weapon from another inside pocket. 'So don't make a false move.' Phoebe Shadbolt gave an abrupt laugh which made JB jump, then replaced it.

'You're not for real.'

'I've spent so much time on desolate digs with pick and plaster, I now find the complexities of human nature quite tedious.'

'You don't know how lucky you are. Stick with the dinosaurs.'

'I will as long as the powers that be come up with the funds. Things are getting tricky though, JB. I may have to go to charm school yet.'

'Let's hope they don't find out you helped me.'

'Why not, dear boy?'

'I'm a Group Indigo agent, Dr. Shadbolt.'

'Group Indigo?'

'We investigate UFO sightings and that sort of rubbish.'

'Rubbish?'

'Mostly, but not always.'

'And the "not always" has caught up with you?'

'Something like that. We made contact, but World Security took over. They want to bomb the aliens out of existence.'

'Could they?'

'They could.'

'Oh dear,' sighed Dr. Shadbolt. 'Mind you, I'd probably feel happier with heavy artillery if I had to meet Tyrannosaurus Rex.'

'Have you got this thing about tyrannosaurus?'

'A great aunt of mine was a direct descendant.'

'What?'

'Sorry. Mind wandering. Please go on.'

'There's not much more. Nightingale, the Senior Controller, managed to get away as well. We'll no doubt keep running from pillar to post until we're caught.'

'Yes,' agreed Shadbolt. 'That would make me absent-minded enough to walk off cliffs and have nightmares.'

'You believe me?'

'I believe as much as you've told me. But there is something else, isn't there? They wouldn't have brought out Air Search if you weren't important.'

JB gazed absently at the crystal for a moment. 'Oh dear heavens! Demsel!' He toppled from his chair in a dead faint.

As she had started to rub the encrustations from a fossil as they talked, this took Phoebe Shadbolt unawares. She hastily wiped her hands on her apron and went to JB. He was out cold. A quick examination with the first aid scanner satisfied her that it was not due to concussion. There were few other things he could have done so effectively to convince her of his integrity. To the palaeontologist's straightforward mind, people capable of fainting that dramatically had to be honest.

She lifted JB onto her bed and made him comfortable, then resumed cleaning the fossil.

He was unconscious for half an hour. During that time JB's whole life, and quite a slice of eternity, progressed by.

Guessing as much, Dr. Shadbolt pushed a warm drink into his hands as he woke. 'Remember the nightmare this time, JB?'

'Yes,' he murmured.

'Tell me about it, then I can get back to my humdrum life.'

JB rubbed the crystal, which he was still clutching, against his cheek. 'I was a child, about eight. When I slept I met these aliens. They seemed all right. Told me to take something to the strange woman my mother worked for on this large rambling estate. Before I reach either of them, I see my mother blown to pieces. I don't know how.'

'How awful, dear boy. Do go on.'

'Ten years later I meet that strange woman. I tell her I'm able to talk to aliens in my sleep, and ...'

'And?'

'Orange blossom - Bertha Mooney! It should have come back to me then.'

Phoebe Shadbolt hardly understood what he was muttering. 'You need to rest.'

'No, I'm all right. Just feel a little strange. I don't seem to remember any more, Dr. Shadbolt,' JB lied.

'Well, that sounded bad enough. Just as well it was only a nightmare. Drink up, your clothes must be dry by now.'

JB didn't feel like leaping into action after a being struck so suddenly by the full horror of his life. It was far too comfortable in Dr. Shadbolt's makeshift HQ, but he would only endanger her if he stayed.

As he rested back, he laid his hand on his chest and was suddenly aware of the pendant he had worn for as long as he could remember. The Lictanan transmitter key was so familiar he had never asked himself where it came from, in the same way people live with birthmarks. Its removal would have only reminded him of its existence. JB knew he had to get rid of it. Yanking the alien jewel off then and there and hurling it into the sea would have made even this palaeontologist suspicious.

'The water's damaged my phone, Dr. Shadbolt. Where's the nearest call station?'

'Half a mile from here. But as soon as you use your card they'll know where you are.'

'I don't have any choice.'

'Use my phone.'

'Has it voice security?'

'Yes. I'll pass on any message you're willing to trust me with. No one will be any the wiser.'

'I don't like asking you to do it.'

'You don't have any choice.'

'I have to get away from here.'

'I can hide you.'

'The dinosaurs looking for me aren't politely fossilised. I won't let you take the risk.' There was the tone of the martinet in his voice. 'Perhaps if I left you Nightingale's check in number, though.'

'Check in number?'

'I don't know where the machine is located. It's automatically checked every hour for messages. It's totally safe. Calls can't be intercepted.'

'What do I say?'

JB thought carefully. 'Tell her, "It's all right, JB lifted the package."'

'"It's all right, JB lifted the package."' She smiled wryly. 'All right, JB.'

The agent found a small space on the whiteboard filled with the locations of her fossil finds to chalk the number. 'Erase it as soon as you've made the call.' He stood back to view the full board. 'Wouldn't it be easier to use an automatic easel?'

'Too damp. The batteries won't recharge themselves.'

JB remembered what the water had done to his phone. 'You've really chosen a desolate pit to work in, haven't you?'

'That's as maybe, but I think you would stand a better chance staying here, myself.'

'I daren't risk being caught.'

'You should get rid of that jacket. From the air, that silver strip will make you look like a firework display.'

'I can't.'

'And you think I'm stubborn for living in a dinosaurs' graveyard? You secret agents certainly believe in making life difficult for yourself.' Dr.

Shadbolt pulled an old grey raincoat from a cupboard. 'Put this on,' she told him, and as he opened his mouth to protest, 'No, it can't be traced back to me. It was washed ashore. Probably from some oriental cruise ship. Confuse the life out of them with a bit of luck.'

'Thanks.'

'And have a shower and something to eat.'

'But ...'

'Do as you're told, dear boy. You don't want body odour and a rumbling stomach to attract their attention, do you?'

In the face of such practicality there was little JB could do but obey.

Nightingale's second in command looked rough enough to be a Natural Living Campaign activist by the time he darted away with the map Phoebe Shadbolt had sketched from her most up to date record of the region's fossil beds.

CHAPTER 22

Clinically manipulated for twenty years by Tim Tharby! Just so Nightingale could feed the Lictana intelligence about Earth!

Now JB Sendall was away from the safety of Dr. Phoebe Shadbolt's curious world, the full horror of what had happened descended on him like a lead duvet. It was hardly surprising that the medic would sooner freak out than admit he knew anything about it.

But why did Nightingale do it? There was no sensible explanation for the Senior Controller going to so much trouble to let her number one give away Earth's secrets. Nothing Nightingale did made sense. She was the only one who could supply the answers but JB doubted that he would ever see her or Tim Tharby again.

He gave up trying to understand Dr. Shadbolt's map based on the district's fossil beds and just kept to the cover of the roadside trees.

Over the years, World Government had made sure everyone could be accounted for on a multitude of surveillance systems. Benefits being, the lost were rapidly found, whether they wanted to be or not, the criminal had nowhere to hide and all citizens belonged to an address of some sort. It was virtually impossible to enter a town or new conservation sector without a scanner picking up their body heat and brainwave patterns. Few disliked the system because it gave them a sense of security. Even fewer went out to enjoy this wonderful countryside for fear of their activities being noted down by behaviourists.

JB had travelled no more than three kilometres, and was probably still inside World Security's search net, when he had to stop and think. What was he doing, apart from putting as much distance as he could between Dr. Shadbolt and himself before Nightingale read his message? He now trusted Nightingale as much as a frog in the fishing bait.

Jonathan Benjamin Sendall decided to do things his way.

He had left Demsel's crystal with Dr. Shadbolt as a token of his appreciation, though it would probably disappear and crop up in his pocket at the most inconvenient moment. That still left him with the problem of what to do with his mother's pendant. JB pulled out the Lictanan transmitter key and gazed at it. All the suppressed memories of the time he had spent as a fly in Nightingale's sinister web welled up.

No longer taken in by the beguiling scintillation of the jewel, JB would have hurled it as hard as he could into the overhead branches. With a bit of luck, some enterprising magpie would inherit the bauble and scare the life out of Dey and Hysle.

The sound of a siren stopped him. Directly above, a starling was mimicking a security alarm. He swore at the bird, then pulled himself together.

JB knew what needed to be done next, but only Nightingale could operate the self-destruct sequence at Group Indigo's HQ.

The fugitive should have been more concerned about breaking a hidden security beam as he moved on. His mind was on other things, though.

A spasm of nausea welled up and JB stopped again. He recalled what the Lictana had done to the humans they abducted. If the aliens were annihilated before Dey and Hysle's technicians managed to shake the worlds free of each other, so what? Perhaps the disc carrying the location of the one-way portals should fall into the hands of Gita Medlock. She would certainly fire the missiles that made sure the Lictana ended up as molecularly confused as the human specimens in those jars. Jeff Devlin must have worked out the sequences required to open Nightingale's one-way portals from the master computer by now. Some bad tempered deity was no doubt up there, sitting on a thunder cloud, using the Demon Devlin to bring back the fiery sword and one or two uncomfortable absolutes.

JB Sendall had been too consumed in the battle between his determination and delicate qualms to notice where he was going. He found himself walking alongside a canal. A remotely operated barge gently chugged up behind him. It had already been scanned and sealed at source, so the vessel would unhurriedly carry its cargo northwards without any security system stopping it.

JB made up his mind. He glanced about. Apart from a pine marten looking down from a conifer and the guard dog on the barge frantically wagging its tail, no one was watching. The dog had either just had its meal from the automatically timed dispenser or didn't know that it was meant to be ferocious.

JB decided not to leap on board in case the deck had pressure sensors. He pinched the tiny disc from his collar insignia and dropped it into a small, ornately painted bucket dangling from a hook as the barge passed. It lay on the red paint, sparkling like a rainbow sequin. By the time the cargo reached its destination, the Lictana would have shaken their planet molecularly free of the Earth.

The guard dog continued to wag its tail until the barge was out of sight.

No longer weighed down by the responsibility of wiping out an entire alien species, JB sighed with relief. All he needed to do now was keep out of sight until night fell.

Something blue caught his eye as he made his way across the nearest road to find denser cover. It was his car.

Obviously a trap. Security must have been tracking his movements ever since he blundered through some surveillance beam or other.

JB Sendall was tired of scurrying about in a raincoat so shabby some seaman had risked pollution prosecution by dumping it overboard. He pulled it off and let his silver braid gleam. Damned if he was going to play the mouse in this game any longer! If the World Security cat wanted a real chase, it could have one.

He told himself to think straight. Then that vengeful demon that he had kept down for so long lurched into life. Why should he sit shivering in some bush waiting to be picked up? He took the ID from his pocket, flattened it as best as he could, then bounded from the cover of the branches.

Not only had the car's body been polished, the engine was fully charged. To his relief, the lock accepted the crumpled card and the door opened. With a ferocious crackle, not usual in electric cars, the engine sparked into life. Seconds later, JB Sendall accelerated towards the section border before any surveillance monitor could register that the vehicle had been snatched.

As it purred past scanners, they picked up his body heat, recorded his brain wave patterns, and could have counted his blond eyelashes for all JB cared. He was travelling! It was an exhilaration he had never dared feel before.

A rotoplane buzzed overhead, stabbing the falling dusk with shafts of light. This only heightened JB's determination. Group Indigo's maintenance would have had a fit if they saw the way he handled the controls of the vehicle. The car was probably quite surprised as well! It had only ever known a rigidly precise hand, secure in the knowledge its fibreglass shell was not at risk from unsightly dents or gouge marks.

Somehow the chaotic journey continued until night fell. JB's nerves started to jangle at having to constantly swerve out of the rotoplane's searchlight.

Suddenly, a car without lights rammed his. Until the impact, he hadn't been aware of it. JB kept going. With some dangerous manoeuvring he lost the vehicle, but dare not switch off his lights. He still had qualms about killing innocent wolves or night hikers.

From nowhere, another vehicle rammed his car's near side. The transmission was dislocated and power rapidly drained from the engine. JB stopped so abruptly, the two pursuers shot past him. It gave him the chance to leap out of his vehicle and double back down the road. He was surrounded by four uniforms before he could dive into cover.

'Now don't be foolish, Sir,' a mechanically mild voice implored. 'We have instructions not to harm you.'

'Well they're not mutual!' JB was amazed at how well he could growl.

It would need more to intimidate the two agents behind him. They tried to seize his arms. He span round and delivered blows to their jaws in quick succession. The security team may not have been trained pugilists, but they did know how to fire a tranquillising dart. As it took effect, JB was gratefully aware that he'd inflicted far more damage than he had received.

* * *

Dr. Phoebe Shadbolt happily trudged up the beach with yet another crate of fossils to chip and dissolve from their matrices.

Not the sort to be easily perturbed, she was astounded by the appearance of a woman even more eccentric than her. Apart from being an odd colour, the visitor was over two metres tall and had a shock of curly grey hair that must have brushed most insulated ceilings. She was concealing a weapon in the folds of her long black coat. Despite being at least seventy, the woman obviously knew how to use it.

The palaeontologist put the crate down, removed her

headscarf, and mopped her brow as she observed her from a safe distance.

Nightingale withdrew the gun from her coat and pointed it skywards. 'Strictly for uniforms. You don't happen to have an infestation in these parts?'

Dr. Shadbolt had been expecting the arrival of JB's superior, not one of the Four Horsewomen of the Apocalypse driving a magenta car. The palaeontologist had encountered a few heavily armed renegades on her digs and wasn't quite so intimidated as the Senior Controller had anticipated. 'Been a lot of them up and down the coast lately. Are you pest control?'

'I'm Nightingale.'

'Oh yes?' Phoebe Shadbolt was surprised that the other wanted criminal was so blatant about her identity given that she couldn't have easily been disguised by some sailor's discarded raincoat. 'How did you manage to get this far?'

Nightingale casually flicked the safety lock on the gun and it clicked into charging phase. 'I kill on sight - they have to get permission first.'

'Oh.' Dr. Shadbolt wondered if similar creatures existed alongside the allosaurids and oviraptors in the ancient rock strata.

'Mean a very messy inquiry if they shoot me. Don't worry about World Security. I've got enough on that lot to have them disbanded.'

Shadbolt believed her. The towering septuagenarian was apparently a one-woman army with her own spy network, as well as vengeful on a Biblical scale.

'Where is that wretch, Sendall, then?'

The palaeontologist picked up her crate. 'Come inside. You may not be worried by World Security but, over the last two days, a few good reasons have presented themselves to me.'

Nightingale hadn't thought the woman could be disconcerted by anything unless it refused to be chipped out of some rock or other.

She replaced the safety lock on the gun. 'That's all right. They can't pick me up on their scanners.' She strode after the Doctor into the hut. The teeth on a megalosaurus jawbone suspended from the lintel almost combed her crinkly hair.

It only then occurred to Phoebe Shadbolt what she had said. 'What?'

'I took the precaution of ensuring they couldn't years ago.' Nightingale opened her coat to reveal her black body suit. 'This outfit gives their heat sensors the readings of a rabbit.' She pointed to her head. 'In there, a plate which can scramble my brain waves to look like a mechanical toothbrush.'

Phoebe Shadbolt would never allow anyone to call her eccentric again. This visitor could well have been alien.

She switched on the solar stove to warm some soup. 'I'm afraid I don't know where JB went. Why didn't you get him fitted with all this paraphernalia as well?'

'Oh, he's got an implant in his brain - not for the same reason - and I'd never have been able to get him to wear thermal black.'

Dr. Shadbolt lifted a pterodactyl wing fossil from her chair and sat down. 'I'm afraid he couldn't have got far. He was in quite a confused state when he left. Remembered this nightmare about seeing his mother blown up. Quite upset him.'

'Expect it would.'

'Like some soup'

'No thank you.'

Dr. Shadbolt looked at Nightingale intently. 'Apart from being in such a pickle with World Security, I'm sure there was something else bothering the dear boy.'

'Probably is.'

'Please stop agreeing with me.'

'Make the most of it. I don't do it very often.'

'Well, are you going to rescue him or aren't you?'

'Of course.' Nightingale looked at her watch. 'As soon as I've got a minute.'

'They could do him serious harm by then.'

'They won't torture him.'

'How can you be so sure?'

'One of World Security's many heads promised.'

'Apart from making agreements with multi-skulled monsters, what else have you been doing since you escaped? What about the rest of your staff?'

'I sent them all on holiday.'

'But that means ...'

'I knew World Security was about to take over? Of course I did. That's why I'm the Senior Controller.'

Shadbolt shut her eyes for a moment. 'This is all beyond me. Just what are you up to?'

'Making the world a safer place.'

However much she had empathised with JB Sendall, the palaeontologist wasn't so sure about Nightingale. 'World Security seem to make a reasonable job of it. Not much gets past them, even though they are a bunch of crocodilians.'

'Blowing up alien civilisations and cocooning our own in a tasteless fudge of personal security is not "safety".'

'You're really talking about freedom, aren't you?'

'Am I? What a quaint old-fashioned soul I must be.'

'It was too much freedom which sent civilisation spiralling down in the first place.'

'Really? I thought it was self-interest, too many antibiotics, and ratifying ecological treaties no one had any intention of keeping to.'

'Look, as much as I'm enjoying this highly suspect philosophical discussion, shouldn't you be looking for JB?'

'Yes,' agreed Nightingale, 'I should. I can see that you're a busy little beaver as well.'

'I've only two more months to move as many fossils as I can.'

'Climate Control going to alter the tides?'

'Conservationists.'

Nightingale gave a wide, sinister grin. 'Don't you worry about a thing, Doctor. Don't worry about a thing.'

Dr. Shadbolt wasn't sure she wanted to know what Nightingale meant. She watched the visitor stride back to her vintage Amethyst car and drive off in the rising sea mist like some deity from the deep. Then the palaeontologist took a sip of her soup.

CHAPTER 23

JB Sendall was only half-aware of being whisked away into the sky, and his explosive rage couldn't help him resist World Security's sedatives.

When he came to, he was in an isolated stone building once used as a secret clinic. He felt so angry and bloody-minded, no pain would have made him admit where he had hidden the disc. He assumed that was what they were after. It would have been a lot of hassle just to find out the name of his tailor. The security team must have known that extracting information without the prisoner's co-operation was going to be problematic. Any brain probe would activate the plate in his cerebral cortex and freeze his vocal cords.

But there was something JB had not counted on. It was smooth-skinned, dark-haired, and intensely good-looking. JB and Tim Tharby regarded the man as little further up the evolutionary ladder than rat turd and Jeff Devlin was wearing that malevolent expression which said that he had every intention of proving them right.

Two guards hustled the dazed captive into a small bare room and handcuffed him to a pillar before he could recover and sock them on the jaw. JB was allowed to sit, so he assumed that the interrogation was going to take some while. Through leaden eyelids, all he could make out on the floor was a pair of shattered spectacles and somebody's bloodstained ID.

As his senses returned, JB tried to place the building's location in case there was a chance to escape. It must have been near Group Indigo's HQ. Devlin would need to be near the action, but far enough away to keep what he was doing from Gita Medlock.

Devlin strolled up and down, brandishing a thin rod, impatient for JB to look reasonably alert. Capable of delivering a minor blow to thousands of volts, the weapon described a fiery trail as it slashed the air. Trust the man to have collected an antique like that. He probably had a wide range of torturer's devices for use on everything from dumb animals to agents with rigorously toughened minds.

JB needed time. He pretended to half sleep for as long as he dared. Sensing he was faking, Devlin touched his cheek with the rod and applied a small charge. It helped his prisoner remember how angry he was. JB's leg lashed out and caught the back of Devlin's knees. He crumpled to the floor. The interrogator quickly got up, increasing the weapon's voltage. It struck the flagstones. Sparks crackled furiously, scorching both of them.

The worried expression of the guards reminded Devlin of Gita Medlock's orders. Before either of the men could protest, he folded the rod into its insulated handle and tucked it into a pocket, then went to a shelf where there was a recorder and paper file. He set them out on a small table in a businesslike way. The guards wanted to believe that he wasn't a psychopath after all, just sorely tested. Not so long ago, JB Sendall had been their superior. Now, whether they liked it or not, it was Jeff Devlin.

'Daris, Shultz - find something better to do!'

The guards reluctantly left.

By the way the old iron clad door slammed shut, it was obvious the room was sound proof.

Devlin immediately pulled the electric rod from his pocket and opened it with a cavalier flourish. 'Alone at last.'

JB sneered. 'My God, I've never known Nightingale make a mistake like this before.'

'Like what?'

'Trawling the sewers for personnel.'

Jeff Devlin lounged against a cast iron pillar, swinging the rod as though trying to electrocute flies before they could settle on the steel shutter that divided the room. 'You know what I'm after, of course?'

'Women usually, but they seem to have better sense than you give them credit for. Or was that more to do with the treatment Tim Tharby recommended?'

JB expected the man to erupt. Instead, Devlin gave a hard, humourless smile that was far more unsettling.

'I can't help being an old-fashioned soul. My real problem is, I'm too romantic.'

'By that standard, so are diseased dogs.'

Devlin pointed the rod at JB. 'Don't count on me accepting this level of conversation much longer.'

JB refused to flinch. 'That's all you're going to get. You don't honestly think you can intimidate me with that thing, do you?'

Devlin had limited options in a game of high stakes. Though no poker player, he was ominously relaxed. 'What did you do with the disc carrying the locations of the one-way transmission portals?'

'Search me.'

'We have. Very thoroughly.'

'Then I must have lost it somewhere.'

'Well you'd better remember where it is in the next ten minutes ...'

The prisoner laughed. 'Or what?'

Devlin increased the charge of the rod and the air about it shimmered. 'I knew nothing so crude as torture would make you talk, so I took a little precaution.'

JB didn't want to know what the man's sick mind had cooked up.

Devlin gave a cruel smile. 'Medlock may have allowed you and Nightingale to walk out of HQ, so I found someone else.'

His calculating malice was like a sabre-toothed kitten taking perverted pleasure in torturing a mouse. Even at his most vicious, the man's easy manner almost reassured JB that he couldn't have done anything too terrible. Perhaps it was because he was still unable to work out why he found Jeff Devlin so familiar.

Devlin pushed a switch and gave a chuckle as though about to reveal some Jacobean tableau. The shutter dividing the room rattled upwards.

The sight of the mouse this cat had already had such fun with, made JB's stomach muscles clench in horror.

The victim's pink hair fell in damp strands over his face and neck and his heavily freckled body was disfigured by long angry weals. The only thing that kept Tim Tharby upright was the beam above his head to which his wrists were fastened.

Nausea and rage battled with JB's digestive tract and he wasn't able to say anything.

'Why?' he eventually demanded.

Jeff Devlin gave a boyish laugh. 'Well, to save time of course. Now you realise what can happen to your fat little medic if you don't tell me what I want to know, we won't waste any time by either of you being wonderfully brave.'

'Why didn't you torture me?'

'Because meddling Medlock insists I've not to harm a silver hair of your head.'

'Tharby couldn't tell you anything!'

'Of course he could. He knew where Nightingale kept the disc.'

'You must already know that!'

'True. I'm not that stupid, Sendall. I just wanted to see if this little shit would tell me.' Devlin pushed up his sleeve. 'And look, the little snake bit me.' He made a token lash at Tharby with the rod.

The medic winced, too exhausted to avoid it.

JB smiled wryly. 'So he didn't tell you a thing?'

'Nothing. But now you're here, he doesn't need to be brave any more.'

JB closed his eyes and tried to think. If he revealed

where he had hidden the disc too soon, the Lictana wouldn't be ready to shake themselves free of the molecular bond with the Earth. On the other hand, Tim Tharby was in no condition to suffer the consequences of his superior's stubbornness as well as his own.

'Don't tell him,' Tharby faintly pleaded.

Devlin hit out with the rod and a charge of several thousand volts slashed across the medic's body. Somehow Tharby suppressed a scream.

JB was at his wits end. Should he save the assistant who had spent over twenty years filling him with mind bending drugs or the Lictana who had spent even longer breaking up and experimenting on human beings?

He had to play for time. 'Aren't you worried about Gita Medlock finding out what you're up to?'

Devlin laughed. 'As long as that disc is found, she won't ask how. Tharby's of no importance to anyone.'

'Except Nightingale.'

Mention of the name markedly dampened Jeff Devlin's excitement.

JB drove the message home. 'She'll kill you when she finds out what you've done to him.'

'She'll never get the chance.'

'You haven't caught her yet, have you?' He knew Devlin would never dare confront the woman. 'And then they'll be me to contend with.' JB flashed a menacing smile.

'I'll have too high a rank for you to reach me.' Jeff Devlin sounded as though he believed it.

JB Sendall chuckled. He knew the machinery of World Government would reject Devlin with all the other worn cogs and faulty connections.

But mentioning Nightingale's name had backfired. With an irrational burst of fury, Devlin repeatedly lashed out at Tim Tharby.

'Stop it! You'll kill him!' JB screamed.

'Where's the disc?'

'I lost it!'

As Devlin struck the medic again, Nightingale's number one realised that there would be a stroke for every evasive answer he gave.

'Where?'

'On the canal.'

Tharby tried not to wince at the next blow.

JB's resolve snapped at his assistant's unexpected courage. 'On a barge going north. I dropped it into one of the nearside buckets.'

'No,' groaned Tharby.

'What was it carrying?'

'Chemicals of some sort.'

'If you're lying-'

'I'm not! Let Tharby down.'

'When I have the disc.'

Devlin snatched up his recorder, opened the heavy door, and dashed out. The metal crashed shut and resealed the room.

Tharby coughed and blood trickled down his chin. 'Why did you tell him? Do you know what you've done?'

JB wasn't sure whether they were being monitored. 'Yes,' he whispered. 'The Lictana are planning to shake themselves free of the Earth. He may not be in time.'

'You remember everything?'

'Everything.'

'I'm sorry,' sobbed Tharby. 'I had to do it.'

'But why?'

'Nightingale insisted I give you those drugs.'

'I told an alien species everything that Group Indigo knew. If I hadn't been under the influence of that poison I would have broken the link with the Lictana.'

'I don't understand why she did it ... Perhaps she's mad...'

'Perhaps she is.'

The air in the portal was buzzing like a cloud of gnats as Nightingale entered Nichols and Hazlewood's subterranean complex. Safe in their underground lair, her two moles had been isolated from the upheavals at Group Indigo.

Nightingale noticed the ultraviolet glow in the transmission portal and knew that they were engaged in Earth moving enterprises of their own. 'What's going on?' she demanded.

Hazlewood had no intention of closing the portal because of her arrival. 'The Lictana are going to separate the planets.'

'That could rip a hole in the Earth!'

'They have to rush things!' Nichols snapped back. 'If World Security finds the location of those one-way transmission portals you set up ...'

Nightingale's eyes narrowed. 'How did you find out about them?'

'It does not matter. I have no doubt that is why you are here.'

Nightingale slumped into a chair.

'What is the matter?' demanded Nichols.

'Sendall had the disc they're recorded on.'

'Good! Where is he?'

'That's what I came here to find out. He's not responding to his call signal. I think he's been picked up by Gita Medlock's security.'

'Would he tell them?'

'Why shouldn't he?'

Hazlewood was agitated. 'We have to find him!'

'The plate in his cerebral cortex carries a transmitter which I can monitor from this receiver.' Nightingale slapped the case hanging at her side. 'I need an aerial. The one you have on the top of this mound will do.' She reached out and pressed the end of a flex into Nichols' hand. 'Plug it in!'

Never having had to deal with anything so low-tech, Nichols looked in disbelief at the naked end of the cord for a moment, then quickly clamped the one pin connection of the dish to it and plugged it in.

Nightingale tuned its reception. 'Start due south.' She pulled a rolled map from her coat, unfurled it on the floor, and carefully marked off each radial as the receiver drew a blank. 'Hold it there!'

Hazlewood was baffled. 'You only have one reference line?'

'I've got an imagination.'

Nichols hadn't. 'You had better be right.'

'Don't threaten me!' Nightingale warned darkly, then continued to pick her way along the line on the map, millimetre by millimetre.

Hazlewood was too agitated to worry about threats. 'Just get on with it! We have got to find him!'

'We?'

'We will be coming with you,' Nichols announced.

'You'll have to use your own car.'

'Do not worry. We are not going to risk getting shot by someone aiming at you.'

Nightingale went back to the map and, after a painfully long pause, mused, 'Must be there.'

'Where?'

'An abandoned clinic World Security once used to "treat" criminals.' She rechecked the location on her receiver. 'Distance seems to be about right.'

'Well, let's go then.'

Hazlewood hesitated. 'But our transmission portal ... if we do not shut it down, the atomic imbalance caused when the Lictana break free could destroy this planet.'

'There is no time. I am sure Nightingale will find the disc long before that happens. Why did you need to put the locations on a disc anyway?' Nichols asked her acidly.

Nightingale gave her a cold, hard glare. 'Were do

you suggest I kept the information? On Group Indigo's hard drive where all the world and its gerbil could have hacked into it!' She scooped up her map, yanked her equipment free of the aerial, and strode out of the complex into the lift. Her two agents hurtled after her.

Once in their car and out of earshot, Hazlewood blurted out, 'What are you thinking of?'

'I know what I am doing,' said Nichols. 'I have always had the feeling she was double-crossing us.'

'It is too risky. This planet could implode!'

'Shut-up and do not let her car out of your sight.'

The journey Nightingale led Nichols and Hazlewood on was uneventful, apart from smashing through unattended toll barriers and leaving tyre marks on the velvet lawns of several landscaped domes. It was often difficult for them to keep sight of her Amethyst. For some reason, no doubt chemical, the car kept fading along dimly lit stretches of road as though the night had suddenly thrown a cloak over it. Even Catseyes blinked as it approached.

Eventually, Nightingale pulled up near two unattended security vehicles. She had already broken into one of them and stolen its starter beam before the other two joined her.

'What are you doing?' Hazlewood demanded.

The Senior Controller pointed to a partly demolished out building. 'You two take cover behind that wall.'

'But?'

'There aren't any sensors near it.'

Nichols and Hazlewood had no choice; Nightingale had switched off conversation mode. When they were out of sight, she took two cases from her car and loaded them into one of the security vehicles. The Senior Controller then flicked its battery switch onto full charge and closed the door.

With her companions well hidden, Nightingale returned to her car for a gun. She swung it onto her

shoulder and nonchalantly strode through the
surveillance beam surrounding the clinic. Its heavy
door immediately swung open. Nightingale was in
firing position before the guards could react. The
Senior Controller was the last person they expected to
see.

The younger man just managed to pull his finger
from the trigger in time. 'Boss!'

'Daris! Shultz!' Nightingale slowly pointed her gun
skywards.

'We could have killed you!'

'You might have got a medal for it.'

'What's happening?' demanded Daris. 'We had a
directive from World Security to take orders from Gita
Medlock.'

'Not kill me?'

'No. Just keep you out of the way.'

'What's going on?' Shultz insisted. 'Jeff Devlin's
been buzzing in and out of here like a wasp with a sore
arse.'

'You'll never know how accurate that description is.
What's he been up to?'

'No idea. He ordered us to take Mr Sendall inside,
then get out.'

'What else?'

'We only arrived with Mr Sendall. The rest of the
place is locked and we can't get in.'

'Prepare for a little demolition, gentlemen.'

'But you can't do that!'

'If you help me I won't need to.'

Daris and Shultz looked at each other.

'What's the matter? Haven't you always wanted to
disobey World Security?'

'Well yes. Is it worth the risk?'

Nightingale seemed to grow taller. 'If you don't,
nobody will be bothered about putting you on a charge
where we all end up.'

Nightingale wouldn't joke about Armageddon, yet

they still hesitated.

'Who do you think knows more about the danger this planet is in? World Security or the Senior Controller of Group Indigo?'

They were both Group Indigo guards and didn't need convincing.

'Come in!' Daris led her through the building to the metal security door.

'Melt its lock,' Nightingale ordered.

Shultz took a beam cutter from the wall and the ancient metal had soon pooled itself on the floor.

Nightingale kicked the door open. 'After you, gentlemen.'

Weapon drawn, Daris darted ahead. He had trouble taking in what confronted him. 'Hell!'

Nightingale barged past. She was momentarily staggered by the sight. Tim Tharby had been at her elbow for so long, she was unprepared for the sight of this barely recognisable, bloody mess. Then there was an upwelling of cold fury.

'Who did it?'

JB Sendall recognised the gravelly tones. He thought he was dreaming, but Nightingale could never be that nebulous.

'Jeff Devlin!'

Shultz and Daris carefully released the disfigured body of Tim Tharby.

Shultz was near to tears. 'We didn't know, boss! I swear we didn't know!'

Nightingale desperately tried to find a pulse on the medic. 'Is he still alive?

Daris had more luck. 'Just! We'll have to get him to hospital quick.'

'Use the white vehicle.'

'Why?'

'I want the other one.'

Neither of the guards argued.

Two unfamiliar women peered into the room.

'Don't mind those two! Get Tharby out of here and give me the keys for Sendall's handcuffs.'

Daris tossed them to Nightingale and she released JB.

Daris and Shultz wrapped Tharby in a blanket as though he were a piece of bone china that hadn't already been smashed, then they carried him out.

Nightingale pulled down JB's eyelids. 'Slept at all?'

Her number one snarled. 'I should kill you!'

'I know, but you've left it too late. I own your soul.'

'How could you let that happen to Tim Tharby?'

'Tharby should have been in his little hut by the sea. What the hell was he doing at HQ?'

'Probably following me.'

'What the hell were you doing at HQ?'

'I had a sudden attack of memory!'

'How much?'

'I told the Lictana about the one-way transmission portals.'

'And?'

JB exercised his neck, then rubbed his wrists. 'And Jeff Devlin knows where the disc is!'

'What?!' roared Nichols. 'How could you have done such a thing?'

'He was killing Tim Tharby!'

'So what? The man was of no importance.'

If there had been any feeling in JB's fingers she would have felt them on her throat. 'Who are these vultures?'

'Nichols and Hazlewood.'

Hazlewood was on the verge of panic. 'Stop this time wasting! We have to get to your HQ. World Security is about to launch those implosives at the Lictana.'

JB was beyond caring about the aliens. 'Why bother? They're nothing but body-breakers. He stooped down to pick up Tim Tharby's blood-spattered ID card and smashed glasses.

Nightingale was getting impatient. 'We're wasting time. I'll meet you two outside. Make sure the cars are charged.'

Nichols and Hazlewood sprinted out like two overweight rabbits.

The Senior Controller pulled JB up. 'Have you slept?' she asked again.

'Probably two hours, but it was difficult with Tim Tharby dying in front of me.' He rubbed some of the dry blood from the medic's ID card and put it in his pocket.

'There's something you have to do.'

'What's that?' he scoffed. 'Save the Lictana?'

'No, save this planet.'

Despite everything, JB couldn't resist the command in her gravelly voice. 'What are you on about?'

'As soon as the Lictana wrench their planet free, it will rip a hole in the atomic structure of the Earth through the two-way portals.'

JB Sendall wasn't used to driving security vehicles at night or wearing uniforms. Fortunately no one stopped him to ask awkward questions. World Security now had other things to worry about.

As he drove onto the green pedestrian area, there was greater danger in negotiating the perimeter of the massive cave-in now surrounded by temporary statues representing world unity and wind power. Finding the entrance to Nichols and Hazlewood's underground complex by the dim light of the cave-in's warning lamps was even more hazardous.

Shouldering his knapsack, JB left the vehicle. He managed to find the lift lobby by the light of his body lamp and consulting Nightingale's plan of the layout. One of the keys she had given him opened the surveillance cabinet so he could check the monitor of each level below to ensure it wasn't registering body heat. No one was about. The complex was mainly storage space and automatic production lines. As there was no public road into it, unauthorised entry was virtually impossible.

Nightingale's security card took JB down in the lift to two floors above Nichols and Hazlewood's control. He would never be able to find his way out of the maze in a hurry, so he adjusted the nearest control to flood the levels below with light. It would be too late by the time some sleepy patrol above registered the burst of photons on their scanner.

Nightingale's pass allowed JB through several security doors without any problem. The way they all slammed shut behind him was unnerving. Just in case it had slipped her memory to mention the resident Minotaur, he switched his beam cutter onto full charge.

When he reached the heart of Nichols and Hazlewood's bunker, JB was taken aback by the array of monitors and computers siphoning off and sifting information intended for the most secret World Government departments. There was no time to stand and gawp at Nightingale's aptitude for espionage. He had to get back to HQ. Running this errand for her, however imperative, was also conveniently keeping him out of the way.

The shutter securing the transmission portal wouldn't open with Nightingale's pass. JB used the beam cutter to melt its hinges and then pushed it in. The ultraviolet light inside the portal intensified.

He froze. Something was taking shape in the buzzing particles. Sickening recollections from JB's childhood put his presence of mind on hold. He was unable to pull the case of explosives from his knapsack, let alone set the detonator.

A familiar figure in a magenta suit was forming. She reached out from the portal to JB, inviting him to join her.

Every molecule in his mind wanted to believe that his mother was still alive and some demented reflex made him step towards the apparition. While his senses insisted that she was real. His rationale told him that she had been blown apart when he was eight. He had only been kept from that memory by Tim Tharby's drugs.

The thought of the medic made JB step back. He pulled out the explosives and snapped the case open.

The figure still stood, arms outstretched. Then it realised what he was about to do. The creature pretending to be his mother reassembled its molecules. An alien figure fleshed itself. The sight was unearthly and nauseating.

'Hallo, little minnow. So this is what you really look like. Did we manage to reduce you to that?'

JB had acquired a complex about his insipid appearance long ago. Not even Hysle's comment could make that worse. He was horrified because he could understand the creature. In the desperate activity of the last day, he had forgotten to remove his mother's transmitter key. He fished inside his borrowed uniform to tear it off.

'Keep listening to me, little minnow.'

'What do you want, Hysle? There's nothing you can say that will stop me.'

'We are ready to shake our planet free.'

'And World Security now have the locations of Nightingale's one-way portals. They are about to obliterate you.'

'You told them?'

'Yes!'

'But why, little minnow?'

'Tim Tharby was worth more than your unnatural species of body-breakers. He could have betrayed you and saved himself. He knew where Nightingale kept the disc. Jeff Devlin half killed him, yet couldn't even make him admit that.'

Hysle hesitated in disbelief. 'What a strange creature? Why did he do it?'

'I don't know. I never have understood Tharby, but I fail to see why he should put his life on the line to save you.' In a spasm of anger, JB took the medic's blood soaked ID card from his pocket and threw it into the portal. 'Here!' he spat. 'He was ready to give you his life; you might as well take his identity!'

'So you valued him more than our friendship?'

'You used me! Nightingale used me! As I can't have revenge on her, you'll have to do.'

Hysle picked up the ID that contained Tim Tharby's DNA map and brainwave patterns. 'Oh little minnow, we were fond of you. Is blowing up our planet any way to repay us?'

'You're about to rip a hole out of ours!' JB set the detonator's timer.

'You know we cannot destroy her one-way portals?'

'I know. Whatever else Nightingale might be, she

was never a fool.' JB suddenly realised what Hysle was inferring. 'You want me to destroy them, don't you?'

'It could be done from Nightingale's portal control at your HQ.'

'Why should I save you?'

'We may be more considered in activating the molecular disruption which will break us free.'

'I don't trust you.'

'I know.' Hysle chuckled wryly. 'Save yourself and your planet, little minnow. Let us see who can destroy the other first.'

The alien faded into the portal's ultraviolet glow, briefly leaving his outline in the atmosphere.

JB reduced the time on the detonator. Not even the Lictana would be able to work out how to disarm Nightingale's explosive in five minutes. There would also be no reprieve for him if the lift malfunctioned or the security doors refused to open. His beam cutter could only cope with one at a time.

JB synchronised his watch with the timer. He pressed the bomb to the portal wall and activated it. Then he hurtled back the control room.

Two of the inner security doors opened with Nightingale's pass. The last one had been booby-trapped by Hazlewood. JB knew he would never find the correct override in time even if he had dashed to the console, so he shot out the explosive mining the security door. Metal eight centimetres thick was ripped open and shrapnel cut through the air.

Shaking and deafened, JP didn't realise that he had been struck several times as he reached the lift, only that his fingers still worked. He frantically programmed it to ascend. With painful slowness on reduced night power, it crawled upwards. JB only had forty seconds.

He wrenched down the alarm lever in the control box as soon as he reached the lobby, then sped out towards his security van. The wailing of the siren drowned out his efforts to jolt its engine into life. With ten seconds left, he had it lumbering back over the dome to the nearest road.

The implosion in the bowels of the hill was cavernous, like an almighty, muffled hiccup.

Nothing happened for several seconds. Then came the inevitable whirr of a fast moving patrol vehicle.

JB stayed long enough to see the hill collapse, making a hole as large as its neighbour.

No recognisable fragments of Nichols and Hazlewood's complex would remain at the bottom of that. The failure of the hill would be taken by the Natural Living Campaign as just another signal that Nature resented meddling humans trying to improve on her. Nightingale would probably set up another residence for her moles anyway – if she survived the night.

CHAPTER 26

A circular field of rust red leaves slowly sank into the ground. The strawberries had been jammed for export weeks ago and the most vigorous runners pinned to the soil. The vast circle then slid aside and rumbling welled up from the bowels of the Earth. It was followed by a high pitched whine as an eerie strike force rose like deadly hoverflies.

* * *

Sirens wailed like scolded cats as soon as Nightingale and her companions entered the grounds of Group Indigo's HQ. Spikes shot from the Tarmac and lacerated the wheels of their cars.

Snatching as much equipment as she could carry, Nightingale leapt into her recently cropped jungle on foot, beckoning Nichols and Hazlewood to follow. She didn't let the panting women rest until they reached an island of foliage the automatic scythes had spared. The two agents were unused to so much fresh air and craved the controlled environment of their underground bunker. It didn't help that the heavily laden septuagenarian they were following was hardly out of breath.

They gratefully rested in a stand of laurel.

Hazlewood assumed that Nightingale had a plan of action. 'Is there another way into your HQ?'

'There is only one way. The front door.'

'Was that wise?' snapped Nichols.

'It seemed a good idea at the time.'

Nichols broke cover to snatch a glance at the well-illuminated porch. 'Would they shoot us if we walked in?'

'I gambled that Daris and Shultz would be tame. They were Group Indigo security. Jeff Devlin is probably in charge of the crew over there.'

Hazlewood was beside herself. 'Well do something!

We cannot sit out here.'

'Oh yes you can!' Nightingale looked at the time. 'For about ten minutes.'

'But?'

'I have to make a phone call.'

If it hadn't been so dark, the odd couple would have noticed how much the Senior Controller relished leaving them in the sodden undergrowth to stew.

Nightingale's apparel was the perfect camouflage as she darted through the remaining vegetation as though it was her natural element. Tim Tharby had fed the seventy-year-old with enough vitamins, minerals, stimulants, and preservatives to keep her nimble for the next twenty years. The odd twinge reminded her that he was no longer there. Though it was probably only well deserved arthritis, Nightingale was surprised at how much she was going to miss the little monster.

Keeping low, on the edge of a small clearing she opened a case and rapidly assembled a directional transmitter receiver.

Inside Group Indigo's basement control, World Security's communications channel to the weapons base suddenly spluttered.

Jeff Devlin jumped. 'What was that?'

An operator at the balcony console surrounding Nightingale's laboratory was trying to clear the interference. 'We're being jammed, Sir.'

Gita Medlock took her attention away from the transmission portal. 'Impossible! No one else can operate on these frequencies.' Then the illegal transmission became coherent. She instantly recognised the husky voice.

So did Devlin. He panicked. 'She must be outside! I'll take a squad and-'

'You'll stay here!' Medlock went to the communications operator. 'Give me a mike and patch me through.' One was immediately placed in her hand. 'Nightingale, what the hell are you up to?'

There was a wicked chuckle. 'I said I'd be back.'

'You're too late. The missiles are airborne and the countdown has started.'

'Now that is clever.'

Gita Medlock took a breath so deep the brooch on her blouse tinkled. 'What do you mean?'

'You've programmed the missile trajectories to enter the one-way portals?'

'Of course. And don't tell me the locations on your disc were wrong. I won't believe you.'

'What about the one you're sitting right next to?'

'Don't be a fool. We'd annihilate ourselves.'

'Not if the Lictana get in there first.'

The senior official hesitated. 'Speak sense.'

'The aliens are about to set up a vibration that will wrench our planets apart. When they do, the atomic imbalance created through that portal will rip away this side of the Earth!'

Gita Medlock went hot, cold, and then numb. 'You're lying! Anyway, as soon as our missiles strike, the aliens will be destroyed.'

This time Nightingale's laugh was deep and sinister. 'Oh no they won't!'

Medlock turned to Devlin. 'Have you any reason to question the accuracy of the portal locations?'

'No, boss. The computer read them off the disc.'

Nightingale heard the discussion. 'I hate to interrupt your little conference, but you'd better give me clearance to come in. While you're wondering about the wisdom of that, ask Devlin how he managed to find the disc.'

The transmitter clicked shut.

'Well,' demanded Gita Medlock, 'How did you manage to get your hands on the disc?'

'I never had any choice ...'

His superior didn't need to hear it. She opened a channel to door security. 'Give Nightingale clearance to come down here.'

Devlin froze. His crime would soon be out in the open.

Gita Medlock had other things on her mind. 'Test the transmission portal.'

Devlin hesitated. 'What? That one?' He glanced unsurely at the darkened laboratory below and the transmission portal. 'You know that's never been active.'

'Just do it!' snapped Medlock.

Devlin left the balcony and went down to the portal's controls. He carefully turned on the power. There was a low ominous hum as it gradually flooded with ultraviolet light.

'It's operative!'

Gita Medlock groaned. 'Why must Nightingale only tell the truth when it's most inconvenient?'

A minute later, the answer was towering above her.

She looked up at the deity too devious to be owned by any civilised mythology. 'Well, Nightingale. Can you prove that the aliens are about to slice this planet in half?'

'You'd better ask those two.' Nightingale pointed to Nichols and Hazlewood who were scuttling about the balcony console looking for something.

'Portal controls,' Nightingale pointed to where Devlin stood. 'Down there!'

The blood drained from Medlock's face. 'What are they doing here? I thought we agreed ...'

Nichols overheard. 'Agreed what?'

Devlin was obviously not part of this conspiracy. He backed away as Hazlewood approached. 'Shall I let them near it, boss?'

'Come out of there and shut up, Devlin!' snapped Gita Medlock.

Nichols and Hazlewood immediately took his place.

Nightingale continued to be infuriatingly nonchalant about impending annihilation. 'Well, ladies, you didn't really believe that World Government would allow you to siphon off every secret and vital decision which affected the security of this planet, did you?'

Nichols and Hazlewood were silent. They obviously did.

Gita Medlock realised that she was still clutching the microphone and pushed it back to the communications operator. She glowered down at the two women. 'We vetted everything that passed through your complex. Now perhaps you will tell me if it's true that the Lictana are going to vibrate our planets apart?'

Nichols and Hazlewood stepped into the transmission portal.

'It is!' Nichols declared. 'The Earth has only minutes to live!'

'Our missiles will detonate in seconds!'

Nightingale caught Medlock's arm. 'No they won't.'

The portal began to fill with ultraviolet light. Everyone rose and stared down in disbelief. Nichols and Hazlewood were no longer human. They had been transformed into four-legged aliens with large multi-faceted eyes.

Then they faded.

Nightingale saluted mockingly. 'Goodbye Tamble. Goodbye Datch.'

The portal was still. Everyone started to breathe again.

'Well,' demanded Gita Medlock. 'Why won't the missiles detonate?'

'Because there aren't any transmission portals for them to hit!' Nightingale announced.

'What!'

The Senior Controller scratched her angular chin. 'I set up the Lictana. I set up World Security. There have never been any more portals than the two you already knew about.'

Medlock jumped on the spot with rage and her corsage shattered. 'You liar! There must be!'

'I've no doubt you would have discovered the truth if I'd given you time to find out, and launched your missiles at the portals which did exist. Damn Sendall and Tharby! They nearly buggered everything up by being gallant.'

Nightingale was so matter-of-fact, Gita Medlock became even more enraged. 'I don't believe you! You're mad, woman!'

'I conditioned Sendall's mind to tell the Lictana virtually everything they knew about us. He had no choice but to pass on what he discovered here. It persuaded them to stop gathering information for themselves by experimenting on us. How do you think they managed to transmute Datch and Tamble? I should have learnt to cook.'

'Why did you do it?'

'Why? Because you idiots wanted to destroy the Lictana before the planets parted naturally. It wouldn't have crossed their minds to shake themselves molecularly free if your security hadn't kidnapped that lunatic Sendall and shown him the missile launchers.'

'He couldn't have remembered anything about that?'

'Maybe he didn't, but little Ben did.'

'Little Ben? What have antique clocks got to do with it?'

'They're still pretty accurate. Do you know what time it is?'

Gita Medlock froze in horror. 'We're totally defenceless.'

'Not quite.' Nightingale strode down to the transmission portal and programmed a code into its controls. She then lifted a concealed handle and swung out a large panel. An intense red light inside flashed on and a sickening howl shook Group Indigo's HQ. In every office, lab, and cupboard, lights pulsed "EVACUATE".

'You've got four minutes!' Nightingale bellowed above the siren. She punched in a sequence of instructions under the panel. 'It can't be countermanded!'

Everyone was outside and running within thirty seconds. Gita Medlock scuttled into the grounds like an excited trifle, losing some pink frills to a cupboard handle on the way. She glanced back to see if Nightingale was following. There was no sign of her. Suddenly, hurtling from the opposite direction, came a familiar figure, bruised and splattered with blood. She grabbed him before he could run into the building.

'Nightingale has set the place to self-destruct.'

JB Sendall's eyes were wild. 'Where is she?'

'Still inside.'

They looked at each other.

He wiped away the blood trickling into his eyes. 'I should want her dead.'

'I know the feeling.'

JB shook himself free and dashed to the entrance.

Nightingale was staggering out of the lift, clutching a heavy piece of artillery one of Devlin's guards had dropped. 'Get out of here, you lunatic!'

'What happened?'

'I wrenched my bloody back picking this thing up.'

JB caught her by the waist and hauled her outside. 'Why must you have that?'

'They took my weapons when I came in.'

'You are mad, woman!'

The Senior Controller stopped dead. 'There suddenly seems to be a plethora of people several decades younger than myself who think they have the right to impugn my sanity.'

'How soon is HQ due to explode?'

Nightingale looked at the time. 'About thirty-five seconds.'

Gita Medlock dashed over and helped push Nightingale into an armoured van. With the acceleration only an electric motor can provide, it catapulted them out of range to where other personnel were already taking cover. They toppled out of the vehicle and followed suit.

'She's not right in the head,' Gita Medlock cursed. 'Her brain must have curdled after trying to keep track of her own intrigues.'

JB turned on Nightingale. 'What is the matter with you?'

'Devlin!' Nightingale growled.

He wondered how he had managed to forget.

'Devlin?' asked Medlock.

'He tortured Tim Tharby to make me admit where I'd hidden the disc.'

Gita Medlock said nothing. She had heard the primary detonation deep inside the large building. With an ear-bursting roar, Group Indigo's HQ exploded. For several moments night became day and a hail of debris crashed about the grounds. Eventually the fire had nothing left to consume.

Nightingale pursed her lips as she checked the time. 'Thirty seconds late!'

'At least we're still here and the transmission portal isn't.' Then Gita Medlock had a stomach churning thought. 'What about the one Nichols and Hazlewood had?'

'I blew it up,' JB announced.

'I've never known such proficient saboteurs.'

Nightingale clutched her back and winced. 'Why should you? Your lot banned anything pyrotechnic thirty years ago when letting off fireworks became socially offensive.'

Medlock ignored the Senior Controller. She rose and pushed the creases out of her chiffon skirt. 'I'll send some medics over to pick you up.'

'No you won't. I'm perfectly all right.' But Gita Medlock had walked away.

JB tried to snatch the weapon off Nightingale.

'You're in no fit state.'

His superior clung onto it as though it was ten years rejuvenation. 'And you look as though you've had an argument with an automated scythe.'

'I've got as much reason to kill Devlin as you have.'

'And even more reason not to.'

JB hesitated. 'Why not?'

'Don't ask me.'

'Then give me that weapon.'

He seized it but Nightingale threw him off. 'You stubborn imbecile! Can't you take my word for anything?'

'Not any more.'

The Senior Controller rubbed the sweat out of her eyes. 'You won't thank me for telling you this.'

'I'm prepared to face the music for wiping that vermin off the face of the Earth.'

'It won't be music you hear at your trial.'

'Either tell me why I can't kill him, or let me have that weapon.'

There was nothing else for it. 'Devlin is your father!'

Jonathan Benjamin Sendall sat back on his heels. 'How?'

'The usual way. He was your mother's lover. He was taken by the Lictana when she was killed and held in suspension for forty years.

'You're lying!'

"Why should I?'

JB hesitated. Nightingale never wasted effort on creating a lie unless it was necessary. The truth could be just as devastating. It was so impossible, it had to be the truth. Despite his wan looks and prematurely white hair, JB had to admit that he had enough resemblance to Jeff Devlin for it to be plausible.

'What was Tim treating him for?' he suddenly demanded. 'Was it something to do with Devlin wanting to kill him?'

'You inherited the mutated virus from him. Tim

Tharby didn't only pump you full of drugs because I told him to. He worked for years to perfect a treatment to inhibit its progress. It's a pity he may never know how well he succeeded.'

'Gita Medlock bragged that World Government could cure anything? You told me you authorised Devlin's treatment yourself?'

Nightingale smiled. 'I signed the authorisation that made sure Devlin wouldn't be able to pass the mutation on. It was incurable for those he infected.'

'Then my mother would have died anyway?'

'I'm afraid so.'

'Did Devlin know?'

'It wouldn't have bothered him. I suspect that over fifty women have died because of it.'

'I want to kill him even more.'

Nightingale took his arm. 'Neither of us could strangle a chicken at the moment. I'll see to him as soon as my back is fixed by Thar-' She stopped. 'Perhaps sooner than that.'

The ensuing chaos had been a gift to Jeff Devlin. As Gita Medlock's creature, he was able to commandeer a security van and its weapons.

Jeff Devlin knew he had made his last bad career move. He still had a debt to settle, though. Any of the weapons in the van would have done the job. He selected the lightest. His quarry must have nursed a mutual desire to kill him: there would be no second chance if he were too slow.

From his hidden vantage point, he guessed what Nightingale and JB Sendall were talking about him. This was the only opportunity he would get to kill both of them. They would be taken as casualties of the confusion carrying on all over the estate. It would be easy for a guard to fire the shot by mistake. All of them knew JB and Nightingale were security risks. He put on gloves and charged his weapon.

'What now?' JB asked Nightingale to try and stop

himself thinking about how a rat like Jeff Devlin took
in his mother.

'We'll set up Group Indigo somewhere else.'

'You honestly think World Government would let us
have a new HQ after what we've done?'

'Of course. There's no guarantee that there aren't
other aliens showing interest in us. After this, World
Government will now be scared shitless enough to give
us whatever we want.'

JB had a more straightforward view of the world.
He suspected they would rather take away
Nightingale's vitamins and put her in a cage.
However, despite his help, she had managed to save
the planet.

'What can we do without any records? They've just
gone up in that conflagration.'

'Everything was duplicated by Tim Tharby onto an
independent system before World Security barged in.'

'Did he know what was going on?'

'Not about Gita Medlock's take-over. Poor little prat
was bursting with suspicion when I sent him on leave.'

'You'll never cope without him.'

Nightingale let her weapon slide to the ground. 'Nor
will you.'

This was the chance Devlin had been waiting for.

By the time Nightingale glanced up and saw him, it
was too late to retrieve the gun. She pulled her
number one to the ground and threw herself over him.

There was a volley of shots. Then silence.

Tentatively, JB moved, expecting to push away
ribbons of lacerated flesh.

Nightingale was still alive.

Devlin towered over them for a few seconds then,
peppered with holes spouting blood, he crumpled to the
ground.

Gita Medlock was standing directly behind him.
'Never did like that man.' She switched her small
handgun off and replaced it in her sequinned bag.

'Now there are a few more molecules that won't bother anyone again.'

JB would never get the hang of politics. 'But he was your agent?'

Gita Medlock nodded to the blackened ruin in the distance. 'That used to be a listed building.'

Nightingale grunted. 'After what your barbarians did to the grounds, it wasn't worth keeping.'

'Security precautions.'

'Bloody vandalism!'

'That's more your department.'

'It bought us time. While you were preparing missiles on the basis of useless information, our worlds were slowly slipping past each other. Two more years - that's all we needed, but you load of bureaucrats wouldn't believe it! Every calculation I sent to you was filed with the waste paper.'

'I wondered why you stopped sending them.'

A couple of medics dashed over and were about to scoop up Devlin's body.

'Not him! Leave it for the birds.' Gita Medlock pointed to Nightingale. They looked apprehensive. 'Refer any breakages to me. World Government always pays up.'

Through the distant cacophony, a voice suddenly rang out from the devastated building. 'Boss! Boss! Over here.'

'I can't you bloody fool!' Nightingale bellowed back. 'What is it?'

'We've found something!'

'What?'

'A container of some sort! Right in the middle of the basement. We're sure it ain't Group Indigo's. Looks like a fancy perfume bottle, only feels like stone - cold stone - and you need protective gear to touch anything down there.'

Nightingale groaned. 'Oh dear Lord. Bring it here! I'll adopt it.'

A firefighter scrambled out of the ruins and jogged over clutching a small cone about the size of a liqueur bottle. He gave it to Nightingale. She brushed the ash from it. The ornament was a light cream colour veined with silver. There was something about it.

JB instinctively knew who it belonged to. 'It's Tim Tharby's. He collected odd mineral shapes from the beach.'

Nightingale dropped the cone into his hand. 'You'd better let his father have it.'

'Is the old man still alive?'

'Oh yes. Chas Tharby still does the odd turn for the community.' She groaned again. 'Get me out of here you two.'

CHAPTER 27

Nightingale's back was repaired after several months of therapy and she resumed command of Group Indigo. JB Sendall was at last relieved of trying to communicate with all the eccentric connections Nightingale had built up over the years. He went down to the landscaped copse in the grounds of their new HQ with an illegal bottle of peach brandy to watch the sun set. There, for the first time in his life, he got drunk.

The hangover was worse than coming off any drugs Tim Tharby had ever prescribed. The bad dreams about having four legs and living in a toadstool had gradually faded. Now they were all about Nightingale.

As JB lay recovering in his darkened office the next morning, Nightingale's rasping voice added to the weight of the leaden cloud over his head. JB turned to look her straight in the kneecap.

'If you had to get drunk, there are plenty of poisons which don't give you a hangover.'

JB clutched his head and sat up. 'I need a hangover to stop me wanting to touch the stuff again.'

'At least you'd be in a fit state to work on the new records bank. Tharby would have had everything collated by now.'

'How is Tim? Nobody will tell me anything.'

'I had the same trouble. Had to blow out a few interfering connections.'

'Why wouldn't they let me see him?'

'No idea. We'll soon find out though. His father's on the way here. Pull yourself together. We don't want him to think his son worked with a team of social misfits.'

JB would have laughed if the effort wasn't so painful. 'He already knows that.'

Nightingale thrust a bottle of tablets into his hand. 'Got these from Tharby's cabinet. Take a couple and tidy yourself up.' Then she strode out.

For the first time JB realised that a sliding door could slam.

After ten minutes, the tablets had taken effect. He had a shower and changed into a suit that didn't look as though it had spent a night in a ditch. He had been wearing the other crumpled jacket and trousers when he mindlessly meandered the grounds at midnight. Even then, he still believed he had every right to get drunk.

As JB Sendall's wits returned, so did paranoia. Once again he tried to work out the politics that had persuaded World Government to give Group Indigo premises larger than the one Nightingale destroyed instead of sending her to a secure institution for geriatric delinquents. Dr. Phoebe Shadbolt had also been granted her own team of palaeontologists and now, safe from conservationists, had as much time as she wanted to remove the district's fossil population, as well as search for her archosaur hominid.

Nightingale had lied, set up everyone in Group Indigo, World Security and an alien species, not to mention destroy a couple of major landmarks. It never occurred to JB that she was so accomplished at blackmail as well. Cheating, homicide and demolition -certainly! It was obvious by the number of strawberry jam crates arriving at HQ, someone had a reason to keep her quiet.

Being responsible for this new HQ, however briefly, had driven JB to his wit's end. He had tried to apply for a minor post in Regional Funding. Unfortunately, there were few positions for clerks qualified to chase UFOs. This tempted him to fill in his next application to Northern Water Control somewhat eccentrically. Fortunately, Nightingale got to it before World Security; otherwise he would have ended up in the same secure hospital as Tim Tharby.

JB had no idea why the medic had been sent there.

Tim Tharby, despite his pink perms and tantrums, was a tough little bird. Even after what Jeff Devlin had done to him, it was unlikely the balance of his mind would have been affected. If he hadn't been so occupied, JB would have been more suspicious at not being allowed to see him. Now Tim Tharby was at home with his father. Not even he had been allowed to talk to anyone until now.

JB looked out of the window at the HQ's tidy parkland and wondered how long it would be before Nightingale allowed it to lapse into jungle. The stack of cans containing bright orange and green paint just outside was enough to bring back his nausea. They were the colours of the rapidly expanding Natural Living Campaign. Nightingale was deliberately stamping on the toes of World Government by having her HQ painted in them. Perhaps it would do them good to believe that she was becoming an eco-rebel. He hoped he would be paralytically drunk when that collision took place.

By the time Chas Tharby arrived, JB Sendall looked as though he wouldn't touch anything more alcoholic than ginger beer.

"The Amazing Chas Tharby" was a small agile man with an amiably crumpled expression too quick for his seventy-plus years. His manner suggested that he was used to being in front of an audience. He deftly took a silver box of peppermints from his waistcoat pocket, flicked it open and offered it around.

Nightingale tried not to look circumspect at his performance. 'No thank you.'

JB also declined. Chas Tharby popped a mint into his mouth before using sleight of hand to make the box disappear.

JB was unsettled by the man's bravura. 'How's Tim?'

As the conjurer shook his head, he could see the resemblance to his son. 'He seemed to be doing well enough. If his mother were still here he might have improved more, but she passed on some years back. Caught in a tornado. That was before they could do anything about them of course. Best way a test pilot could go I suppose, but it was hard on both of us all the same.'

'He never mentioned that to me.'

'Our boy can have a secret way with him. Couldn't always tell what he was thinking. Might have been able to prevent it if I'd known what was going to happen.'

Nightingale frowned. 'Prevent what?'

'When Tim saw that cone thing Mr Sendall gave me, he wanted it opened. Quite a job it was, but I thought it might help. He went back to being a child y'see. No trouble though. He was never any trouble. Looked after himself quite well given what had happened. Cope with anything our Tim could.'

'I thought that cone was a mineral of some sort?'

'So did I. So did I. But Tim knew it was a container. That's what made me think it was his.'

JB had also been convinced that it belonged to the medic. 'Wasn't it then?'

'Well, it couldn't have been, could it?'

'Why not?'

'There's no lock, weld, bolt or fastening the Amazing Chas Tharby hasn't been able to get into. 'Specially the old-fashioned sort. Still do a healthy business for antique dealers.' He shook his grizzled locks. 'This was something else, though. Bit wary at first. When I held the thing it was like cold marble. When our lad touched it, it warmed up. Weird it was. Anyhow, I still have a small compressor and electronic saw from the old days. Used to saw a mate of mine in half I did, until he put on weight and couldn't get into the box.' By the stony expressions on the faces of his audience it was obvious they set their entertainment levels a little higher. 'Anyhow, I spent hours searching for a way to unscrew the bottom or unlock the top. It was like some huge quartz seed, just waiting to open. If it weren't for Tim I would have left it, but he knew what he wanted. So I put it in a vice and fretted a groove in its base. Now this seemed to liven it up a little. Vibrated faintly it did, like a purring cat.'

'Then what?' asked Nightingale.

'Oh, I took it to Tim in the hope he would be satisfied.'

'Was he?'

'Seemed so, and I didn't fancy doing any more work on it. It might have hatched out a bloody triffid.'

'Triffid?' asked JB.

'Three-legged vegetable,' Nightingale muttered, but he was none the wiser.

'Anyhow, seeing as you know about molecules and things, I thought you were the ones to tell about it.'

'Where is he now?'

'At home - mostly.'

'Mostly?'

Chas Tharby shrugged mysteriously. 'He comes and goes. Comes and goes.'

Nightingale wasn't amused. 'You let him out? The hospital released him on the understanding that he doesn't leave your living section.'

'No harm in it. No harm in it,' Chas Tharby added hastily. 'He seems so much better, like his old self. Come and see what I mean.'

* * *

Chas Tharby's home had a huge living room that looked out onto a garden and swimming pool that were once an ancient football ground. Relics from the performer and his wife's past were everywhere; costumes, banjos, faded photos, plasticized press cuttings, masks, dangerous-looking swords and some stage curtains draped across the windows at the far end. Tim Tharby's collection of lace fans covered a wall.

At the touch of a button, the heavy curtains swept dramatically aside and the triple glazed wall slid open. Nightingale and JB followed Chas Tharby into the large garden.

Hardly higher than Nightingale, were two ancient prop aircraft and, covered by wisteria, the wing of the last experimental machine Tim's mother had tested. There was also a sizeable workshop and living module with a spacious sun lounge in the distance.

'Our Tim's place is over there. Likes it out here he does.'

The low wall separating the garden from the rolling downs beyond worried JB. 'Aren't you bothered about him wandering off?'

Chas Tharby laughed. 'Wander off? Our Tim? He loves it here. I could leave him all day and he would sit out there looking through albums and picture books. Didn't use the monitor much, though. Doesn't like computers for some reason.'

Nightingale was getting impatient. 'Well, is he here now?'

'Could be. Could be,' was all Chas Tharby would say.

They walked down some steps and through a rockery where automatic weeders were pecking at the thin soil. The swimming pool, shaped like an artist's palette covered with cobalt blue, caught the light and sparkled invitingly below. It was a large jewel set in the emerald lawn bordered with beds of yellow and orange daisies.

The sunlit ripples reminded JB of something. 'Didn't Tim like swimming?'

'Used to. Used to, but since-' Chas Tharby shrugged. 'He was never that strong again, and I couldn't pull him out if he got into trouble.'

'Just what did happen after you left that container with him?' Nightingale demanded.

'Well ...' The old man faltered. 'The first hospital
were a bit puzzled. That's why they sent him to that
secure place. And, of course, they wouldn't tell anyone
about it. I had to complain to the regional council
before they let me see him. He didn't seem changed
that much. And there wasn't anything they could do
about it anyhow. So they had to let him out in the
end.'

'Do about what?' asked JB.

'He seemed a lot brighter for all that. Tim still
didn't speak much, but he had changed. Like there
was this bubble of light about him.'

'Literally?'

Chas Tharby stopped for a moment. 'Perhaps there
was. Perhaps there was.'

Nightingale lost patience. 'Go on!'

'Suddenly everything seemed all right with him.
Different person he was.'

A tingle of apprehension skittered up JB's spine.
'How do you mean?'

'Never seen him so happy, as though he had some
secret.'

'Secret?'

'You know, Meaning of Life, philosopher's stone,
that sort of thing.' Nightingale snorted in disbelief.
Chas Tharby went on. 'He was changed. For a while
he was so lively, then he started to sit and think more.'

'It was wearing off?'

'Oh no! If anything, he was even more content, like
one of those Zen monks.' Chas Tharby hesitated,
suddenly ill at ease. 'Didn't need so much to eat
neither, but never seemed to lose any weight. Then I
started to notice it as well. The hospital had warned
me, but I never paid no heed. Didn't think it was
possible.'

Even Nightingale began to suspect something
sinister. 'Notice what?'

Chas Tharby nimbly descended the remaining steps

and led the way to Tim's sun lounge. The other two followed him inside.

This couldn't have been Tim Tharby's room. There was no clutter of notepads, useless ornaments or jars of make-up. It was as clinically clean as his lab at the old HQ. Even his favourite koala-shaped mug sat on a shelf, polished and unused.

Chas Tharby pressed the switch that drew the blinds. 'Helps if there isn't too much light.'

'Doesn't Tim like the light?' asked JB.

'No, it's just easier to see him.'

'What?' murmured Nightingale.

JB caught sight of the small cream and silver cone. The bottom of it had come cleanly away. He picked it up.

Chas Tharby gave a small giggle. 'Nothing ever inside it I reckon.'

Then the truth crashed home. 'Oh yes there was!'

'Go on?' Nightingale demanded.

'Soolain.'

'Soolain? An ancient Moslem prophet of some sort?'

'No. The Cone of Soolain. I expected it to be the size of a city.'

'It can't be peach brandy talking, so try making sense. We might understand.'

'The Lictana! I told Hysle how Tim Tharby had tried to save their planet. I didn't think it would bother them. The Lictana must have put the cone in the portal before HQ went up!'

'How did they know it would get to him? It didn't have his name on it.'

'Oh yes it did. I threw his ID through the portal at Hysle. They had access to everything that made up his biological identity. They must have tagged it in some way so when I saw it, I would realise who it belonged to.'

'Not possible.'

'It wouldn't have been a problem for the Lictana.

They can manipulate brainwave patterns like we can
pheromones.'

Nightingale grunted. That was one of the reasons
she had a security plate fitted inside her skull. 'Tell
me about it ...'

'But that's not the point. It's all to do with-'

'Start spouting Zen and I'll hit you.'

'Can't you see? It would have been easy for the
Lictana to make a recognition device like that.'

'Why would they go to the bother? They had more
pressing things on their minds. Anyway, if they had
cooked up a cure-all for Tim in their dimension, there's
no way it could have been married to his atomic make-
up in ours.'

Chas Tharby suddenly raised a finger. 'He's here! I
can sense it.'

JB could hardly believe his eyes. 'Tim!'

Tim Tharby looked younger, slimmer and hardly
freckled. His hair was a natural, youthful colour, so
healthy it seemed to have a halo around it.

JB reached out to touch him. Nightingale pulled
him back.

The medic was so transformed he glowed.

In fact, to the Senior Controller's critical eye, he was
glowing more than was natural for any human being.
'Can you hear me, Tim?'

Tim Tharby nodded.

'Can you understand what has happened?'

He nodded again. 'Have you any sensation?'

He shook his head.

'Memory?'

Tim Tharby smiled noncommittally.

'Does it matter?'

He shook his head.

JB began to shake uncontrollably. 'What's
happened to him?'

Nightingale clasped his shoulder.

Chas Tharby smiled fondly at his son. 'He don't talk

no more. Like he don't need food or to stay in one place.
Go anywhere now he can.'

Tim Tharby held out his hands to JB and
Nightingale.

Then he stepped back and dissolved through the
wall.

THE END

www.ingramcontent.com/pod-product-compliance
Lightning Source LLC
Chambersburg PA
CBHW051558030726
47592CB00001B/346